AWAKEN

Copyright

Paperback ISBN-13: 979-8-9929818-0-3
Hardback ISBN-13: 979-8-9929818-1-0

Cover design by: Image generated by Shelley Watters using Canva
Printed in the United States of America

Trigger Warnings

Sex depicted on the page
Rape/attempted rape
Child death
Suicidal ideation

AWAKEN

SHELLEY WATTERS

Contents

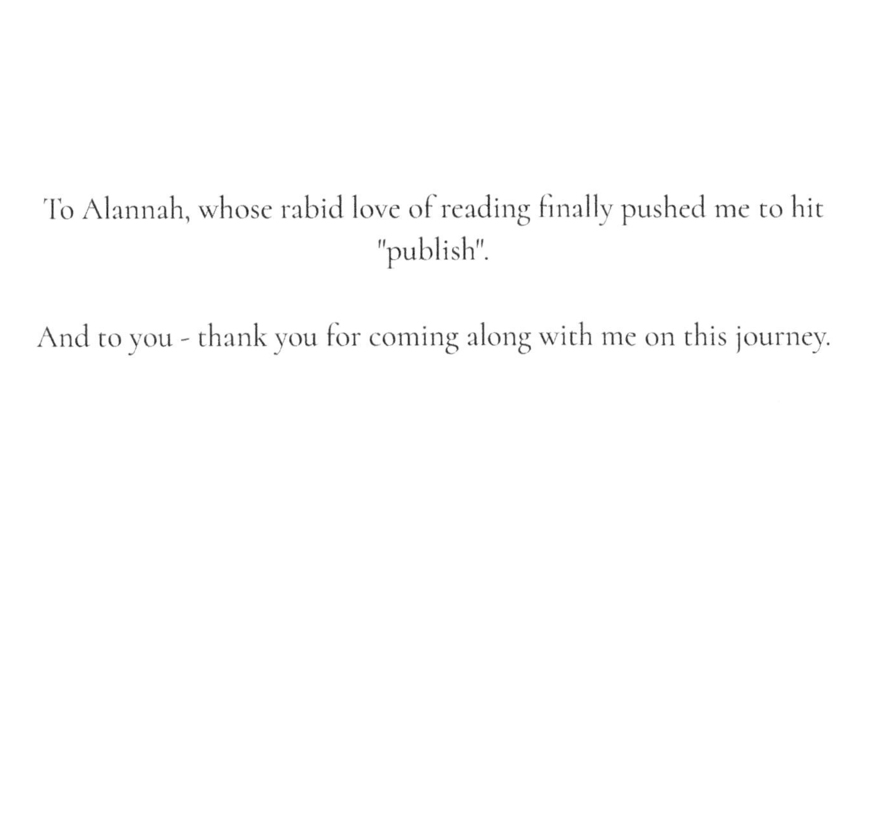

To Alannah, whose rabid love of reading finally pushed me to hit "publish".

And to you - thank you for coming along with me on this journey.

1

Chapter One

A cold tingle of anxiety rushed down my spine, while my heartbeat thrummed in my ears, drowning out the obnoxious slap of my flip-flops against the shiny marble as I dashed toward security. I briefly considered launching over the security barricade in a hurdle-leap, but that would not only guarantee I missed my flight but add a bit of jail time to my already tragically ruined summer.

My sandals squealed as I skidded to a stop on the highly polished floor, my eyes flitting between the lines. I whispered a prayer for forgiveness as I cut off an elderly woman heading for shortest one. I ignored my name being called from somewhere behind me and tossed my bag and shoes on the conveyor belt. My heart skipped a beat as the agent slowly waved people through, occasionally waving someone to the pat-down area. *Please, please don't let that be me.* There were still a few other kids from the Seniors in London trip in the neighboring lines, so at least I wasn't the only one cutting it seriously close.

"Hey! Pay attention!" I glanced in the direction of the voice, only to find the security lady glaring at me from the other side of the metal detectors, waving at me with irritation to pass through. I barely stepped into the detector when a shriek emitted from the arch above me, making my stomach drop. *Oh no.*

"This way." The woman ushered me roughly into the involuntary pat-down area. *Dear God, kill me now.* I stood in front of the guard with my arms outstretched, my bare feet clammy on the polished marble floor. The other kids snickered about getting felt up as they passed, making my cheeks blaze. Go figure that out of all of them, *I* was the one who got selected. Like fate hadn't already made me its bitch so far this summer.

Claire, the quiet girl who sat behind me in calculus, smiled sympathetically as she passed. "Too bad you didn't get the that one," she whispered and nodded to the way-too-hot-for-government-service guard who flashed a confident smile at me.

"Yeah, too bad," I joked and tried to pretend like the elderly woman's latex-gloved hands sliding over every inch of my body didn't make me feel completely violated.

"You're clear," the old lady grumbled and shoved the bin containing my personal items toward me like I'd wasted her time.

I fought the sarcasm that sprang to my lips and quickly toed on my flip-flops. I slung my messenger bag over my shoulder and patted gently, reassured that the firm rectangle of my favorite book was still in the side pocket. A tingle of shame flamed my cheeks. Obviously, I was too old to have a "woobie", a nickname Mom lovingly used for our comfort objects, but I just couldn't leave it behind. But if someone found out... Without a backward glance, I sprinted toward the terminal. I tried not to remind myself of what I was running *to*, since the thought of being wedged in a confined space breathing recycled air and hurtling through the sky with only two man-made engines holding me aloft made it hard to breathe.

"Tor! Wait for us!" Casey screeched from somewhere behind me.

I sighed and slowed my pace a little, glancing back at my little sister in annoyance. She was barely putting her shoes back on after coming through security. "I don't have time!"

Casey rolled her chocolate eyes and stuck her tongue out. "You act like you're the only one going on this trip."

An immature move, I know, but I returned the gesture, sticking my tongue out and wrinkling up my face at her. I stopped short of saying that if I had my way, I *would* be the only one going on the trip. Just because Mom was the president of the PTA didn't mean that Principal Miller was obligated to offer the opportunity to chaperone the trip to her. I had the nagging suspicion he did it maliciously. All because of a tiny incident involving the lap pool and a few hundred goldfish. I mean, seriously. It wasn't like he had any proof that I was the mastermind behind the junior prank. Besides, we had to show up the seniors' prank. My mistake had been to put the receipt for two-hundred-and-fifty feeder goldfish in my wallet instead of burning the evidence. And further, he had no proof that I put the fish there, only that I bought them.

"Will you just relax, Tori? You're not going to miss the plane," Mom chided a little out of breath, as they caught up to me. She clutched Casey's arm and dragged her along behind her, proving she too, was worried we weren't going to make our flight.

I rolled my eyes and picked up my pace, turning my attention to the terminal just in time to glimpse vibrant green eyes a moment before I slammed into a hard wall of muscle. My bag flew from my shoulder and the contents went sailing across the floor. I muttered an apology and scrambled to gather my stuff -- ChapStick, book about medicinal plants, a hairbrush, a few tampons. I cringed as I snatched them up and deposited them in my bag, praying no one saw those.

"Sorry about that," a familiar male voice from my daydreams murmured. Brandon? My heart fluttered. Our heads bumped as we reached for my treasured book at the same time.

"Ow!" I squeaked and straightened. "Sorry!" I stammered, heat blossoming on my cheeks. My stomach did the flip-flop it always did when I saw him. Brandon's green eyes flashed and a blinding white smile stretched across his sculpted face. He pushed his floppy blonde hair out of his eyes and I couldn't help but watch the way his t-shirt stretched across his bicep with the movement. I'd never admit it, but he was what I pictured Prince Charming in my favorite, albeit a bit immature to still love fairytales at my age, book -- The Little Briar Rose by the Brother's Grim -- looked like. He pretty much *was* the epitome of Prince Charming: Painfully handsome. Captain of the football team. Uber popular.

"My fault. Sorry I have such a hard head." He smirked and held out my book.

I stared at his lips. I'd spent so many nights imagining how they'd feel. Then he was dipping his head towards mine, his lips slowly inching closer, his breath brushing across my lips as he whispered "Awakened with a kiss".

"Tori?" Brandon studied me with a puzzled expression.

I blinked. "Oh, um." My cheeks warmed. I was a complete idiot.

Wait a second – he actually knew my name? And why did my voice sound pathetic?

He held the book out to me again. My skin tingled when our fingertips brushed as I took the book. I winced, hoping he wouldn't look at the title. It was bad enough I had to carry the thing around with me everywhere, I didn't need him thinking I was a dork for still reading fairytales. My gaze shot to his. "Thanks." I quickly tucked it in my bag.

"So you're going to London too?"

Was he actually trying to talk to me? "Huh?"

He chuckled and the rumble made my stomach tingle. He inclined his head toward the gate behind him where a group of our classmates had assembled, waiting impatiently to board the plane. Dad and Casey perched on the benches facing them and Mom paced while frantically pointing to each student and quickly marking something off in her notebook. I cringed.

"London?" he repeated slowly, as if I didn't speak English.

I nodded.

A group of girls shoved between us, and a shoulder slammed into me, sending me off balance. I stumbled a bit but regained my footing and glared at Bianca's retreating form. She turned and lowered her sunglasses, a satisfied smirk lifting one corner of her painted lips. It was the universal "Yeah, that was on purpose, what are YOU going to do about it?" look. Her eyes flitted to Brandon for a moment, and satisfied that his eyes were on her, she turned and sauntered away.

A ridiculous tingle of jealousy sparked across my skin. I ground my teeth. *Bitch.*

Bianca's shoulders stiffened and she turned.

Crap. Did I say that out loud?

She raised a delicately pruned eyebrow and eyed me from head to toe, her face screwing up in disgust. "Trash."

Adrenaline rushed through my body and I opened my mouth to respond.

"Tor, come on!" Casey appeared beside me and grabbed my hand. I turned back to Brandon, whose eyes were back on me.

"Don't mind her. Money can buy popularity, but it can't buy a personality. And she's obviously lacking there... Is this your sister?" A dazzling orthodontist-for-a-father perfect smile flashed and he winked at Casey.

I stifled a snicker and nodded. It was nice to know Bianca didn't have everyone under her spell. Casey blushed and tugged on my arm. I yanked it away and nodded to my parents. "I'll be there in a sec!" Casey pouted and flounced off to sit back down, kicking her legs out like the little kid that she was.

I turned my attention back to Brandon, who, for some unfathomable reason, was still trying to talk to me. "Sweet. Are they coming too?"

I sighed and nodded. "Unfortunately."

Another blinding smile. "I think it's cool your family gets to come. I'm going to miss mine like crazy."

I flinched. He thought it was cool that my family was coming along? Seriously?

"So, um, what are you doing here? Not that you aren't allowed to be here. I mean --" I snapped my mouth shut. If someone had been standing behind me, I would have asked them to kick me. I sounded like a babbling idiot.

"I'm going too." His bewildered look made my stomach drop.

"Oh. Right. Duh." For having a crush on the guy, I apparently wasn't very good at the whole stalking thing. I snorted, then blushed because I snorted.

His smile melted from his face as he rushed to continue. "I figured it was a great chance to get some traveling in before college, you know? I've heard there's some awesome hiking on the daytrips."

I smiled, and he did in return. "That sounds like fun, hiking in Europe." The picture of us hiking together through a dense forest and finding a hidden waterfall that no one else knew about filled my head. And as the water rushed over us, he leaned in to press his lips to mine. But before our lips touched, his voice interrupted my fantasy. "Besides, I need the credits."

My face flamed with embarrassment. I had just daydreamed about the guy *again* while he was staring at me. From the surprised look on his face, maybe I'd actually said the whole thing out loud. I said the first thing that came to mind to cover the trail of my thoughts. "Yeah, school is hard." I rolled my eyes. Might as well have tattooed a giant "L" on my forehead.

"Come on, Tor!" Casey shouted from her seat beside Dad.

"Well, I should let you go. Maybe we'll talk later?" He nodded towards Casey, who looked like she was about to bounce out of her seat.

"Right. See ya later." My stomach tensed at the promise in his words. Later. Really?

He smiled, showing off his blindingly white smile again before crossing the terminal to the seat beside his best friend. He leaned over and whispered something into Darien's ear, whose copper eyes darted up from his iPad and locked with mine. In that moment, all of the air from the room disappeared. It was the first time he'd made eye contact with me since he started school last year. And his eyes were as stunningly copper as Brandon's were green. I stood there, gaping like an idiot at him before my sister's voice broke into my consciousness.

"Tor! Stop drooling!"

I winced. *Please, tell me he didn't hear that.* I dropped my gaze to my feet and pretended she didn't exist as I crossed the terminal and slumped into the seat beside Claire, which was as far as I could possibly manage from my family.

Claire leaned over. "Brandon seems to have made quite an impression."

I rubbed my head. "Well, he does have a hard head."

Claire snorted. "That's what I've heard."

I gaped at her. We hadn't spent much time together outside of Calculus, but she was the closest thing to a friend I had on this trip, since none of my friends from school were interested in summer school, regardless of the opportunity to travel or not. I had no idea she had a sense of humor. Especially a dirty one.

She chuckled and nudged me with her shoulder. "Lighten up, Bookworm. We're not in Calculus anymore."

This might turn out to be the trip of a lifetime after all.

2

Chapter Two

My hands shook and my mouth felt like I'd been sucking on sand as I made my way toward my assigned seat. I made it a point to select a seat two rows back from my parents in the middle of the center aisle, flanked by an empty seat on each side. Supposedly the safest place in a plane, according to my Google search prior to booking. My breath hitched when Brandon and Darien made their way down the aisle, their overstuffed backpacks slung over their shoulders. My heartbeat accelerated as they neared. How lucky would I be if I had to sit between two of the hottest guys in school for a fourteen-hour flight? It'd be an awesome distraction from the horrors of being stuck in a metal tube hurling through the air, that's for sure. I silently prayed they'd stop at my aisle. My heart sank when they loaded into the row behind my mom, and I mentally kicked myself for even having the idea they'd be sitting next to me. I was Irish, after all, and had the luck to prove it.

I sighed and tucked my bag under the seat in front of me. Out of the corner of my eye, a pair of Louboutin's stopped at the end of my aisle. *Oh please, for the love of God, no.*

"Hey look, someone forgot to clean the trash out of our row." Bianca's valley-girl copycat voice was straight out of Mean Girls.

I straightened up and eyed her. "Excuse me?"

"Those are *our* seats that you're contaminating. Besides, aren't you supposed to be sitting over there with Mommy?" She glared at me through the biggest set of sunglasses I'd ever seen.

I shook my head and refrained from giving her the bird. "I don't think so."

Her cheeks reddened. Apparently she wasn't used to people standing up to her. Ever.

"Flight Attendant!!" Bianca shrieked.

God, how I'd love to smack those dumb glasses off her stupid face.

A Patricia Adams look-alike in an airline uniform strode up and glared at me before turning a sweet smile to Bianca. "What seems to be the problem?"

"This *trash* is in my seat and refuses to move."

"No, I'm not." I didn't budge.

The flight attendant's nasally voice echoed through the cabin. "May I see your ticket, please?"

I could feel every pair of eyes in the plane on me. "Whatever." I rifled through my pack and pulled the boarding pass and shoved the ticket at her. "Here."

"And yours?" the attendant turned to Bianca.

Bianca smiled sweetly and handed over the ticket without even glancing at it.

I watched the attendant study the passes, her black eyes darting between the papers. She handed my pass back to me. "I'm going to have to ask you to move."

My eyebrows shot up. "Excuse me?"

The attendant's hands hit her hips. "If you're going to be difficult, I'd be happy to have you removed from this flight."

"I'm not being difficult. This is my seat. Why do I have to be the one to move?"

"Apparently the airline double booked this seat. Your pass is dated two days after hers. Therefore, *you* are the one who must move." Her black eyes flashed at me, daring me to argue with her.

Someone's hand landed on my shoulder, and even without turning, I knew exactly who it was. "What's going on here?"

The attendant glared at my Mom. "None of your concern, please go back to your seat."

Mom's hand stiffened on my shoulder. "I'm this group's chaperone. So, it does concern me."

The attendant sighed; her anger clear on her pale features. "The airline double booked this seat. This girl's ticket is dated two days after this one. Airline policy states that the person with the ticket that was bought first gets the seat. Therefore, this girl needs to move, and she is being difficult."

I could almost hear Mom's teeth grinding behind me. "I understand. Well, there is empty seat in my row. Can we move her there?"

I could tell the attendant had "no" on the tip of her tongue, but after a moment to think, a look of almost satisfaction flashed across her face. "Fine."

I sighed and hefted my bag from between my legs and swung it over my shoulder, almost hitting the attendant with it. Bianca and her cronies' giggles followed me up the aisle as I made my way toward Mom's row, the words "pathetic" and "trash" biting the back of my neck like bee-stings. I pointedly avoided everyone's gaze as I marched my way up the aisle and flopped down into my new seat.

The back of my seat flexed as someone pulled on it. Darien's voice -- which I was only familiar with because we were in the same AP biology class -- filtered through the crack between the seats. "We'd rather have you sitting by us than Bianca anyway."

I smiled and settled back into the cushions. Maybe sitting next to my Mom wasn't the worst thing that could happen, after all.

##

Like mounds of whipped cream, clouds stretched out for what seemed like eternity beneath my window. I longed to watch the deep blue of the Atlantic as we soared over it, but the cloud cover hadn't let up since we'd left Newark Airport. Being a desert rat from Phoenix, it would have been the first time I'd seen the Atlantic. I'd hoped to catch a glimpse of a whale or two beneath us as we soared towards London.

"It's not that bad, sweetie. I promise you it's down there."

I frowned and turned to face her. "You know I hate flying. It would've been nice to take my mind off of this."

Mom snorted and nodded to the tattered book I clutched so tight my fingers were numb. "Why don't you just lose yourself in your book for a while? I promise I'll wake you up when we get there."

I loosened my death grip on my treasured book. "Yeah, sure."

"Are you still mad we came?"

My eyes flitted to Dad and Casey sitting in the center row where they were playing some game on the iPad. My sister tapped the screen and smiled triumphantly at Dad, who studied the screen with mock frustration. After a minute of contemplating his move, he tapped the screen and then sat back with a smug grin while Casey pouted at the screen.

My gaze shifted to the rows behind us where my fellow classmates were seated. None of whom had their over-protective families tagging along for the trip. "I could've handled this on my own, Mom. I *am* seventeen, after all."

Mom nodded. "I know, sweetheart. But someone had to chaperone the senior trip. Besides, Principal Miller *asked* me to. Come on. It's a free trip to London, how could we pass that up? It's not like you'll see us *that* much anyway." She picked up her bottle of water and took a swig.

I shrugged. "I guess I'm kinda glad you're here. It makes calling home to ask for more money easier."

Mom snorted. "Well I'm kinda glad I had the opportunity to come along. I'm not ready to let you go just yet. I still have a little longer to get used to the thought of you not being around as much before you go off to college and then medical school." She raised her e-reader in front of her, which was her universal sign that she was finished with what she had to say.

Thank God. With a sigh of relief, I fluffed my pillow and settled into the corner between the window and the seat and cracked open my book. That tingle of shame that feathered across my skin every time I touched the yellowed pages reminded me of how immature I must be to still be reading a kid's book. But Mom was right. There was no better way to get my mind off the fact that we were thousands of feet in the air -- trusting two ear-numbing engines and a human pilot to keep us there -- than to lose myself in my favorite book for a few hours.

The sounds of the noisy cabin fell away as the story sucked me in, even though I'd read it a billion times. I fought through the brambles with Prince Charming as he uncovered the hidden castle. I felt the stone steps beneath my feet as we climbed the tower to search for the princess. My breath caught with him when he parted the curtains to find her sleeping form. But even though I knew exactly how the story would end, I was always anxious to get to the part where Prince Charming kissed Briar Rose and woke her from her enchanted sleep. Where he bends, ever so slightly, his gaze fixed on Briar Rose's ruby lips. He hears the witch's crackly voice replay in his head. "The spell will be broken with true love's first kiss." He cups her cheek and his thumb brushes across her bottom lip. Her skin's so soft, so delicate, he fears she might crumble into dust in his trembling hands. I mouth the words along with him as he whispers "awakened with a kiss" and dips his head, his lips inching towards hers.

The world lurched and my book tumbled into my lap. My gaze shot up as the cabin shuddered beneath us again, making the bottom of my stomach drop out from the turbulence. I snatched my book off my lap and glanced out the window, trying to anchor myself to something stationary outside the shaky cabin, but the clouds beneath us churned like potion in a witches' cauldron. What had started out as fluffy, sunlight-tinged cotton balls had turned a angry gray, darkening until I could barely make out where cloud ended and wing began. The plane lurched again.

"Mom?" I gasped and instinctively grabbed for her hand.

Her hand gripped mine, cutting off the blood flow to my fingertips. "It's just a little turbulence, sweetheart. It'll pass."

The bottom dropped out of the plane before finding its stride again, and I clutched my mom's hand with all the strength I had. "Please make it stop," I pleaded. Tears burned my eyes and I squeezed them shut in a vain effort to stop the rattling in the cabin.

"I can't, sweetheart. It'll be okay, I promise."

The cabin jolted and frantic flight attendants scrambled down the aisles shouting directions. Not one of them took time to console the frightened passengers when they tried to stop them as they passed. The creepy black-eyed attendant caught my eye for a fraction of a second, and I swear a look of satisfaction crossed her harsh features as she rushed past. A ding echoed through the cabin and the seat belt light glowed overhead. My fingers were ice as I struggled to strap myself in.

Mom's calm voice filtered through the chaos. "It's going to be okay. It's going to be okay." Casey's terrified crying sliced through my fear. I glanced at Dad, who was buckling my ten-year-old sister into her seat. Mom leaned across the aisle and held her hand. "It's going to be okay."

The entire cabin shuddered and then, like a gift from God, everything stopped. My breath of relief caught in my throat when the world around me shook like an earthquake. A male voice echoed through the cabin. "Ladies and gentlemen, this is your captain. The storm has blown us off course and has damaged our equipment. We're currently somewhere over southwestern Ireland. We will be making an emergency landing momentarily. Please brace for impact." Before he finished his sentence, the whole world lurched forward, and I flinched when an air mask dropped down from the ceiling above me.

"Mom!" I grabbed for her hand.

"Put it on, Tori!" she grabbed the mask and helped me put it over my head like she'd done with hers. The cabin shuddered and I braced my hands on the seat in front of me.

"This isn't happening. This isn't happening," I chanted. I was only seventeen. I wasn't ready to die. I panted in an effort to keep what little food I had in my stomach down as the panic overwhelmed me.

Mom grabbed my hand again and squeezed it tight. "Look at me, Tori!"

I turned my terrified gaze to hers. "Please tell me this isn't happening!"

Mom squeezed my hand harder. "I love you."

Tears streamed down my cheeks. "I love you too."

She nodded, her tears making inky mascara streaks down her cheeks. "You're going to make it through this. Do you understand me? You're going to be fine."

I nodded, trying to believe her. But she didn't know. She didn't know how this was going to end. At that moment, I wished with all my heart my family hadn't come with me on the trip. Now they were going to die in an airplane crash that should have only claimed me. A trip they shouldn't have even been on.

The rattling intensified and screams built on screams. The plane leveled off just a bit and then jolted, causing my teeth to smack together with the impact and my stomach lurched violently. Eardrum-shattering screeching beneath our feet added to the deafening chaos around me. Pieces of ceiling sheared off in chunks at the front of the cabin, sending mangled luggage, twisted pieces of shrapnel, and insulation into the cabin and out into the sky. With a sudden lurch my seatbelt snapped open. I screamed as Mom's hand ripped from mine. Pain exploded on the side of my face and white light blinded me when I connected with the seat in front of me.

Silence.

3

Chapter Three

The warm, wet taste of copper filled my mouth, like the way wet pennies smelled. I brushed the wetness from the corner of my mouth and fought to open my eyes. The pounding in my head intensified as my eyelids parted, the inky darkness replaced by blinding rays of sunlight slicing through the destroyed cabin like white-hot knives. My groan echoed in the silence as I struggled to un-wedge myself from between the seats. My blood chilled and my ears strained against the silence. Not a breath, not a whimper, nothing. Panic tightened my chest and I slowly raised my gaze to Mom's seat. The seat was empty. Hope gave me the strength to extract my battered body from between the mangled seats. Mom was alive.

"Mom?" I called as I stood. I gasped at the sharp stab of pain from my ribs. Half the cabin was gone.

Row upon row of empty seats. Air masks dangling from what was left of the ceiling. Gaping, jagged holes where the cabin had ripped apart. Insulation and wires hung down from the openings. Sparks shot from the wires every now and then, making me jump when their electrical arc broke the silence. Baggage littered the floor.

"Dad?" I cautiously moved into the aisle, stepping over a shoe and an inhaler. My knees nearly buckled at the sight of Dad's Ipad in his seat, and Casey's bear lying on the floor. I picked up the toy. They had to have gotten out, right? Not a drop of blood was on any of their seats. The only blood, in fact, was the smear of blood where I'd collided with the seat in front of me. My eyes were drawn to the vibrant blue sky through the gaping holes in the roof. It was painfully blue. I flinched when the frayed electrical wires sparked again. The faint sound of scratching somewhere near the galley broke the silence. Fear tingled through me as I slowly hobbled toward the noise, dodging hanging wires, clothing and twisted pieces of airplane. *Where was everyone?*

The sound intensified as I reached the bulkhead. I peeked around it into the galley. It was like in one of those zombie movies where the heroine would hear the scratching, think it was someone trapped, and open the door and bam! Brains! I rolled my eyes and followed the sound to a tall cabinet. The scratching became frantic and my hand hesitated for a moment on the handle. I was being stupid. Someone could be trapped in there and I was worried about zombies. I took a deep breath and turned the handle, easing the cabinet open a fraction of an inch. The door flew open and I screamed, protecting my face with my hands and reeling backwards into the cabinets behind me. The sharp edge of the counter gouged into my back, but the scuffle as something scurried past my feet had my toes curling. I peered through my fingers down at the creature. An offended squirrel chattered at me before scampering away. I fought to control my galloping heart, my head pounding in time with its frantic pace. What the heck? I peered into the cabinet and found a hole in the wall of the plane where a fallen tree had jabbed into the side.

Everyone had to be around here somewhere. There was no blood. No bodies. Why'd they leave me all alone in this plane while everyone had gotten out? I frowned and picked my way through the rubble toward the bulkhead door. It was still closed, latched from the inside. How had they gotten out? I turned the latch and shoved with all my might to open the door. It swung open and crashed against the side of the disabled plane. I shaded my eyes from the bright light and struggled to see where we'd crashed. My head swam from the rush of fresh air that engulfed me. I clutched the doorway with both hands and struggled to fight off the dizziness. Lush grass, which had never seen the blades of a lawn mower, undulated in the gentle breeze in the meadow before me. Beyond that, towering pines stretched out for miles in every direction. Birds chattered in the trees. But, like the plane, not a single human sound.

"Mom?" I called out. "Dad?" People didn't just disappear. Especially from the scene of an airplane crash. "Casey?" Had they really just left me? Where was everyone? Blood pounded in my ears as fear and anxiety overwhelmed me. "Mom!" I jumped the short distance to the ground and waded through the grass to the other side of the plane. They had to be here. They wouldn't have left me. They wouldn't have. But no one was there. Just more trees and a mountain, with its peak disappearing in the clouds. "Mom!" I screamed. "Anybody! Please! Help me! Please!" I clutched my aching ribs, which protested sharply at my scream.

My gaze scanned the forest surrounding me, the terror searing a path through my veins and clutching my heart in a vise-grip. My head spun and I sunk to my knees to keep from passing out, forcing myself to breathe deeply, to pull huge lungs full of painfully fresh air into my lungs. Tears streamed down my cheeks, and I clutched the whisper-soft grass in my fists, ripping the innocent vegetation out by its roots. I crammed the heels of my palms against my eyes to stop the tears from falling.

I had to figure out where the hell I was and why they left me here. Maybe they thought I was dead. Which made sense, right? Why drag a corpse through the wilderness while trying to find help? My breathing calmed. I opened my eyes and the grass fell from my clenched fists.

What the hell was I wearing?

The red brocade sleeves formed a point over my hands, the swirls of gold in the pattern twinkling in the sunlight. I jumped to my feet and looked down. Where was my Jack Skellington t-shirt, shorts and flip flops? Who the heck changed me into this Renaissance fair nightmare, and more importantly, why? I tried to think back to the plane, to what I was wearing when I woke up. Nothing had felt weird, but what I was wearing hadn't really been on the top of my priority list. Besides, what freak weirdo would change me into *this*? I glanced behind me in the direction I'd come, back to where the plane should be. Only trees stretched out behind me.

What the ...?

My feet were lead as I made my way back through the knee-high grass in the direction I'd come from, where the wreck should've been. I broke through the tree line back into the meadow. Only more meadow stretched out before me. And more trees beyond that. Fear constricted my throat. Not only had I just been in a plane crash, but now was lost, by myself, in only God knows where, with no supplies and no idea where everyone else was.

I forced myself to take in some calming breaths and assess the situation. Okay. I was alone. But there had to be civilization somewhere around here. The pilot had said something about Southern Ireland right before the crash. From what I remembered from geography class, that area was highly populated. I could probably hike in any direction and eventually come across civilization. That's likely what the other passengers had decided to do as well. Hope surged through me. Mom, Dad and Casey were probably fine and headed toward civilization right now. And when they brought help back and didn't find my body, they'd realize they'd made a huge mistake and send search crews after me. Helicopters. They had to have helicopters in Ireland, right?

With hope strengthening my resolve, I turned around and eyed the forest, determined to hike my way out of this mess. I would simply find a local who had a phone and have them call for help. I could be with my family by dinner. I gripped the hideous dress in both hands, hiking it up enough to walk unimpeded, and marched into the grass. I'd deal with whoever the nut was that thought it'd be a good idea to change the poor "stiff" into a pretty dress once I found my parents.

After what felt like hours trudging through miles of meadow and forest, my heart skipped a beat when I came to the first sign of civilization. A rustic wall surrounded rows of what looked like apple trees. My stomach growled. I scampered over the wall and my feet landed on the soft earth inside the orchard. In every direction, only more grass and trees stretched out before me. It might still be a while before I found anybody to help me, and even longer before I got any food. This time my stomach rumbled louder, sufficiently making up my mind about taking an apple or two from the orchard.

I meandered down the rows of trees until I came across a tree with a ladder propped against it. The branches around the ladder were laden with shiny blood-red apples. My stomach grumbled again as my gaze fell upon the most beautiful apple I'd ever seen. Golden light reflected off its shiny surface like something straight out of a commercial. My mouth watered as my hands and feet found the rungs of the ladder like they had a mind of their own. When the apple was eye-level, I stretched out, reaching for the perfect fruit. My fingertips brushed its glossy skin, but I couldn't get a grip on it. I stood on my tiptoes and leaned over, stretching until the apple settled firmly in my palm.

"M'lady!" a girl cried out.

I let out a startled gasp as my fingers slipped off the rung on the ladder, and then I was falling, the air rushing around me until my breath was knocked from my aching lungs when my back hit the soft ground.

4

Chapter Four

"M'lady? Are y'all right? Had a bit of a fall, y'did!" A young woman asked.

I tried to open my eyes and grimaced when the throbbing in my head intensified. A gentle hand wrapped around my arm and tried to pull me up. "M'lady?" My eyes fluttered open. The light behind the lady's head lit her hair up around her face like a halo. She looked like an angel. How many times could a person hit their head before they had permanent brain damage?

I sat up and grabbed my head to stop the spinning and wrapped my other arm around my ribs to ease the stabbing pain each breath caused. "I'm okay, I think." I blinked at her, trying to focus on her blurry face. "Did the rest of the passengers come this way?"

Realization dawned on me as her face came into focus. "Oh my God! Claire!" I scrambled from the ground and hugged her with all my might, my bruised ribs screaming in pain at the sudden movement. I didn't care. "I knew you guys had to have made it out! Thank God! Where's Casey and my parents?"

She gently eased me away, her cheeks reddening. "His lord be at the castle. Come, we must be getting you to the healer. Hit your head hard, didn't ye?" She glanced around like she was worried someone would hear and whispered: "Are ye bewitched?"

"What the heck are you talking about? A healer?" I frowned. "Why do you keep calling me m'lady?" The rest of her words filtered into my brain. "What do you mean my father? What about my mother and my sister?"

Claire quickly averted her gaze to study the ground before her. "We're forbidden to e'er speak of your mother. And you d'na have a sister."

I grabbed Claire, my fingers digging into her shoulders. "Have you lost your freaking mind? Why the heck are you talking like that? And you know I do, Claire! You were sitting right in front of us on the plane!"

Tears sprung to her eyes and she shook her head, her voice barely a whisper. "We must get to the healer, m'lady. Ill, you must be." Her eyes locked on the ground before me.

There was something seriously wrong here. I released her and let my gaze drop from hers. "I'm sorry," I muttered and stepped back. Here Claire was the first person I'd seen from the accident, and I was manhandling her. Who knows, she'd probably hit her head too and had amnesia or something. I glanced back to where I'd fallen. The ladder lay on the ground beside the trunk of a massive tree. A basket of apples lay on its side, its contents strewn about the ground. The smell of fresh turned earth and grass filled the air.

Claire nodded. "Whatever were you doin' in the orchard anyway? At your lessons, you're supposed to be."

I blinked. "What are you talking about?"

She clicked her tongue and brushed the grass off my skirt. "Auch! Her highness won't be happy to see the grass stains on your gown, and we must get you to see the healer, mind."

Yep. Definitely hit her head too. She was obviously in some sort of delusional state. Poor girl. At least I still had my sanity and I'd hit my head. Twice.

Claire brushed the grass from the vibrant fabric, and I hadn't noticed until that moment that she wore the same renaissance festival crap I did. But unlike mine, which was crimson shot through with swirls of shimmering gold, hers was a drab brown and white. *Maybe she was the nut who'd changed me?*

She grabbed my hand with her calloused one. "Come, we must get back before she notices y're missing."

I yanked my hand away. "I'm not going anywhere until someone tells me where my family is and what the hell is going on here."

She wrung her hands before her. "Please, m'lady... A beatin' I'll get if she learns y'were out here doing work I should be doin' m'self."

"Oh my God, *please* stop calling me that. Where is my sister? Casey?" I called.

"You d'na have a sister. I promise. M'la... Um. What shall I call you, then?" She toed a bruised apple with her shoe. If you could call that thing a shoe. It was brown, with laces, but looked hand-sewn.

There was so much about this situation that was so very, very wrong. "You're actually serious?" I sighed. "Fine. Victoria. My friends call me Tori."

"Aye, Lady Victoria. But I'll only call you that when we're alone. Beaten, I'd be if anyone heard me." She tugged again at my arm, ushering me towards the end of the orchard where it opened up into a lush green field.

"And my sister?"

Her wild mass of dishwater blonde curls bounced around her face when she shook her head.

I took in a slow breath and looked at the orchard around me. Golden rays of early-morning sun filtered down through the branches of the apple trees, lighting up the dust motes floating in the air like tiny fireflies. The breeze smelled fresh and clean, like apples and grass. Where was my family? Claire had to know. She didn't just climb out of that wreck by herself. Had she? Suspicion tingled along my skin. I couldn't give up until I found out what happened to them. But standing in this orchard wasn't helping me get any closer to the truth. "Fine, let's go."

We stepped under an arbor overgrown with climbing rose vines and into the meadow. The scent of roses permeated the air and mixed with the fresh scent of grass and sunshine. I closed my eyes and inhaled deeply, savoring the sweetness in the air. The bright sunlight painted my closed eyelids a bright, cheery yellow. Save for the throbbing in my head and ribs, it felt like Heaven.

My eyes popped open at the sound of Claire clearing her throat. Delusional *and* bossy.

"Come, Lady Victoria. We must hurry. Your stepmother is probably already looking for you."

I waited, expecting her to lead the way. But she stood, watching me, like she expected me to go first. I waved my hand and shrugged. "Well? Aren't we going?"

Claire frowned slightly, but still didn't move. Finally, when she realized I wasn't budging until she did, she sighed, grabbed my hand and pulled me through the tall grass. I stumbled every few feet. Hadn't they heard of lawn mowers in Ireland? "You really don't remember the crash?"

She shot me a confused look and continued to cut a path through the grass.

"Are we dead? Is this Heaven?" I felt ridiculous for asking.

She snorted. "Nay. This isn'a Heaven. At least, not for m'self." She cleared her throat again and marched in silence before me.

I frowned and matched her footprints through the grass. So much for that theory.

My heavy skirt swished against my legs as we hiked up the hill. Claire stopped at the top to let me catch up. I wheezed to catch my breath and tugged desperately at the laces that held the dress closed.

She gently brushed my hands away. "Please, Lady Victoria. D'na do that."

"I can't get a deep breath because this thing is so tight."

She rolled her eyes and knelt before me, loosening the ties a little. "'Tis a corset. And y'*always* say that."

The second the knot was free my vision cleared and I could breathe.

I gaped as I took in the white stone walls of the castle in the valley before me. It was like I stepped inside one of the fairy tales I loved. A turquoise river ran from one side of the valley to the other, passing around the castle on both sides. Scarlet flags on top of bleached-white towers rippled in the wind. Eagles soared across the sky above the castle. Little thatched-roof cottages dotted the lush green valley. Rustic stacked wood fences made up pens where sheep grazed on the thick grass.

She pointed a sun-darkened hand towards a little cottage with a colorful garden and a pen of pigs. "M'parents live o'er there in the village with m'brother Connor. I be livin' in the servant's wing of the keep."

I couldn't help but smile at the quaint little cottages dotting the hillside, reminding me of the Shire. I half-expected Claire's fictitious brother to come bounding out of the house with huge hairy feet.

The breeze ruffled my hair and sent it swirling around my face. I reached up to shove it behind my ears when my skin caught my eye. The scar on my right arm, from when the neighbor's dog bit me, was gone. In fact, every freckle, mole and blemish was gone. My flawless pale skin shimmered in the light. I held my hand out. My fingers were longer, with neatly sculpted nails. It didn't even look like my hand. I caught a lock of my hair and studied it. The pale golden strands glittered in the sunlight. It didn't look like my hair either, which was normally boring dishwater blonde on a good day. Hadn't the pastor at church said something about a person's physical flaws being erased in Heaven? I couldn't remember, but my heart did, and squeezed at the thought. Maybe I *was* dead...

"I need a mirror."

Claire moved beside me. "A what?"

I sighed. Of course they wouldn't have those here either. I wondered if my face even looked like my face.

A thundering sound approached and Claire pulled me to one side. It took a moment for me to place the sound. Bass thumping in passing cars? The high school marching band? Horse hooves? That was it! The ground rumbled and dust filled the air as the riders passed.

"You've got to be kidding me," I gasped.

"Hold!" a familiar male voice called from the center of the group.

The horses skidded to a stop and the dirt flew up around their hooves. One rider circled around and stopped before us. He slid from his horse and handed it to the other rider that approached.

My gut clenched in recognition. "Seriously?" I groaned, but my heart fluttered like it always did when he was near.

Brandon's blonde hair glistened in the sunlight and a slight smile played across his features. His grass-green gaze studied my face for a moment. "'Tis a marvelous day for a stroll, m'lady. I see you're out on another one of your adventures?" *Dear God, not him too.*

I refrained from an eye roll. *Had everyone knocked themselves senseless during the crash?* I sighed. It was easier to play along than to argue. "Tori. And apparently."

A warm smile crossed his face, softening his angular features, his handsomeness tugging at something inside me. "Would m'lady care for a ride back to the castle? I imagine her highness the Queen is anxiously awaiting your return. 'Tis nearly time for your lessons, and you know how dedicated she is to furthering your education."

"Um, okay?" I glanced at Claire, who nodded.

In the second I turned to glance at Claire, he swung back up into the saddle, then swooped me up and settled me in front of him. His strong arms wrapped around my torso and he grasped the reins.

"Claire?" I squeaked. His body pressed into mine, each ridge of his chest pressed against my back. It was hard to remember why I was so upset when every inch of my body was squished against his like that.

"My man will bring her. No fear," he purred into my ear.

His deep voice sent chills racing over my skin. I turned in the saddle. "So you're in on this too?"

A half-grin spread across his face, revealing perfectly straight, blindingly white teeth. "Fell off the ladder in the orchard again?"

I scowled and turned back around. "Actually I did."

My stomach clenched when he leaned into me a little more. His lips brushed my ear as he murmured into it. "I am pleased you're safe, Lady Victoria."

5

Chapter Five

The rumbling thunder of hooves ricocheted off the stone walls of the castle that loomed up before us. While there were only about ten riders and horses, it sounded like an army stormed the castle.

Brandon pressed the hard wall of his chest against my back and his hot breath puffed against my ear. "Welcome home."

Home. Right. Unless my parents and my sister were in there, I doubted it. I chewed my lip and gazed up at the impenetrable fortress. Thorny vines dotted with puffy white roses meandered up the white stone walls and wound their way around turrets topped with steeple-like roofs and scarlet flags. The whole place reminded me of something straight out of *The Princess Bride.*

The drawbridge's thick wooden planks rumbled as we crossed. I peered over jagged wood planks at the crystal river below. The rocks on the bottom glittered like change in a wishing well. Rainbow-hued fish darted between the shadows.

"Let me guess. You live here too," I said. Maybe we'd flown through some sort of time-space continuum rip when we were crashing and traveled back in time. That'd explain the crazy castle-horses crap, but what about Claire and Brandon? Why didn't they remember anything?

A deep chuckle rumbled in his chest. "You d'na remember?"

"I can't remember anything about this place." Boy, was that the truth.

He brushed the hair from my neck and murmured into my ear. "Aislin is *your* family home, not mine. I traveled quite a long distance to visit your father from Crell. See those mountains?" He pointed to the snow-capped mountains rising up to our left. "Crell is just beyond them."

"Halt! Who goes there?" the gate guard called.

I rolled my eyes. The next words out of the guard's mouth were sure to be "What is your name? What is your quest? What is your favorite color?" Maybe I was still knocked out cold, and this was some crazy drug-trip in the back of the ambulance on the way to the hospital.

"Raise the gate! I have returned with the prodigal daughter Princess Victoria," Brandon called.

Chains rattled and the thick wooden gate pulled up into a pocket in the wall. We barely made it beneath the door when it rattled back down and sealed with a crash. Chills raced over my skin. The sound reminded me of the plane hitting the ground when my seatbelt broke and sent me flying.

"Cold?" Brandon rubbed his leather gloved hand across my forearm.

I shook my head. His touch only made the goose bumps worse.

We crossed the courtyard and rode through a market where haggard peasants in threadbare clothes sold their various wares. The air was thick with the stench of livestock. Stray chickens scampered out of the way of the horse's hooves. I cringed when we passed a butcher's stall with freshly killed fowl and pigs hanging from strings. I searched the faces of the children playing between the stalls and in the courtyard for any resemblance to Casey, but none looked like they could have even been remotely related to her.

We stopped in front of a set of steps leading up to two of the biggest doors I'd ever seen. Brandon slid off the horse, wrapped his hands around my waist, and lowered me to the ground.

His eyes burned with intensity as he gazed at me. His sandy blonde hair fluttered in the wind and fell onto his forehead. Every inch of him reminded me more of Prince Charming than the Mr. Popularity I remembered from school.

A female voice bellowed my name from behind the closed doors. I cringed. That, apparently, would be the wicked stepmother, if this were my mind's odd recreation of the fairytales. And, if this was a dream, I just had to wake up, right? I closed my eyes and pinched the inside of my arm hard.

Claire rushed to my side and tugged at my hand. "M'lady, please! Her highness beckons!"

I glanced at Brandon.

He lifted his gaze from my arm and winced when Queen Marcilena bellowed again. "'Twas an honor to provide you with a safe escort. I pray I shall see you again soon." He held a hand out and I put my hand in his like I'd seen done in the movies. A sexy grin crossed his face and his gaze never left mine as he lowered his mouth to my fingers. His lips were soft and warm against my skin.

On Marcilena's third bellow, which had grown in pitch to more of a banshee scream, he straightened and released my hand. Then he bowed before spinning on his heel, waving for his men to follow him through a side entrance.

I didn't blame him. I probably would've avoided the scene if I could too. Anyone who could shriek like that was bound to make my life a living hell. God, how I missed my mom. Even in the face of a broken curfew, a dinged fender, or forgetting to pick Casey up from ballet, she'd never screamed at me. Not once.

A pair of jittery servants kept their eyes lowered as they pushed open the massive doors. Light spilled into the cavernous hall. The marble floors gleamed as if someone's sole job was to make sure they shined like glass. Cut stone pillars trimmed with carved wood soared above the hall into gothic peaks.

A statuesque woman stood at the base of a grand staircase. Her bodice dipped low and her heaving boobs practically popped out the top. Her tightly cinched corset followed her narrow waist, dipping to another deep V where thick skirts piled over her slight hips. Her hair was pulled back into a severe style, with pearls and velvet entwined in the braids. As she turned, her face came into view and I gasped. It was the bitchy flight attendant!

Her face was an extreme version of a heart-shape, with wide temples and cheeks, narrowing to the tiniest chin I ever saw. Out of the flight attendant uniform, she was exquisite, and while striking, the cruelty in her face would no doubt haunt many a child's nightmares, including my own. My jaw must have been dragging on the floor and I snapped it shut.

So, either all these people were having mass-delusions brought on by the stress from the crash, or I was dead or this was a dream, or I was in a coma. Most likely it was some weird delusion brought on by whatever medications they were pumping through my veins.

Her midnight eyes bored into me, but her voice was melodic and saccharine. "Princess Victoria, there you are, my dear. Wherever have you been?"

Regardless of what exactly was going on here, it looked like playing along was the least painful mode for the time-being. I glanced at Claire for help, but found I was alone. "I, um, went for a walk and tripped and hit my head?"

A growl escaped her lips. She coughed and covered her mouth with a long, dainty hand. "Of course you did. You look atrocious." Her eyes narrowed as she took in my dress. "Your father entrusted me with ensuring you become a proper lady, yet you fight me at every turn. Is it so much to ask that you attend your lessons on time and do not embarrass me?"

I opened my mouth to speak, even though I was unsure what my answer should be, but snapped it shut at her frosty glare. Apparently it was a rhetorical question.

"Go clean yourself up before your lessons." She jutted her chin towards the stairs. I nodded and breezed past her while the scorching heat of her black gaze burned into me.

She caught my arm and her cold fingers dug in painfully. "I wonder if I should prohibit you from taking walks alone. You do seem to have two left feet." Her sickeningly sweet tone slinked along my skin like worms. She caught my chin and forced me to look at her. Her thumb stroked my jawline, her eyes trailed over my face with what almost looked like envy in her dark, soulless eyes for a moment. "Such a waste." She studied my face for a moment longer, then blinked, as if realizing I was watching her. Her face tightened with anger and dropped her hand from my chin, but kept her death grip on my arm. "I pity your future husband. You shall probably die from clumsiness before you can give him an heir."

I bristled, biting my tongue at the sarcasm that rose to the occasion. My real mom would have rolled her eyes, but I could picture Queen Marcilena screaming "Off with her head!"

"I'm sorry, your highness. It won't happen again." I awkwardly curtsied, effectively escaping her pincer-like grasp.

Her eyes narrowed to slits. "See that it doesn't. Otherwise, I am sure my guard Antonio would *relish* in escorting you on your little escapades." Her heels clicked delicately on the marble as she marched across the hall.

I took the stairs two by two, or at least I tried. The stupid red curtain Claire insisted was a dress threatened to trip me with every step. I bounded around the corner and stifled a scream when a hand closed around my arm. I spun around, my arm cocked and ready to swing.

"M'lady!" Claire snapped.

"You scared the crap out of me!" I lowered my arm, a blush heating my cheeks at the thought I almost decked her. "Thanks for throwing me under the bus back there. Where the heck did you go?"

She looked confused for a moment. "Seen me with you, had she, we'd have been beaten." She ducked her head. A faint scar peeked from beneath her collar, which looked suspiciously like the lash scars they showed in movies.

"Oh." My stomach churned. Had she gotten those scars because of me? Wait – what the heck was I thinking? This obviously couldn't be Heaven. People didn't get beaten in Heaven. So I wasn't dead. So this must be a dream. A sliver of hope shot through me. If this was a dream, maybe my family was alive. And all I had to do was wake up. But how? "Can you show me where my room is?"

Claire shot me a bewildered look. "See the healer, you should. 'Tis not a good sign that y've lost your memories." She shook her head in frustration and led me down the hallway flanked by suits of armor. It felt like all the helmets turned to watch as I passed.

The pair of massive doors near the end of the hall groaned open. My jaw dropped. My 'room' was the size of our entire house. The fairy-tale like bed, complete with a canopy and curtains sat in the center of the room across from a massive fireplace. Everything was trimmed in red and gold, from the curtains to the tapestries hanging on the walls. Bright morning light filtered in through the open windows, sending cheerful rays of light across the thick carpets.

"Change you before your lessons, we should." Claire flung open the heavy wooden doors on the wardrobe and rifled through it.

"What lessons?" I peered over her shoulder at the rainbow of fabrics flowing out of the wardrobe. I sighed. Not a pair of jeans or a t-shirt in sight. Big surprise there.

"Music, dancing, needlework, languages, etiquette, reading, and political relations. But her highness said needlework and etiquette should be priority."

"Seriously?" I sighed. Even in my drug-trip dream world, I couldn't get a break from school. And there was no way any of the crap "lessons" I had to take here would help get me into med school.

Claire turned around with a pile of forest green chiffon draped over her arm and a triumphant grin plastered across her cherub-like face. "A bit of a wash up first, then I'll be helping you get into this."

She lifted her arm slightly to indicate the dress. "Now, then, how shall we fix y'hair?"

"What's wrong with my hair?" I plucked a perfect lock from my shoulder and inspected it. It was beautiful. Even in my wildest dreams, I couldn't have imagined this shade of light golden blonde. I could see the hair color companies trying to bottle this shade to sell to the masses. Though, I had a funny feeling my trademark blue streak was mysteriously absent from my perfect hair.

"'Tis proper to wear it up most of the time. Her highness is quite particular about how y're to dress at all times. Said y'must set an example for the rest of the kingdom, or some such nonsense."

I raised an eyebrow at her. Proper and I didn't get along. Even back in reality, I shunned what was socially acceptable in favor of practicality and comfort. I wouldn't say I was a tomboy, but give me a good worn-in pair of jeans and a soft t-shirt and I was happy. All this primping and dressing up was going to get old *real* fast.

With a ton of help, I managed to escape the red brocade death trap. An army of servants came in lugging a metal tub. A sigh escaped my lips when I stepped into the steaming water. The scent of roses drifted around me as I sunk into the brew. I closed my eyes and slipped under, letting the velvety water soak every inch of my hair. I sat up and squealed when a pair of hands touched my head.

"I apologize, m'lady. Gave you a bit of a scare, I did." Claire worked something lavender scented into my long hair. The self-consciousness of having someone see me naked quickly passed and I leaned back against the tub, enjoying the sensation of someone washing my hair.

My eyes slid closed and I envisioned my view of the castle from the top of the sun-drenched hill. "Tell me about how things were before Queen Marcilena married the king."

"Wish'in I could, m'lady. But I was only seven when she came into power. We're the same age after all."

A twinge of guilt twisted my gut. We both might have been seventeen, but her life of hard labor left her old beyond her years.

Her rough fingers kneaded my head and soothed gently over what felt like a goose egg on the back of my skull. "Even if I knew, we're forbidden from speakin' of the time before she ruled."

"What?" I spun to face her and water sloshed on to the stone floor.

Claire grabbed a towel and mopped up the water, avoiding my eyes.

"So you can't tell me about my real mother?" Well, my mother in this drug trip fairy tale anyway. My *real* mother was hopefully sitting beside my hospital bed right now crying her eyes out with my dad and Casey safely tucked by her side.

Claire shook her head. "Rinse."

I leaned my head back and allowed her to pour clean water over my head. She held out a robe and I stepped from the tub and followed her to a dressing table with brushes, combs, and other things I barely recognized.

I watched her in the small slab of polished metal as she slid a carved comb through my long, perfect hair. A pair of almost-familiar eyes stared back at me in the reflection. My eyes had always been a shade of smoky blue-gray, reflecting the colors I wore, which was usually black. So most of the time, they were a boring shade of gray. The eyes staring back at me from beneath a thick fringe of black lashes were vibrant blue with swirls of my old smoky gray.

My gaze followed down a perfectly straight nose, across flawless golden cheeks to a pair of full rose-colored lips. It was like I was staring at a photo-shopped version of myself. My breath caught in my throat. Would my gap be gone too? My lips parted in a half-smile, half-grimace, revealing perfectly straight, white teeth. And no gap.

"Yep, I'm definitely dreaming."

Claire shook her head and continued combing my hair. "If this was a dream, things would'na be this bad." She leaned in and whispered softly into my ear. "And Marcilena would be dead." She coughed and glanced around, like the room had eyes. "Excuse me m'lady. Had a bit o'grass in your ear, y'did." Claire's wide-eyed gaze caught mine in the mirror and I bit my lip at the fear clear in her eyes.

6

Chapter Six

It was bad enough the footman, or doorman, or whatever the heck he was called, had to announce my entrance to the room. But it was the muffled giggles that really peeved me. I was supposedly the princess, yet these girls regarded me with hatred in their eyes.

I self-consciously brushed my hands over the forest green chiffon dress Claire squeezed me into. I swear she broke the rest of an already bruised rib when she cinched the herringbone corset tight. The bodice was way too low-cut, and with each curtsy I worried I'd pop right out the top. My head throbbed from the tight coil of braids Claire pinned to my head in an intricate pattern. God, what I wouldn't give for a t-shirt and jeans right now.

I slowly made my way down the aisle, past the girls perched on either side of the heavy wooden tables. They reminded me of pampered Pomeranians at a dog show. Each of them wore a different vibrant color from the next, their hair perfectly styled, without a hair out of place. Blondes, brunettes, red-heads, all perfectly painted and each face with the same scowl of disapproval.

My stomach soured when I locked eyes with the statuesque brunette in a vibrant red dress. A self-satisfied smirk screwed up Bianca's perfect features and her blue eyes shot icy daggers at me.

Well, at least *some* things stayed the same...

Bianca's snotty voice broke through my consciousness. "Is there something you require, my lady?" I flinched at the venom that dripped from her use of the phrase "my lady".

I dropped my gaze and quickly made my way to the end of the hall, where the royal family was supposed to sit. Marcilena sat at the head of one table, and apparently, I was supposed to head the other one.

I plopped down onto the high backed chair at the end of the table. My stomach lurched when snickers erupted from around the room.

Marcilena let out an angry hiss. "Princess Victoria, where are your manners?"

I shot to my feet and glanced at her. Her porcelain features were flushed, her chest heaving at the confines of her way-too-tight bodice.

"I'm sorry, your highness?" I was clueless what I was supposed to do.

"How dare you!" she hissed. Her eyes narrowed into slits, the whites of her eyes seemed to change to black. Color stained her cheeks.

"I'm sorry?"

She nodded to the bench at her table, where one empty seat remained. A girl sat beside the empty seat in a pumpkin colored fluffy dress and sent me a sympathetic smile. Danielle? I hadn't known her very well in school, but I liked her already.

I blushed and rushed to my place, silently wishing I'd paid more attention to Claire's lecture about my responsibilities while she combed out my hair. At least she'd stopped nagging about seeing the stupid healer.

The headmistress came and sat in the seat I hastily vacated. I blushed when she caught my eye. She looked every bit as grouchy as Marcilena. With a nod, the ladies broke into groups and disappeared in different directions.

Apparently, the groups were divided by table, with each table a subject. I sighed when we stepped inside the needlework room and I realized Marcilena was the teacher for the lesson. That and the lesson would last the entire morning. I now longed for the one-hour classes at my old high school, where at least we had some variety.

The morning crawled, full of boring instruction about needlework. The only highlight was getting to spend it with Danielle. While she gave me the "are you crazy?" look when I asked her if she remembered the crash, she was the only nice one out of the twenty ladies in the hall, and she discreetly helped me whenever I was having trouble. I got the brilliant idea that pricking my finger might wake me from this dream and stabbed myself not once, but twice for good measure. I didn't wake up, but did catch a strange twinkle in Marcilena's eye when I sucked the thick drop of blood off my finger.

I was elated when we finally broke for lunch, or as they called it, the midday meal. Danielle and I walked into the dining hall where heavy wooden tables had been arranged for a grand feast. Huge chandeliers filled with candles dotted the cavernous ceiling, illuminating the room with a warm glow. I followed Danielle to her table, trying to blend into the organized chaos. But it felt like every eye in the room was on me.

Danielle looked confused and shook her head. "You c'na sit here."

"Oh." I frowned, the uneasy knot settling in my stomach again.

She shot me an apologetic smile. "'Tis not that I d'na want you to. But you know how angry her highness gets when you d'na follow her rules. Besides, someone is waiting for you." She nodded towards the main table.

I followed her gaze to where Marcilena sat next to an empty throne. My heart stuttered when I recognized Darien sitting beside her. But it wasn't the fact that he was here too, but the way he was staring intensely at me with his coppery eyes that made my cheeks flame and the bottom of my stomach drop out. I quickly glanced away. On the other side of the empty throne was a smaller empty throne. My heart leapt into my throat when I saw Brandon seated beside it.

Danielle winked. "He is very handsome. Wish I could have such pleasing company to take my meal with."

"I'll, um, see you later?"

"Aye. We have a riveting afternoon of fiddle lessons with Mistress Elandir." Danielle rolled her eyes.

I smiled. In an act of defiance, I'd insisted on taking violin lessons rather than piano when I was a kid. Hopefully the fiddle was similar enough to my old violin. Who'd have guessed an act of defiance would actually come to my rescue? "That doesn't sound so bad."

"You c'na be serious. Mistress Elandir's favorite pastime is berating you about your horrendous playing!" Danielle's dimples deepened with her wide smile.

"I might have a little surprise for Mistress Elandir." I winked. "I'll see you after lunch." I turned and headed for my table.

"After what?" Danielle called after me.

I sighed. We all might be speaking English, but we definitely didn't speak the same language.

My gaze flicked to Darien. Like a moth drawn to the flame, I couldn't help my sigh when a slight smile crossed his face, deepening the dimples in his sculpted cheeks. My stomach flip-flopped and my gaze darted to Brandon, who was also watching me intently. My skin tingled self-consciously. His green eyes widened when he saw me, matching the exact color of my dress. A smile lit up his face. He kicked his chair back and stood, bowing as I passed.

"Princess Victoria." His smooth Irish accent caressed my name, almost to the point where I forgave him for using my full name.

I smiled over my shoulder as he slid the chair beneath me. "Thanks."

"You look stunning. I love that color on you." His eyes twinkled and he raised his eyebrows suggestively.

The blood rushed to my cheeks. I grabbed my goblet and brought it to my lips to hide my blush and practically sloshed the liquid onto myself in the process.

"I appreciate her highness gracing us with her presence." The artificial sweetness in Marcilena's voice could have satisfied the sweet tooth of every diabetic in the country.

I snagged a clump of grapes and popped one into my mouth, successfully avoiding making eye contact with her. The flavor was nothing like the grapes Mom brought home from the store. It was like someone picked these fresh from the vine and put them on the table. Casey would've loved them, as grapes were her favorite. My appetite waned at the thought of my mom and sister.

Marcilena leaned across the empty throne and grabbed my arm, her fingers digging into my wrist, her voice barely a whisper. "I'd be careful if I were you."

I met her black gaze head-on. The hair stood on the back of my neck at the threat clear in her words. "You don't scare me," I lied. Mom taught me the best way to deal with a bully was to stand up to them.

Her eyes flashed with anger and indignation. She obviously wasn't used to being challenged. "Then I am not trying hard enough," she spat back.

I smiled sweetly and turned back to Brandon. The air was practically vibrating with the hostility rolling off Marcilena's slight frame. I shot Brandon, who looked like he was about to have a panic attack, an innocent smile. "These are wonderful." I popped another grape into my mouth.

He smiled weakly and handed a plate of meat to me.

I eyed the table, looking for a fork, but the only utensil I found was a dagger. I glanced around and found everyone using their hands to eat, using the dagger for cutting or poking a piece to put into their mouths. I grabbed my napkin and laid it across my lap and reached for a piece of what I hoped might have been chicken. "Thank you."

Brandon nodded and put the plate down.

It was the first chance I'd had to talk to Brandon since he delivered me to the castle that morning. I leaned over and whispered into Brandon's ear. "Please tell me you remember."

His eyes shot to mine. "Of course."

A white-hot arrow of hope seared through me. Maybe this *was* some mass delusion brought on by the plane crash and my parents were somewhere right now getting help. "Where are the rest of the victims from the plane crash? Did they try to hike out of here? Is my family with them? What's going on here? Why did you stay?"

The color drained from his face and his eyes widened. It was like I'd started speaking a different language. "I d'na understand. A plane crash?" his lips stumbled over the words, like they were foreign to him.

My heart fell. He had no clue what I was talking about. And now I had to backtrack to avoid them dragging me to the healer for being possessed. I took a deep breath and blinked back the tears of frustration that sprung to my eyes. I shook my head. "It doesn't matter. So, um, tell me about your home, Prince Brandon of Crell." I bit my lip and hoped I didn't sound ridiculous.

A chuckle rumbled from his lips. "Ah, Crell. Majestic snowcapped mountains on one side, waves crashing onto the beach on the other. 'Tis nowhere else in the world I'd rather be." He lowered his voice. "Besides here with you, that is."

I couldn't fight the blush that started at the top of my chest and crept up my cheeks. "It sounds beautiful."

"I would love to show you one day." A mischievous half-grin crossed his handsome face. He seemed to enjoy making me blush.

His grin was like a punch in the stomach. "I'd love to see it."

"Perhaps I shall petition his majesty to allow you to escort me back to Crell when I leave. You would bring your ladies, of course." He nodded to Claire, who at some point had come to stand behind my chair. Her chocolate brown eyes focused on Brandon, and I swear she sighed wistfully when his eyes caught hers for a brief moment.

Marcilena's shrill voice broke my train of thought. "That will not be possible. Princess Victoria could not possibly take a holiday without falling sorely behind in her lessons."

I turned and eyed her warily. Her porcelain cheeks were flushed, but her face was the picture of sweetness.

Brandon's face fell. "Perhaps another time then."

"Perhaps," she purred. She motioned to a guard behind her, who I guessed was Antonio. At one time in his life he might have been handsome, but it was hard to look past the jagged scar that crossed over his cheek and screwed up one side of his mouth into a permanent grimace. He kind-of reminded me of the Joker. I fought a shudder as his dark eyes trailed over me when he leaned forward to listen to whatever vile thing Marcilena was whispering into his ear. Probably instructions to stalk me. Or murder me. Or worse. Were there such things as restraining orders in this backwards place?

I chewed at my lip. Was she to dictate every second of my life? What if I never woke from this nightmare? Would I ever see my family again? Would I ever find out what happened to them? I contemplated Claire's promise that this wasn't a dream.

I turned my attention to Brandon, who was watching me with a confused expression on his face. The same expression I'd encountered so many times since I woke up in this crazy, drug-trip of a dream. It made me sad to see it on his handsome face.

I took a sip from my goblet and coughed as the wine burned my throat. I covered my mouth with one hand and whispered: "Where is the king?"

Brandon cleared his throat and brought his goblet to his lips. "His majesty seldom leaves his chambers," he whispered from behind it.

"Oh. Why?"

He eyed me like I'd completely lost it. Then he kicked his chair out behind him and stood. "Now I must depart, I have an urgent matter which must be attended to," he said with more bravado than necessary. He took my hand in his, bowed and kissed it. My stomach clenched at the contact of his lips on my knuckles. "Another time," he mouthed.

I nodded and glanced at Marcilena, whose coal-black eyes bored into mine.

7

Chapter Seven

After lunch I caught up with Danielle on the way to the music chamber. Our small group settled into our seats, beside which was something that remotely resembled a violin. Mistress Elandir was a plump old woman with frizzy gray hair piled high on her head, who reminded me of a cheerful grandmother. I wondered whether Danielle was exaggerating the woman's disdain for me. She didn't look like she had a mean bone in her body.

"Silence! Now, I trust you have been practicing since our last lesson." Her voice was a sweet as any grandmother's should be. I half-expected her to whip out some fresh-baked chocolate chip cookies from underneath the piles of blue ruffles she wore.

I stifled a giggle at the mental picture.

Her gaze zeroed in on me, and I coughed at the rage in her once cheery features. "Excuse us, your highness, do you have something to say?" Her lip curled in disgust at the title and her fist clenched around the baton in her hand, her knuckles almost white.

Maybe Danielle wasn't exaggerating after all. "No, Mistress. Something got caught in my throat."

Her eyes narrowed and her jaw clenched. "Well then, care to grace us with a demonstration of your talents? I think song from the last lesson would do nicely."

I glanced around the room at the other girls. Bianca smirked at me. I glanced at Danielle for help. She nodded towards my instrument and mouthed *play*.

I tentatively picked up the fiddle and bow. It wasn't that different from my old violin. I could do this. "I actually have a different piece I'd like to play, if you don't mind."

Surprise crossed Mistress Elandir's features before she regained her composure and nodded sternly. Was every teacher here so grouchy? I longed for my old science teacher, Mrs. B, whose goal in life was not only to help us learn, but to make us love science in the process. It was because of her that I'd decided on a career in medicine in the first place.

I drew in a shaky breath and tucked the instrument under my chin. I stretched my fingers and drew the bow across the strings. A vile noise emitted from the instrument, resembling a cat in heat. Snickers erupted around the room, but Mistress Elandir silenced them with a hiss.

Heat rushed to my cheeks. I closed my eyes, took a deep breath, and pictured the fingerboard in my mind. I was in my parent's study, my sheet music set up on a stand before me. Another deep breath. The scent of the Pledge my mom used to dust the wooden bookshelves, the old leather on the books, and the sweet, wet smell of the first days of summer filled the air.

A pang of homesickness twisted my stomach. Without opening my eyes, I drew the bow across the strings and a somber note rang out. My fingers moved on their own, easily remembering each note of my favorite song from childhood. The Aaran Boat song was somber and melancholy, kind-of like my mood since I woke up in this dream world. I could almost feel the breeze brush my arm as Casey twirled around the study in her little tutu in time to the song. I played for the song for her. Just for her.

Each note resonated deep in my soul as it sang out from the instrument. Chills chased down my skin when I drew out the last note. I sighed and opened my eyes to find myself back in the music chamber with ten pairs of astonished eyes staring at me.

Mistress Elandir's cleared her throat and blinked, as if she were entranced. "Breathtaking."

"Thank you." I set my fiddle down beside my chair, careful to avoid the eyes of everyone else. Danielle caught my hand and gave it a reassuring squeeze.

"Well ladies, you should all be practicing as hard as Princess Victoria, who apparently overnight has learned not only how to play, but play better than every single one of you. Class is dismissed so the rest of you may practice." Mistress Elandir marched out of the room.

I blinked. I suddenly had the rest of the afternoon free.

Danielle giggled quietly beside me. "That was the most beautiful playing I have ever heard."

I smiled, not sure how to respond. We stepped through the door and someone grabbed my arm and pulled me around the corner.

"Shh," Brandon whispered into my ear.

My cheeks flamed and Danielle shot me a sly smile before disappearing down the hall. I turned to face him. "What are you doing?"

"I was on my way to the stables when I was lured in by a beautiful siren song." He reached up to brush a stray hair from my face. "No surprise something so beautiful come from someone so beautiful."

The heat of my blush was enough to catch my hair on fire. "Thanks."

"Now that you are free, would you care to accompany me in a stroll through the gardens?" He studied my face, his vibrant green eyes hopeful.

My stomach flip-flopped. "That'd be nice."

He tucked my hand in the crook of his arm and led me to a side door. Our footsteps crunched as we crossed the pea-gravel pathway to get to the manicured gardens that spread before us like a football field covered in thick grass and meticulously groomed bushes. The air was heavy with the scent of fresh cut grass and orange blossoms.

Another twinge of homesickness hit. The smell reminded me of the orange grove my mom used to take Casey and me to at the end of summer to pick oranges. I'd heft her up onto my shoulders so we could get the fruit from high off the tree. Casey's laughing, freckled face flashed before my eyes, her face illuminated by the bright summer sunlight filtering through the leaves.

Brandon's voice brought me out of my memory. "Have your memories returned?"

I could ask you the same thing. I shook my head. "In fact, I'm pretty sure this is all a dream."

He cocked an eyebrow and leaned down to pick a pansy and handed it to me. "How so?"

I smiled and took the dark purple flower from him, the picture of the talking pansies from *Alice in Wonderland* flashing through my mind. I brushed the soft petals against my lip. "Well for one, we are in a castle, I'm wearing this breathtaking gown, and you look exactly like the Prince Charming I imagined from the fairytales my mom used to read to me." My face flamed at the rambling confession that poured from my lips.

"Prince who?" A chuckle rumbled through him. "Were this a dream, would you be able to feel this?" His gaze searched mine while he lightly stroked a finger down my arm. Goosebumps pricked my skin.

"Maybe..."

His hand closed over mine and squeezed gently. "And this?"

"Maybe..."

We passed under an arch in to a labyrinth made of jasmine bushes. I had the silliest urge to run through the maze.

My eyes twinkled mischievously when they caught his. "Find me."

Something flashed in his eyes and a wide smile crossed his face.

My chiffon dress rippled behind me as I dashed down one path, then another. A childish giggle bubbled from my lips and I covered my mouth to stifle the sound.

Around a corner, and another. I came to a small open area and then it was just me, the birds chirping and the warm breeze rustling through the trees. I inhaled deeply, savoring the sweetness of the air. It was so clean, untainted by the pollution we had at home. Sometimes it was so easy to forget how badly I wanted to go home.

A snap of branches behind me had me running again, giggling the entire time. I dashed under another arch and glanced behind me as I turned the corner. My breath caught in my throat when I collided with someone. Strong arms wrapped around me and kept me from falling.

"Good morrow," the guy said.

"Oh my gosh! Sorry!" I glanced at Darien, whose coppery eyes twinkled in the muted light.

He smiled, revealing deep dimples. "Tis quite all right. You can accost me anytime you wish."

His handsomeness was like a punch in the gut. But he probably was just like everyone else, with no memory of the crash. And his closeness to Marcilena had me on edge.

"We have'na been introduced. Darien of Kovanic, at your service." He bowed, took my hand and pressed it to his lips. "You are Princess Victoria, aye?" his breath brushed my hand as he spoke.

Yep, no memory of the crash. Or me, for that matter. I sighed. "Tori."

"'Tis a pleasure to meet you, Princess Tori." He straightened but didn't let go of my hand. His thumb brushed over my knuckles. "Tell me, do you often go gallivanting through the labyrinths here?"

I shook my head. "This is a first."

"Well the exercise becomes you. So beautiful..."

My skin tingled, but my head was a jumble of conflicting emotions. I pushed away from him at the sound of footsteps approaching. "It's nice to, um, meet you, Darien. But I have to go." I brushed past him and glanced back as I turned the corner.

His eyes locked with mine as I disappeared behind the bush. Neither my pace nor my heart slowed until I hit another clearing with a small rose garden surrounding a bleached stone bench.

My heart leapt into my throat when Brandon's voice rumbled in my ear. "Aha! There you are, m'lady. Now that I have found you, what do I win?"

"This." I wrapped my arms around him and laid a butterfly kiss on his cheek. At least he could chalk the blush on my cheeks up to that and not running into Darien in the bushes.

"Had I known that was the prize, I would'na have let you get so far away!" He chuckled and caught my hand when I pulled away.

I led him to the bench and sat down. "If I had a memory of this place, what would I remember of you?"

He sat down and gazed at me for a long moment before responding. "You truly believe 'tis a dream, aye?"

I nodded. The deeper I got into this world, the more I started to believe it.

He sighed deeply. "Our mothers were dear friends before Queen Katherine died. I have'na been back to Aislin since. When we were but babes, our fathers signed a betrothal agreement that we would be married when we were of age. I came to Aislin a month ago to court you." Pink flushed over his cheeks at the admission.

A knot wound in my stomach. "We have an arranged marriage?"

Brandon nodded.

"Oh." I gritted my teeth. How much of his attraction to me had been purely his duty?

He rushed to continue. "I had no plans of marrying you if you did'na want me. Arranged or nay, 'tis your decision." He nudged a rock with his toe. "The moment I laid my eyes on you, I knew no other lass would ever hold my heart." He raised his gaze to meet mine. "You are the most enchanting woman I have ever met. And your lust for adventure is unrivaled..."

I studied his eyes. Either he was the best liar ever, or he was telling the truth. "But you just met me."

He shook his head. "Nay, I have known you a month. You just met *me*."

I opened my mouth to respond then snapped it shut. He was right. Everyone else seemed to have a history with me, or at least the Princess Victoria I inhabited in this dream. No one else remembered the crash. I was the only one who was new to this world. A dream world...

"But I knew the moment I met you..."

Overwhelmed tears welled up in my eyes and threatened to spill down my cheeks. "Stop. Please." I dropped my gaze to study the crushed pansy in my hand.

"I only speak the truth."

I shook my head, the loose strands of hair falling around my face. "I'm sorry. It's just too much to absorb right now. I need some time."

"I know how overwhelming it must be –"

"Do you? Really?" I shoved off the bench and paced. "This morning we were flying across the Atlantic. All of us. You, me, my family, everyone. The plane goes down, I wake up and everyone is gone. Then I find out everyone I was with on that stupid plane is here, except my family. And no one remembers a thing about the crash but me. I have no idea if I'm dead or dreaming. I don't know what happened to my sister or my parents. And now I find out I'm supposed to get married?"

Brandon looked stunned, like I was rambling in a foreign language. He stood and pulled me into his arms and stroked my hair. "Shh, 'tis all right. I shall'na speak of it again. You have my word."

I sighed and snuggled into his chest. It felt so good, so reassuring to be held in his arms. He held me like that, just standing there, the smell of roses and warm afternoon sunshine swirling around us. I pulled back and looked up at him. Sunlight filtered through the bushes and set off the highlights in his hair, the angles of his face a little sharper, his green eyes more vibrant. He was just like I always dreamt he'd be.

And if this was just a dream, I got to make the decisions, got to tell my dream where to go from here. And at that moment, all I wanted to do was kiss the Prince Charming of my dreams. I slid my hand around the back of his neck and stood on my tiptoes, pulling him toward me.

"Victoria..." He murmured, his voice cautious.

"Please." I lifted my lips to brush his. They were soft and warm, just like I knew they'd be. This was where my dreams always stopped, where I woke up feeling frustrated and unfulfilled.

He pulled back and searched my face, his breath puffing against my lips. "Are you sure?"

I smiled and nodded, brushing his lips with mine again, this time more urgently.

His arms encircled me, lifting me into the air as he pressed his lips to mine.

"Princess Victoria!" My blood ran cold at the sound of Marcilena's shrill shriek.

I reluctantly slid down his body and spun to find a red-faced Queen seething at the entrance to the rose garden.

"How dare you!" Marcilena shrieked.

"I am sorry your highness..." Brandon started.

"Not you, imbecile. Princess Victoria! How dare you!" She jabbed a long finger in the air at me.

"How dare I what?" I snapped.

Marcilena stormed up to me and grabbed my wrist, her nails digging into my skin. Hot trickles of blood pooled where her claws pierced my flesh.

"But your highness!" Brandon argued.

Marcilena shot a glare that sufficiently silenced him. My eyes pleaded with him as she drug me out of the garden. The helplessness in his eyes said it all. She didn't stop her frantic pace, dragging me along behind her, until we reached my chamber.

She threw me onto the bed and marched back to the door. "You shall not see Prince Brandon again without an escort." She took a deep breath, smoothed her gown and hair before looking back up at me. Her voice was sticky sweet. "Princesses do not consort with men without a chaperone."

I wiped at the bloody crescent-shaped cuts on my wrist and stared at the door as it slammed shut behind her.

8

Chapter Eight

"You did *what*?" Danielle squeaked.

I nudged her with my elbow. "Shhh!"

Marcilena shot us a glare from across the room.

A giggle escaped Danielle's lips, which she tried to catch by covering her mouth with her hand. "'Tis why you missed last meal?" She whispered from behind her needlepoint hoop.

"No, she caught us and confined me to my room."

Her eyes widened.

"Don't worry, Claire brought me dinner and kept me company."

"Well, ladies, especially princesses, are not supposed to spend time with men unchaperoned anyway..."

I glared at her. "You sound just like her." I nodded towards Marcilena.

Danielle gasped. "D'na, *ever*, say a thing like that," she snapped and turned away.

"I'm sorry, I didn't mean –"

Marcilena's nasally voice cut me off. "Is something amiss, ladies?"

"No, your highness," we muttered simultaneously and lowered our faces to study the pointless needlepoint we were working on.

It was a few days before Danielle would talk to me again after that, and a week before I was allowed to see Brandon outside of the dining hall. Marcilena kept me occupied with a heavier load of classes than usual, adding etiquette and dancing to my class list. In my spare time I searched the castle grounds, trying to find anything that could give me a clue to what happened to my family, but came up empty handed.

That afternoon, during a much-needed break between music and dancing, I escaped the castle for a walk through the gardens. My fingertips brushed the prickly tops of the hedges as I turned the corner towards the labyrinth. It was the only place I could be truly alone. The crunch of footsteps in the gravel behind me brought the little hairs on the back of my neck up.

I attempted to avoid Antonio, whose leering stares made my skin crawl, at all cost. But it seemed like anywhere I went, he miraculously showed up. It was getting to the point of being stalker-creepy.

The footsteps quickened. I hefted my skirt and picked up my pace. A hand closed around my arm. I whipped around and yanked my arm from the strong grip. "Don't touch me!" I snapped.

Brandon took a step back and raised his hands innocently. "I thought you would be happy to see me outside of your elegant prison."

The blood rushed to my cheeks. "Brandon!" I threw myself into his arms and squeezed him tight. He smelled like sunshine and freedom.

A chuckle rumbled in his chest. "Now that was more the reception I had hoped for." He stroked my hair and squeezed me to his chest.

I sighed. "I'm sorry! Marcilena's kept me buried under a way-overloaded schedule. I barely have time to breathe anymore."

"I suspect 'tis to keep us apart. She has never approved of, or even acknowledged, the betrothal." He pulled back and gazed into my eyes, the color of his eyes reminding me of the deep green of the hedges in the labyrinth. A girl could happily get lost forever in either.

My skin prickled at the mention of our betrothal, but I nodded. That was exactly what she was doing. And she wasn't being very discreet about her disdain for Brandon. At every turn she insulted him, and when the insults stopped working, she pretended he didn't exist.

He pushed a stray lock of my hair from my face as he spoke. "God, how I've missed you. My days are punctuated by the bright moments when I sit beside you in the dining hall, those fleeting moments when your hand brushes mine under the table, when your eyes catch mine, your little smiles when you think no one is watching."

My blood hummed at his confession. I felt exactly the same way. Those private moments, those tiny touches, those longing looks. Seeing him was the highlight of my day. He was like a bright ray of sunshine lighting up my dreary, cloud-filled days of endless lessons.

"Tonight, after your lessons, would you care to take a ride with me?" His eyes blazed as he studied my reaction.

I sighed. "Marcilena would never let me..."

Before I could finish the thought, he spoke. "You would, of course, bring Claire as a chaperone."

My stomach fell at the thought of having to be chaperoned. I *so* missed the freedom of the real world, where every moment wasn't supervised, where I could take a moment and breathe without worrying someone heard me breathing too hard. "I'd love to."

A wide smile crossed his face, which disappeared as he studied mine. Before I could breathe, he tilted his head towards mine. His lips barely brushed mine when heavy footsteps crunched on the gravel behind the hedge.

I flew out of his arms and across the path before the person turned the corner. I tried to slow my breathing, which was difficult in the tightly cinched corset.

"Auch! There you are, m'lady. Late for your dancing lesson, you be. Mistress Belina sent me to find you." Antonio's heavy accent and deep voice made my skin crawl, like cockroaches scurrying over my arms.

My gaze met his dark one without wavering. "I was taking a walk to get some fresh air."

He raised a bushy black eyebrow, which caused his scar to deepen. "Aye, I can see that for m'self." His eyes flitted to Brandon, who glared back at him. It would have been a success if not for the blush that crept onto the sides of Brandon's cheeks.

Antonio closed the distance between us and held out a hand. "Come. I'll escort you back to your lessons."

I grit my teeth and glared at him. "No thanks."

His eyes flashed with anger and he snatched my hand. "T'was na a request."

The sound of metal scraping metal as Brandon unsheathed his sword registered only briefly over the roaring of my pulse in my ears.

I yanked my hand out of Antonio's grasp and slapped him hard across the face. "Don't you dare touch me!" His head snapped to the side and an angry red handprint flamed on his cheek.

He reached for me again and I shrugged out of his grasp and marched away. "I can take myself back to my lessons, thank you very much." My eyes caught Brandon's for a second as I marched past him out of the labyrinth. The pride in his eyes was unmistakable.

My stomach did flip-flops all through the dancing lesson. All I could think about was my upcoming ride with Brandon. My poor partner's toes must've throbbed with the number of times I stomped on them over the course of the lesson. At any moment, I expected someone to come in and carry him to the healer to treat his broken toes. Like I always said, Casey was the dancer in the family, not me. My heart twinged at the thought of my sister. God, how I missed my family.

Mistress Belina's heels clicked across the stone floor behind me. Her tiny hands grabbed my shoulders roughly and repositioned me into the proper stance for the dance. She was, with the exception of Marcilena herself, my harshest teacher. *Who would've thought that someone so tiny could be so mean?*

She swatted me on the shoulder. "Pay attention!"

I winced. The blonde boy who was unlucky enough to be my partner blushed. I bet he enjoyed my punishment. God knows how much pain I'd inflicted on him over the past hour.

We spun around the room, hopping and tapping. The dance was so complicated I tried to just match his steps, which apparently wasn't the right thing to do, considering the girls had different steps than the boys.

I bumped into Danielle, who fell against another dancer. The next instant, we were a sea of tangled arms and legs in the middle of the dance floor.

A giggle escaped my lips and I stifled it with my hands. I could only imagine how we looked.

Mistress Belina's face, on the other hand, looked like it was about to explode. "'Tis enough for today," she snapped and marched from the room.

Danielle laughed. "At least you are good at getting us out of lessons early!"

I winced. She was the only one who laughed. Everyone else glared at me. "Sorry," I mouthed and helped Danielle off the ground.

Her earlier words exploded in my head. We got out early! "I have to go. I'll see you tomorrow okay?" I lifted my skirt and dashed for the door.

"Where are you off to in such a hurry?" Danielle called.

I was already out of the room and down the hall, heading for my room when I ran face-first into Claire. "Hurry! We're going for a ride!" I grabbed her hand and towed her to my room.

"Aye?" she asked when she caught her breath.

I nodded and rifled through the closet for something reasonable to wear for riding a horse. Claire nudged me aside and pulled out a relatively sensible lightweight blue gown with a draping neckline, flowing sleeves and a built-in hood. A golden cord crisscrossed the chest and stomach in a corset-type style.

I quickly changed and Claire twisted my hair into an intricate weave, while leaving the bottom half unbound. "Do you need to change?" I asked.

"Into what?" A frustrated smile crossed her face. My gaze followed her hand as it swept over her drab brown and white dress. I'd never noticed it before, but with the exception of color, every dress she wore was the exact same.

"Oh." Guilt overwhelmed me. I had so much, while she had so little. "Do you want to wear one of mine?"

Claire's face flamed. "Nay, thank you, my lady. T'would na be right."

I sighed. Always so proper. She should be the one in this princess gown, not me. "Okay," I conceded.

I grabbed her hand and pulled her with me out of my room and down the stairs, practically flying as we launched ourselves towards the main door. *Almost there. Almost there.*

"And where are we off to in such a rush?" Marcilena asked from the top of the stairs.

What the heck, did she have surveillance cameras all over the darn castle? "Claire and I are going for a ride. We'll be back before dark." Didn't need to give her more information than she needed.

Her eyes narrowed as she descended the staircase. "Who will be accompanying you?"

I studied her earrings, hoping I could manage to say Brandon's name without blushing. "Brandon and his men. We'll be perfectly safe."

"I see. I suppose as long as you are properly chaperoned I cannot stop you..." Something about her tone wasn't right.

"Your highness," I purred and curtsied deeply.

Marcilena nodded and her dark eyes locked with mine.

I didn't give her a chance to say anything else. I turned, yanked the door open and marched into the bright afternoon sun.

Brandon's face lit up when he saw us hurrying across the courtyard. He stood beside a towering bay horse, while a dark haired, blue-eyed hottie held the reins to a palomino.

"Let's go. Now," I urged and grabbed his arm. "The warden isn't too pleased. Let's go before she sends the dogs after us."

A wide smile crossed his face and his green eyes glittered mischievously. He swung up into the saddle and settled me before him.

I blushed when his arms wrapped around my waist. "Oh! I thought we'd be riding our own horses."

"I thought this might be more of an adventure," Brandon murmured into my ear and nudged his horse to a trot.

I glanced at Claire. Without a word, Brandon's friend did the same, pulling Claire up into the saddle before him. She shot me a cautious look, her cheeks a deep magenta. Her companion was pretty hot, so I didn't blame her.

The clatter of the horses' hooves across the drawbridge matched the frantic pace of my heart as we raced for the woods. It was like I was escaping a prison. At any second someone would come charging out of the castle and demand I return at once. I glanced back at the open gate. No one emerged.

I breathed a sigh of relief and settled back against Brandon's hard chest. I was finally free, if only for a few hours.

##

After twenty minutes of hard riding, we broke through the trees and entered a grassy clearing. My jaw dropped at the elaborate ruins stretching out before us. Gothic archways wrapped in ivy towered into the sky. Intricately carved windows that, at one time, held masterpieces of stained glass dotted the crumbling walls. Trees grew through the walls, their green tops peeking over the roofline from their foothold inside the ruins.

"What is this place?"

""Twas once the grand Jocelin Abbey, now reduced to rubble" Brandon said.

"It's beautiful!"

He dismounted and helped me down. He had a glint of mischief in his eyes. "I hoped you would like them. This abbey is evidence of a better time in Aislin's history, when the fair and just ruled the land." He took my hand and led me towards the doorway.

We stepped into the abbey, which was little more than walls with no ceiling at this point. Birds nested in the branches of the trees that claimed Jocelin Abbey as their own.

I could barely hear Brandon's retelling of the history of the abbey over the Gregorian chant I could almost hear echoing through the halls. I could almost see the monks, their soft-soled sandals quiet on the ground, their heads bowed reverently, their crucifixes in their hands, the hypnotic chant echoing from their lips.

Muffled giggling from the doorway brought my attention to the present and I turned to see Claire and Brandon's friend, who I think was named Charles, stumble in, hand in hand. I caught Claire's eye and raised an eyebrow. Her face fell and she yanked her hand out of Charles'.

I shot her an encouraging smile. "We aren't within the walls of our prison. Let's just forget who we are supposed to be for now and enjoy being who we are."

Claire smiled sheepishly, a delicate blush crossing her cherub-like features. "Aye, m'lady."

"And for the love of God – just call me Tori!" Remorse washed over me at the tone I'd used. All I wanted was one moment of normalcy, one moment where I could forget this crazy dream and just be good old Tori. The Tori that didn't always do what she was told. Sarcastic, witty, obnoxious Tori.

Claire nodded and disappeared out the door with Charles.

Butterflies fluttered in my stomach when I turned to face Brandon. His green eyes smoldered. "What?"

"I wish you remembered me." He sighed. "Remembered us."

I felt the same way. But for *him* to remember. Warmth crept onto my cheeks. "Us?"

He caught my hand and pulled me to him. "I have'na met anyone like you before. Even before you lost your memory. You are such a contradiction."

"How so?"

"You are a princess, yet you d'na let your servants wait on you like servants should. You always insist on helping them with their chores, even though the queen forbids it. Like Claire picking apples, for example. 'Twas what you were doing when you hit your head and lost your memories, aye?"

I sighed. He was so convinced this wasn't a dream. And I was so convinced it was. "Don't you find that odd? That I don't act the way I was supposed to? Like maybe I don't belong here?"

His eyes pleaded with me. "You belong here. You belong with me. I could make you happy, Victoria."

I shook my head. "This is a dream. At some point I'll wake up, and you'll be gone."

My heart clenched at the pained look that washed over his features. "What if you never wake up? Would you be happy to be with me then?"

I smiled. It was a dream after all. What did it hurt to indulge him a little? "Maybe."

"Maybe I can convince you..." His voice trailed off as he tipped his head towards mine.

I gasped at the urgency in his kiss. But as quickly as his lips were on mine, he pulled away.

"Come, I want to show you something."

I followed him to a crumbling staircase. He grinned at my hesitation.

"That can't hold our weight." I eyed the staircase, mentally calculating how many feet it was to the top.

"It shall." He winked. "Trust me."

I hefted up my skirt and cautiously copied his footsteps up the stairs. Surprisingly, a little balcony was still intact at the top and looked into the valley below. The abbey was perched on the side of the hill, which I hadn't noticed until we were up off the ground. Farms dotted the grassy countryside, separated by what looked like stacked stone walls. Well, they were farms once. The houses and barns were little more than charred shells of what once stood there.

I gasped. "What happened here?"

"Marcilena."

"How?"

"When she ascended the throne, she destroyed the abbey and anyone who opposed her rule. She—"

Charles' deep voice echoed in the hollowed out abbey. "Rider coming!"

"Come, quickly!" Brandon pulled me back down the stairs. We rushed out of the abbey and ran to the horses. Brandon swung into the saddle and pulled me up before him. Charles and Claire were already mounted and racing towards the woods.

"Someone followed us?"

Brandon nodded and brought a finger to his lips. "Shh."

We stopped a safe distance away behind a thick outcropping of boulders.

"Who?"

"Antonio."

"Bastard," I seethed.

Brandon raised an eyebrow. "Such language, Princess." He frowned and kicked his horse to a gallop, back towards the castle. The thundering of the horse hooves in the damp earth echoed in the distance as we raced for the castle. It sounded like more than just two horses.

"Damn. The scoundrel pursues us!" He spurred his horse, urging him into a sprint. We darted in and out between the trees.

His breath came in quick pants against my ear as he leaned over me. "We are in danger if he catches us. He knows we were at the abbey."

I turned slightly and stared wide-eyed at him.

His green eyes twinkled mischievously. "'Tis forbidden to go there..."

The horses rumbled across the drawbridge and raced for the stables. Brandon and Charles paused for a moment to slide us to the ground and disappeared inside. Hooves rattled again across the drawbridge. I grabbed Claire and darted for the side door and flew up the stairs. Before the door to my chamber even clicked closed, I was shrugging out of my dress. Claire had another one over my head before the old one hit the floor. I toed the discarded dress under the bed and flopped onto the bench at the dressing table as my door crashed into the wall and knocked a book off the side table.

"M'lady, there you be." Antonio's words came in short gasps. He leaned over and braced his hands on his knees.

My voice was sweet as syrup. "Where else would I be?"

"You went for a ride with Prince Brandon," he panted.

"Yes, around the castle grounds. We've been back for hours." I raised an eyebrow. "And I was properly chaperoned. Isn't that right Claire?"

Claire curtseyed. "Aye, m'lady."

He bowed. "My apologies, m'lady." His eyes narrowed and I followed his gaze to the hem of my dress sticking out from under the bed. A sly smile spread across his face as he met my gaze. "Inform her highness that you are safe and sound then, I will."

My blood ran cold at the sarcasm in his voice, and it was as though icicles fell onto my head when the door slammed behind him.

9

Chapter Nine

I sat up and clutched the sheets to my chest. Muffled crying echoed through my chamber. Flickering light from the dying fire in the hearth sent eerie people-like shadows dancing across the walls. My heart thundered in my chest.

"Hello?" My voice sounded thin and weak in the twilight.

Another muffled child-like cry came from near the door. My eyes strained against the darkness, trying to make out a solid form from the shadows.

"Who's there?"

The figure by the door grew a little clearer, a little more opaque.

"Tor?" Casey's voice was barely a whisper.

Tears sprung to my eyes as I bounded off the bed and skidded to a stop before her. Her eyes were shadowed, and she wore a flimsy hospital-type gown. Tiny tubes were taped to the skin on her arms and floated around her like tiny writhing snakes. Her hand clutched at her heart. Wet trails from her tears streaked down her cheeks.

"Casey, what's wrong?"

Her mouth moved, but no sound came out. Her lips made out the words "Help me."

"Tell me what to do and I will."

She opened her mouth to speak, but instead turned her head to the side, as if she heard a noise behind her. Her face was a mask of fear when she turned to face me. "Hurry!" she mouthed.

"I'll help you. I promise! But I don't know what to do!" I leaned forward and wrapped my arms around her.

Her form exploded into a cloud of mist, which swirled into the air around me and dissipated into nothing.

I screamed and shot up from the bed with tears streaming down my face, my chest heaving against my thin nightgown. It was just a dream. Just a dream. I pulled my knees to my chest and rocked, chanting to myself as the tears rolled down my cheeks.

I had to find out what happened to my family. And in order to do that I had to wake up. I pinched myself and sighed. It hadn't worked any other time I'd tried to do that either. How was I supposed to wake up from this dream when I wasn't even sure it was a dream in the first place?

I slipped from the bed, my bare feet silent on the cold stone floor. If I couldn't wake up, at least I could find out a little more about this world that I'd woken up in. Maybe I could find some sort of clue. Something, anything, to prove to myself I was dreaming. Maybe I just needed proof that this was, in fact, a dream, in order to wake up from it.

I grabbed the candle off the table and lit it in the dying fireplace. I cringed at the deep groan the door emitted when I pulled it open. A quick peek into the darkened hallway proved it was empty. Not a soul, not even a guard.

I eased the door shut and padded down the hall. Down the stairs, past the kitchen and servant areas, was a hallway I'd passed but never been down. It seemed that everyone avoided it at all costs. Maybe they had a reason to...

The air was instantly cooler the second I stepped beneath the arch. My little candle sent a cheery yellow glow across the gray stone walls.

A far-off screech, like the call of a bird, made the hair on the back of my neck stand on end.

The stench assaulted me before I made it more than ten feet into the hall. Mold. Garbage. Raw sewage. The three melded to into a nauseating mixture that had my stomach churning. Maybe this was just where they disposed of the castle garbage. They had to do *something* with it, right?

I spun on my heel and took one step when a muffled pained scream came from behind me. My eyes widened as I spun to search the darkness. No doors, just a long, stinky hallway.

The second scream, this one sounding more like someone was having their fingernails pulled off, one at a time, had my feet flying beneath me as I raced towards the noise.

The further I moved down the hall, the louder the screams got. At first, it was as though a person was being tortured. But with each footstep, it was like another voice joined in the chorus of terror. There had to be a hundred people here somewhere, begging for mercy, screaming out in pain.

Spurred on by pure adrenaline, the hallway ended before I could stop my feet. I ran face-first into the end of the tunnel. The stone held fast, giving me one hell of a headache. I searched the wall for a hidden door, a hidden button to push, anything. There were no doors, no windows in the long hallway to nothing. Nothing. I held my ear up to the stone, trying to pinpoint the source of the screams.

And then all sound stopped. But the stench of death and decay remained.

I have no idea how long I stood there, frozen, breathing in the noxious fumes of death, waiting for the screams to start again. Nothing but silence met my ears.

Had I imagined the entire thing? Maybe I'd been sleep walking?

The chill from the cold stone seeped into my body, and my teeth chattered. I wrapped my robe tighter around myself as I made my way back to my room. What the hell had just happened? What was that hallway used for? And why didn't it have any doors?

I closed and triple checked the lock on my door before settling back into my pillows. But sleep wouldn't come. I stared at my window until the gray light of morning filtered in through the warped glass.

##

It was the first day I'd had off since waking up in this dream world. But instead of enjoying the freedom, my feet dragged as I wandered aimlessly through the castle. My lack of sleep from the nightmares and the sleepwalking had taken their toll. I passed the hallway and chills raced over my skin. Unlike last night, two guards stood flanking the hall.

I ducked behind a column when a haggard kitchen servant passed me carrying a basket of bones and half-eaten food from the breakfast feast and approached the hallway. His trembling was almost pronounced on his bare-bones frame. His features were contorted with fear as he passed between the guards and disappeared down the hallway. Neither guard acknowledged him.

I sucked in a deep breath and marched towards them. I held my head high as I approached the guards, whose gazes flicked to each other warily before locking with mine. They made no move to stop me.

I tore my gaze from them and searched the hall for the peasant, who was mysteriously absent from the long hall, the light fading before it reached the end.

The metallic clank of spears crossing snapped before my face just as my foot crossed the threshold into the hallway.

"Sorry m'lady, c'na go that way," The guard to my right said, his eyes locked on something across the room.

"Because?" I tried to keep the suspicion from my voice.

"Her highness the Queen's orders," the other guard replied. His gaze, like the other guard's, was locked on something across the room.

I moved before the taller, red-headed guard, whose face seemed to flush at my proximity. "Why?" I whispered.

His hazel eyes shot to me before locking back on something across the hall. "C'na say m'lady. We have strict orders to only allow the peasants carrying the garbage access to this hallway."

The other guard spoke up. "Why'd ye want to go down into the garbage chute anyhow?" I glanced at him, and his dull brown eyes were locked on my chest.

"Why are you guarding a garbage chute?"

His eyes flicked to mine for a moment, and his face contorted with fear. "D'na ask questions ye d'na want the answers to m'lady."

"But I *do* want the answer." I sauntered over to him and brushed against his shoulder. "What's down there?"

His eyes locked with mine, his words little more than a whisper from his lips. "Hell."

"There you are, Princess Victoria!"

I spun around at Danielle's cheery voice. "Hey Danielle."

She slipped her arm into mine. "I have been searching for you everywhere! I need to buy some new scarves for my mother. Would you like to accompany me to the market today?"

I glanced back at the guard, whose gaze was locked on the point across the room again. But the flush on his cheeks was still there.

"Sounds like fun," I said half-heartedly.

We wandered through the courtyard toward the market I'd seen when I first arrived at the castle. Colorful tents were set up in rows, reminding me of the little farmer's market my mom bought her produce at on the weekends.

The pungent aroma of livestock filled the air as we neared the market. Bony peasants wearing threadbare clothes with hollow cheeks peddled their wares as we passed, holding out their various merchandise, bolts of cloth, bundles of beets, little beads on strings.

Danielle brushed them away like you would an annoying fly. I smiled at each and said "no, thank you". Their faces fell like a child on

Christmas morning after discovering they received no presents. *Would their families go hungry?* I dug in my heels.

"What are you doing?" Danielle asked when she realized she'd lost me.

"Shopping." I pulled out the little sack of coins that Claire had given me. It was the equivalent to an allowance, apparently. I had no use for it anyway.

I marched back to the first stall to the haggard elderly woman with the bolts of cloth. She could barely hobble off of the folded blanket on the ground.

I held out my hand to stop her. "Please, don't get up. Here." I bent over and pressed four golden coins into her withered hand. "Feed yourself and your family."

Tears sprung to her dull white-blue eyes. "Thank ye, m'lady." A toothless grin spread across her face, and her eyes almost got lost in the wrinkles.

"You're welcome."

I stopped by each stall and pressed a few coins into the hands of each person I passed.

A pregnant woman, who looked so weak she could barely speak, hoisted herself up off of the ground and wrapped her bony arms around me and whispered in my ear. "Thank ye. Ye remind us so much of yer mother. The world was a better place when she ruled."

"Estancia!" An older man hissed.

"Oh hush ye old coot. She should know how much we loved her mother."

He grabbed her roughly by the arm and shoved her back onto her blanket. "Yer going to get us all killed. Or worse, if she hears ye!" The fear was thick in his voice.

I reached for the pregnant woman, as if I could somehow protect her. Danielle clutched at my arm, but I waved her off.

"Princess Victoria! We must go. *Now*!" Her voice was strained with fear.

The clatter of wagon wheels and pounding of horse hooves against pea gravel filled the air. I turned just in time to see two of the ugliest, burliest little men driving a cart that looked more like a prison cell on wheels than a wagon. They looked more like trolls than men.

"The traders!" The pregnant woman gasped and clutched her stomach protectively.

"The what?" I asked.

Danielle grabbed my shoulders and shook me. "Slave traders. We have to go. *Now.* You d'na want to see this."

I shrugged her off and jogged to catch up with the wagon. I glanced back at her. Her face was flushed beet-red, her eyes wide with fear. I waved at her to follow, and she shook her head an emphatic "No".

"Now!" I mouthed. I could almost hear her swallow the lump in her throat as she stood frozen, watching me with wide eyes. Then she dashed forward and hid behind the cart beside me.

We kept out of sight behind the wagon as it turned the corner where it opened up into another courtyard. I'd never seen this one, as it was hidden behind the castle between two of the towering turrets. I'd never had a reason to venture to this part of the castle before, and now I knew why.

In the center of the courtyard was a rectangular platform with what looked like hitching posts. I gasped. Instead of horses, the platform held people. Close to twenty kids were chained to the rings. The oldest one couldn't have been much older than me, but the majority were around Casey's age. If Casey had been here, could she have been one of these kids, sold away to slave traders?

A burly guard marched up to the wagon and the deep timbre of his voice made my stomach churn. "How many will ye purchase today?"

"We shall see." The man driving the wagon replied.

We ducked into the shade of one of the turrets and watched from the shadows. The men inspected each child, checking their teeth, their muscles, their eyes, like they were livestock.

"What are they doing?" I whispered.

"Slave trade. When someone c'na pay their taxes, their children are sold as slaves to pay off the debt." Danielle whispered.

"Why didn't you tell me about this?"

She shrugged. "'Tis always been this way. You know that."

"Who ordered this?"

Her confused and terrified eyes caught mine. "Who else? Marcilena."

I opened my mouth, but no words came out. I had no words for the horror I was watching before me. My blood froze in my veins when the next words fell from the evil troll-like slave traders.

The other troll man finally spoke up, with his nasally voice. "We'll take them all. Thirty coin."

I clutched the bag of coins in my hand. Did I have enough to outbid them? I stepped from the shadows and shrugged away from Danielle's clutching fingers.

I called out in my most authoritative voice. "I'm sorry, but these children are not for sale."

A hushed gasp echoed through the square as the crowd parted to let me pass. By the crowd's terror-filled, tear-streaked faces, they had to be the parents of the children being sold.

"Ye c'na do that," the burly guard called.

"I am Princess Victoria. And I *can*." I shook the coins in my bag and watched the guard's face shift from anger to confusion.

"Whatever the little priss will pay, I'll double it." The troll man spoke. I marched up beside him and stared down at him. He couldn't have been more than five feet tall on a good day.

I gritted my teeth. "I said: these children are *not* for sale."

"Listen little whore, I d'na care who ye are. Slave trading is a *man's* business. And no woman will stand in the way of man's business."

His words stung like bee stings on my face. "Listen to me, you evil little troll. You will not touch a single hair on these children's heads, or I promise you, you'll have to pee sitting down for the rest of your ugly, miserable little life."

He staggered back like I'd physically hit him. "Little bitch." His hand snaked out so fast I was unable to dodge his fist when it connected with my face and sent me crashing into the platform. Tears pricked my eyes and my cheek throbbed.

He nodded to the guard. "Get them into the wagon."

The children's frightened wails filled the air as they were drug across the platform. I scrambled to my feet. "Stop!" I screamed and ignored the throbbing in my cheek.

"Not enough of a lesson for you, eh?" The troll snarled. His sword sung from his scabbard and he leveled it at me.

Fear snaked up my spine and I held my breath. The crowd hushed and the guard paused in loading the children into the wagon.

The vile little man sneered and took a swing at me with his blade.

I didn't have time to get out of the way. I clenched my eyes shut, bracing for the blow. But instead of the searing pain of his blade slicing through me, a metallic clank near my neck made my eyes fly open.

"You dare swing your sword at a lady, and a princess no less?" Darien's angry voice rumbled beside my ear.

"She was interfering with the trade. I was just teaching her a lesson," the little man sniveled, his eyes wide with fear as he took in all six-foot-four-inches of Darien's large frame.

"Perhaps she is'na the one who needs to learn a lesson." Darien's blade arced through the air and the little man deflected the blow, practically falling backwards in the process.

Darien kept up the attack, landing bone-jarring blow after blow on the man's sword. With a well-aimed thrust, he knocked the troll-man's sword from his hand and pinned him to the ground, the tip of his blade pressed against the man's jugular.

"Please, sire, I was'na going to hurt her. I swear," the pudgy man sniveled. Tears welled up in his bulging eyes, his pudgy cheeks rosy from the exertion of deflecting Darien's blows.

Darien's words came out slow and measured. He hadn't even broken a sweat in the duel. "Apologize to the lady."

The man's bulging eyes darted to me. "Sorry, your highness."

I glared at him. An apology wasn't going to set things right.

Darien's copper eyes caught mine. "Are you satisfied?"

I shook my head. "Not until every child is freed."

He nodded to the guard. "Do as the lady asks."

"Ye have no right..." The guard's baritone voice grated on my nerves.

Darien pushed the blade a little harder against the troll's throat, forcing him to let out a pained shriek in response. "Do as she asks. *Now.*"

"Aye, sire." Oddly, the guard's face looked almost relieved when he nodded and started unchaining the children. One by one they ran to their parents, who cried and clutched them in their arms.

"'Tis intolerable," the fat little troll man squealed, reminding me of the pigs I'd seen in the market earlier. If only he was the one trussed up and hung to dry.

The slave traders shot me loathing looks as they loaded into their empty wagon and rumbled from the square. Cheers erupted from the peasants and they swarmed around us. Little arms encircled my waist. What felt like hundreds of kisses on my hands and cheeks. When the crowd eased, I slumped onto the platform and rubbed my throbbing cheek.

"That was amazing," Darien murmured and sat beside me as the crowd began to clear from the square.

I sighed. "It was worth it. I had no idea such horrible things were going on here."

His gaze traveled over my face, and he winced when he saw what I was sure was a hand print on my cheek. "You will make a fair and just queen someday." He brought a gentle hand to my injured cheek and soothed it gently.

I shook my head. "Hopefully I won't be here long enough for that to become a reality."

He cocked an eyebrow and shot a quizzical look at me.

I dropped my gaze to the crushed stone at my feet. "You wouldn't understand."

His hand caught my chin and lifted until I met his gaze. Something inside me lurched to life, like my heart started beating for the first time.

"I would like to," he murmured.

I opened my mouth to respond, but was cut off by a loud call from the side entrance to the castle.

"Darien of Kovanic, her highness the Queen requires your presence at once!"

A pained look crossed his face and his hand dropped from my chin. He held my gaze and bowed deeply before spinning on his heel and marching towards the door.

My skin tingled where he had touched me, while my thoughts churned.

##

My footsteps pounded the stone as I marched towards the King's chambers. His negligence had gone on long enough. Either he didn't know about the slave trade happening in his kingdom, or he didn't care. Either way, I was going to give him a piece of my mind. Besides, I had to find out if Casey was among those kids sold off. And who knows. Maybe he knew where my parents were too.

I turned the corner and skidded to a stop. A burly guard flanked either side of the massive door. Not lanky like those who stood guard everywhere else in the castle, these guys looked like they were slipped steroids. Or given an I.V. line of them directly into their bulging pumpkin-sized biceps.

I swallowed my fear, squared my shoulders and marched forward, my eyes locked on the heavy oak door.

They didn't say a word to me when I stepped up to the door. It wasn't until my hand closed over the cold metal latch that a burly hand snatched my wrist. The huge meat-paw clamped down so hard bones popped in my wrist.

The thug who held my wrist captive spoke, his baritone voice vibrating the space between us with authority. "No one is allowed to see the King."

"According to who?" I glared at him and tried to yank my hand free, but he held fast with his death grip.

"Her highness, the Queen. No one sees the King without her permission."

My eyes narrowed as I sized up the mental capacity of the muscle-bound monkey. I yanked my arm again, still to no avail. "The Queen sent me, you idiot. Let. Me. Go."

The jerk grunted and glanced at the other guard, who chuckled. "Doubtful."

The overwhelming urge to kick him in the balls was almost too much to bear. But I had the feeling that if I tried it with the hand-sewn slippers I was wearing, the only thing that would result was a few broken toes. He probably didn't have any balls anyway. Weren't all muscle-bound guards eunuchs anyway?

I squared my jaw and glared at him. "I demand to speak with my father at once. Step aside, jerk."

The guards straightened and cleared their throats, and for a moment I thought they were actually complying.

Marcilena's nasally voice filled the hallway. "What's this all about?" Her heels clicked on the stone as she sauntered towards us.

I turned as much as I could with my wrist still captive. Her eyes flicked between the guards and settled on the guard's hand on my wrist, a satisfied smile stretching across her usually stoic face.

"M'lady wants an audience with the King. Told her she had to ask you."

She nodded and her beady black gaze locked with mine. Her sticky sweet voice dripped with irritation when she spoke. "Why do you need to see the king?"

"You know why."

A half-hearted chuckle escaped her. "I assure you I have no idea why you need to see the king. But nonetheless, he has been ill and needs his rest. *No one* shall disturb him."

"If he's ill, there's even more reason for me to see him."

She shook her head, the tightly coiled rolls of black hair swinging from the movement. "Nay."

"Has he seen a doctor?"

Her eyes narrowed. "The healer? Of course he's seen him."

"When can I see him?"

"When he is well."

"When will that be?"

A un-ladylike growl rumbled through her and her perfect porcelain face screwed up. "Enough. Get out of my sight."

I wrenched my wrist from the brute's grip. "If I can't see the King, who *should* I talk to about the slave traders I just sent packing? Or the supposed trash chute that screams come from?"

Her snow-white complexion reddened, and I wondered if her face might actually explode. I smirked at the mental image of her head exploding.

She took a few calming breaths, the crimson in her face fading slightly. "'Tis none of *your* concern."

I opened my mouth to argue, when her next words stopped me cold.

"And I would be careful about poking your nose where it doesn't belong, or you might suffer the same fate."

She had all but admitted everything. My blood tingled at the cold indifference in her face.

"Now. This is the last time I will tell you: get out of my sight. And if I catch you trying to gain an audience with the King again, the consequences will be severe."

My teeth ground against each other. "Fine. But I *will* see the King, sooner or later."

Marcilena spun on her heel and stomped towards the stairs. Barely audible, she muttered "That's what you think."

10

Chapter Ten

The door crashed shut behind me as I marched into my chambers. My heartbeat thundered in my ears. Anger thrummed through my veins while I stomped from one end of the room to the other.

Screw her. Screw Marcilena and screw this whole, stupid dream.

I flopped back onto my bed and let out a long breath. With each passing day here, I'd allowed myself to become complacent, to just play along until I either woke up, or the rescue helicopters descended on this insane renaissance fair recreation. But if this wasn't a dream, why hadn't they come? It'd been weeks. The rest of the survivors had to have gotten to civilization by now. Why wouldn't they have sent search parties out to look for us?

So, maybe this really was a dream. Time elapsed differently in dreams, right?

I had to find the crash site. I just had to. I had to prove to myself that this was a dream. Once I was convinced it was a dream, it should be easy to wake myself up. And if this wasn't a dream, there had to be evidence of a search effort at the crash site. Maybe there'd even be investigation and clean-up crews still there. That always took weeks, right?

I sat up and retrieved a cloak from the wardrobe. I'd have to be quick to sneak out of the castle unnoticed, but I might be able to pull it off. I bit back a smile, having finally formed a plan to get myself out of this insanity. Either way, I'd give myself piece of mind knowing either that this was a dream, or that everyone was having one hell of a mass-delusion.

The door creaked as I eased it open. Stupid door. My feet were silent on the stone as I tiptoed toward the stairs. It was a little ridiculous trying to escape from a castle in the middle of the morning, but I didn't have a choice. Today was my only day off from Marcilena's princess boot camp. It was my only chance.

I held my head high and marched through the main hall, striding purposefully toward the door past bustling servants. No one took a second glance my direction as they scurried around doing their work. Perfect.

I ducked through the door into the bright morning sunshine and cringed at the crunch of the pea gravel under my feet. I kept to the shadows the wall cast across the path and walked as quickly as I dared without looking conspicuous toward the drawbridge. My heart sunk at the sight of the armed guards flanking the gate. They'd never let me through. The deep green of the meadow and the forest beyond beckoned to me from the other side of the bridge.

The sound of wagon wheels rattling across the gravel behind me gave me an idea. I tucked myself back against the wall in the shadows when the vehicle passed. My nose wrinkled at the stench drifting over me from whatever was in the back, but it didn't matter. I grabbed ahold of the splintered wood and swung myself into the hay-strewn wagon and ducked down behind the rails.

"Hold!" the guard called.

I held my breath and prayed the sound of my frantic heartbeat wouldn't be audible to the guard, who I could hear just on the other side of the rail.

"What do ye haul?" the guard asked.

"Kitchen scraps for the heap," a haggard, scratchy voice replied from somewhere above my head.

Footsteps approached the back of the wagon. I was about to be caught, trying to escape in a pile of garbage.

"Move along."

A whistle and the clattering of horse hooves and rattling of wheels over wood was like music to my ears. I let out the breath I was holding and instantly wished I hadn't. The meager breakfast I'd eaten of toast suddenly threatened to come back up. The stench coming from the pile I was hiding beside filled my nose. I tried not to look too closely at the pile as I struggled to breathe and peek out from between the slats in the side. As soon as we were a safe distance away, I jumped from the wagon, not caring what I landed on, just grateful to escape the horrendous smell.

I turned to watch the wagon disappear down the trail when something dangling from the back of the wagon caught my attention. A limp, and very blue, human arm.

I had never been more grateful to have eaten so little for breakfast. After evacuating my stomach from its meager contents, I wiped my face and turned toward the forest. I had to get off this road.

I tried not to think about the arm as I weaved into the forest, trying to retrace the path I thought I had taken when Claire led me to the castle the first time. But I couldn't push the sight from my mind. The peasant driving the wagon had said he was hauling kitchen scraps for the "heap". But the stench, and the obvious contents of his wagon, were definitely not kitchen scraps. So why had he lied? Where was he going, and who was the unfortunate person who he was transporting? My mind flicked back to the "garbage chute". Could that have been what the guard was trying to warn me about?

Acid churned in my stomach as I stumbled through the grass, which seemed to grow and snake around me like it was alive.

A snap behind me brought me back to the present. I scanned the trees around me, searching for anything that looked like a human figure, which was hard, because all of the trees seemed to look and feel like people watching me.

I pulled my cloak around me and picked up my pace. The trees thinned and light filtered down through their branches in golden rays, dotting the forest floor with little circles of golden light. They reminded me of little golden coins, laid out before me as if a leprechaun had spilled his pot of gold on his way from the end of the rainbow.

I snickered at my train of thought and grinned triumphantly when the wall of the orchard came into view. I'd made it, at least part of the way, to the crash site. I picked up my heavy skirts and ran toward the orchard, my eyes scanning the forest around it, trying to pick out something that might have felt familiar.

I skidded to a stop when, out of the corner of my eye, something darted between the trees. I squinted toward where I saw the figure and it stepped from the trees and into a ray of light.

My heart stopped beating in that moment. Her chestnut hair tumbled about her face and shoulders in tousled waves, her white t-shirt and shorts dotted with pink flowers. Her pink tennis shoes sparkled in the light, the glitter and rhinestones twinkling like tiny diamonds. She smiled at me, her dimples deepening in her freckled cheeks, her chocolate eyes wide with surprise.

Tears of relief burned my eyes. "Casey!" I gasped. I reached out for her, expecting her to disappear into mist like her vision had done in my dream.

She giggled and darted into the trees to her left.

"Casey, wait!" I shouted and hefted my skirts to my hips and raced after her.

I followed her giggles, catching glimpses of golden sunlight reflecting off her chestnut hair as she raced through the forest. "Casey, please! Wait!" I called out. My lungs burned as I raced after her, her giggles drifting farther and farther away.

I slowed, my gaze searching the darkening forest around me. The trees were much closer together here, blocking out most of the sunlight. The grass was thicker and I trudged through it like I was treading water. "Casey!" I called, my voice a hoarse whisper.

"Are you lost?" A deep voice rumbled from the forest to my right.

"Did you see her?" I asked, out of breath from my chase. I turned towards Darien's voice to find him standing a few feet away from me with a pack slung over one shoulder, a bow over the other.

He raised an eyebrow over those heart-meltingly gorgeous copper eyes. "See who?"

I closed my eyes and fought the tears away. "My sister." I whispered.

"You are the first person I've run into in these woods today, m'lady."

I opened my eyes and studied him for a moment. "Why are you playing along with this?"

"Sorry?" He took a step back.

"This whole act. The renaissance festival role playing act. Why?"

He blinked like I'd slapped him. "I d'na understand."

I sighed. "You don't remember the plane crash." It wasn't a question. No one remembered but me. But my glimpse of my sister, in the clothes she'd been wearing when we crashed, made me hope I wasn't dreaming.

He shook his head, tentatively, like he wasn't sure what he was denying. "What are you looking for out here, m'lady?"

I marched past him, deeper into the darkening forest. "The crash site. I know it's here. I just have to find it."

Darien stepped into line beside me, picking his way through the deepening grass, all the while keeping up with my pace. "I'll aid you in your search, if I may. I pray it provides you with the answers you're searching for."

I eyed him warily. "Why?"

He kept his eyes on the forest before us while he contemplated a response. "Dangerous beasts lurk in these woods, m'lady." He flicked his gaze toward me for a moment, and quickly returned it to the forest. "And seeing the desperation on your face when I came upon you a few moments ago broke m'heart. 'Twould be an honor to be of assistance, if I may."

I opened my mouth to respond, but snapped it shut when nothing coherent came to mind. I settled for walking in silence beside him.

For what felt like hours, we picked our way through the deep grass, winding between the trees. I couldn't stop myself from sneaking glances at him every now and then. He silently walked beside me, keeping me company, more or less, without the need for words. He probably thought I was crazy anyway. I was starting to wonder myself.

Our eyes caught and I missed a step, nearly tripping over the yards of fabric that Claire insisted was a dress. I found my footing and looked up to find myself on the edge of a meadow.

I gasped. "It was here!" My eyes darted around the empty meadow, searching for any sign of the crash. Broken branches, squished grass, scrapes along the rocks, anything to prove that this was the site of the crash.

Darien stepped into the clearing "What was?"

"The crash! It was here! Where'd the plane go? I know it was here. I remember this meadow!" I darted to a fallen tree and pointed an accusatory finger at it. "I tripped over this when I tried to hike out!"

Darien's gaze scanned the clearing. "I d'na see anything out of sorts, m'lady."

I collapsed to the ground, clutching my knees to my chest and sobbed. "It was here. I'm sure of it."

Darien knelt before me and pulled my hands away from my face. He studied me with his coppery eyes full of concern. "I am so sorry you d'na find what you were searching for."

I blinked away the tears and stared at him. "This really is a dream, isn't it?"

He shook his head. "Nay, 'tis not a dream."

I sighed. He might not think it was a dream, but now I was sure of it.

11

Chapter Eleven

The long walk back to the castle didn't strike me as it had the first time I'd been brought to Aislin's walls. Each step away from the barren field where I was sure the plane had crashed was like someone was snipping away at my hold on the real world. Maybe they were right. Maybe I *had* hit my head and *I* was the one who was delusional.

I didn't want to go back. But I didn't have a choice. I didn't have anywhere else to go. My feet grew heavy as we trudged over the wooden drawbridge.

The hair on the back of my neck bristled. Antonio leaned against one of the pylons by the gate, a smug smile plastered across his scarred face.

Great. If Marcilena didn't like me walking through the labyrinth with Brandon for a few minutes alone, she was just going to love my day-long adventure with Darien in the woods.

"Darien," Antonio nodded at him as he passed.

I frowned and glanced at Darien, who kept his gaze locked on the gate.

Antonio didn't say a word to me as I passed, which, for some reason, felt way more threatening than any threat he could've spewed at me.

We stepped up onto the steps leading to the main hall and I nodded at the guards flanking the doors. As always, they ignored me. Darien caught my hand and raised it to his lips. He didn't say anything, simply held my gaze as he brushed his soft lips across my knuckles. My cheeks warmed as I watched him, mesmerized by the muted sunlight reflecting off the gold flecks in his eyes. His gaze said what he couldn't because of the guards. He was sorry. I nodded, a slight smile pulling at the corners of my lips. He straightened and released my hand. I watched him retreat to the stables before turning to face what I was now convinced was simply a dream-induced purgatory.

Oddly enough, Marcilena didn't say a word to me at dinner. I'd expected her to jump at the opportunity to rip me a new one for visiting the abbey ruins, or the confrontation regarding the slave traders. But what bugged me the most was that she hadn't mentioned my escape from the castle, which I was positive Antonio had reported back to her that I had done, considering our interaction on the bridge. So, I was still on edge when I made my way to my first lesson the next morning. The cool morning air was stagnant in the needlework room as we settled into our seats.

"'Tis time to learn a new skill." Marcilena sauntered to the center of the room, pointedly avoiding my gaze. She stopped beside some sort of thing-a-majig that kind-of looked like a steering wheel to a boat without the handles sticking out.

"This, ladies, is a spinning wheel. We use it to make thread from wool." She rambled on about the duty of the ladies to keep their husbands clothed, blah, blah, blah. I *so* wasn't listening. There was no way I was going to make my husband's clothes. Hopefully I wouldn't be stuck in this dream long enough to need that skill.

"Now I have given you the basics, let us have someone come up and demonstrate." My stomach lurched when her beady black eyes locked on me. "Princess Victoria, considering you gave Mistress Elandir such an exceptional demonstration last week with the fiddle, perhaps you shall have a breakthrough with this too."

"No, thank you, your highness. I'd rather give someone else a turn to go first." I rambled.

Her eyes narrowed. "I insist," she snarled.

I swallowed the lump in my throat and stood, grateful Claire had put me in a less cumbersome dress. The lightweight crushed velvet and off-the shoulder design was so much easier to breathe in than the other stuff she usually squeezed me into. But the long, flowing sleeves might cause problems with that wheely thing, considering I *had* paid attention when it started spinning.

If she was going to act like nothing had happened between us, I could too. I refused to show my fear as I curtsied deeply before crossing the room to the spinning wheel. My skin tingled as my fingertips trailed over the large wheel. I sat down on the stool and tried to remember what Marcilena had shown us. If only I'd been paying attention.

I took a bit of fluff from the basket and twisted a little into my fingertips and stuck it into the machine. I gave the pedal a gentle tap. The contraption sprung to life, the huge wheel turning around and around. I smiled triumphantly when the material spun into a thin line of string. I pulled a little more out of the basket and fed it into the machine. It was strangely hypnotic, the sound of the spinning, the slight rocking from depressing the pedal.

Just when I thought I was getting the hang of it, the fluff lumped together and flew into the machine. I lunged forward to grab the lump and my arm yanked into the wheel, the crimson of my long flowing sleeve tucked around the spinning parts.

Stifled snickers echoed around the room. I tugged on my sleeve, but the machine wouldn't give it back. Tears of embarrassment stung my eyes as I tugged in vain. Danielle rushed up to help me get unstuck.

"Well Princess Victoria, it seems you have gotten yourself all wrapped up in your work." Marcilena sneered.

Boisterous laughter erupted from the other girls. Danielle gave a final tug and I was free. I jumped up from the stool, tipping it over in my haste, resulting in another round of hysterics. My heartbeat roared in my ears and my cheeks blazed as escaped the room, my train billowing out behind me.

I skidded around one turn, then another, bumping into warm bodies with distorted faces, tears blurring my vision to the point where I couldn't see at all. I turned the corner and raced for the stairs. Before my foot could make purchase on the first step, the infernal dress of shame tangled around my leg and I landed face-first on the stairs. The startled gasps around me brought on a fresh round of tears. I sobbed into my arms, crumpled against the staircase.

It was all too much to handle. My missing family, the poverty, the slavery, what I was sure was a torture chamber, a stepmother who loathed me, the other girls, who, given the chance, would stab me in the back. Or laugh in my face. I wanted out. I had to get out. *Please, wake up.* Desperate sobs shook my body, and I had no control over myself to stop them.

Strong arms wrapped gently lifted me into the air like I didn't weigh a thing. I didn't look up, just buried my face in his chest and cried. His scent of cinnamon and cloves encompassed me like a comforting blanket. His chest wasn't overly muscled, just enough that I could feel the hard ridges against me. He easily took the stairs with me in his arms, a door opened and closed, and before I knew it, I was lowered onto a soft bed.

I didn't want to open my eyes, to see the pity in Brandon's face. But my eyes fluttered open when a big, soft hand gently brushed my hair from my face.

My heart skipped a beat when I found Darien, not Brandon, gazing at me with nothing but concern in his gaze. Flecks of copper and gold glittered in their depths. There was no evidence of a smile etched on his face, no crinkles at the corners of his eyes. His forehead was creased with concern. His lips parted slightly, like he might lean in for a kiss. I sucked in a shuddery breath and waited.

His deep voice broke the silence. "Are you all right, m'lady?"

I nodded, and wiped my eyes with my hands.

"Are you injured?"

"Just my pride."

"I am glad." He blinked and stammered, "I mean, I am glad you are uninjured, not that your pride is bruised."

I shot him a watery smile. "I know what you meant."

His eyes locked with mine and my stomach did that crazy clenching thing it did when I first met him in the garden. He cupped my face with one hand, brushing away the tears with his thumb. "Who brought these tears to your eyes?"

"A spinning wheel."

"I see." His face was so close, his body pressed against mine.

God. I wanted this amazingly hot guy I barely knew to kiss me. My body ached for him. "What do you see?"

"A breathtaking woman who does'na know her own strength."

My heart clenched. "Breathtaking?"

He nodded. "Every time you walk into the room, 'tis like someone punched me in the chest and I c'na breathe."

The air sizzled between us. It felt like I was the one who was punched in the chest.

"Oh," I murmured. *Kiss me. Please, for the love of God, kiss me.*

I watched his lips as he leaned towards me. He paused right before his lips touched mine.

His breath brushed my lips as he spoke. "Ask me."

"Kiss me," I commanded.

His soft lips were hot against mine as he obeyed. He tasted like he smelled: spicy, exotic, intoxicating. I sighed against his lips when he shifted to lie over me, his hands cupping my face, his lips dancing across mine.

I wanted more. God, how I wanted more. Tentatively, I traced his lips with my tongue. A growl rumbled in his chest. Something ached deep within me when his tongue invaded my mouth. My arms slid around his shoulders, desperate to get closer. He just wasn't close enough. I caught his lip gently between my teeth and tugged.

"M'lady," he warned against my lips.

"Tori," I corrected and brushed my lips against his.

His eyes darkened. "Tori," he growled.

"Darien," I sighed and pulled him back to my lips. His kiss was everything Brandon's wasn't. Wild, fierce, uninhibited, unrestrained. Like he wasn't holding back. I wasn't even sure he could. Or that I wanted him to.

Chills raced through me when his fingers traced over the bare skin on my shoulder. I slid my tongue into his mouth and my hands slipped under the hem of his shirt. My fingers inched over his stomach. Corded muscles flexed beneath my fingers.

He grabbed my hand and let out a shuddering sigh. "Cease." His eyes, darkened with desire, pleaded with me.

I sighed and pulled my hands from his grip. I guess he *could* hold back if he wanted to. I didn't say a word, just returned his gaze and panted to catch my breath.

He shifted off me and got up. "Lord, Tori. You drive me to insanity."

I nodded. He was right. We couldn't do this. Besides, what about Brandon? The picture of his green eyes blazing before he kissed me flashed before my eyes.

Confusion washed over me. I was falling for both of these guys. *What the hell am I doing? Who am I?*

My heart almost jumped out of my chest when a soft knock sounded at the door. "M'lady 'tis Claire. Do you need my assistance?" she murmured through the door.

I cleared my throat and stared at Darien wide-eyed. I got a week in lock down for innocently kissing Brandon in the garden. What would happen if I got caught making out with a guy behind closed doors in my bedroom? On my bed?

"Yeah, I'm fine. Thanks, Claire. I just need some time alone okay?" I called.

Darien smirked.

"Yes, m'lady. If you be needin' anything, let me know." Her retreating footsteps sounded down the hall.

I let out a shaky breath and glanced at Darien, who was tucking his shirt back into his trousers.

He shot me a half-smile and crossed the room. "I should leave." He leaned down and kissed me on the cheek.

I watched him disappear out the door and the latch quietly clicked closed behind him.

I flopped back on the pillows and brushed my still-tingling lips with my fingertips. Had I really let Darien, a guy who I barely knew, kiss me? Even in the real world, we'd barely spoken two words to each other.

But God, he was so hot. And on three different occasions, he'd helped me without any promise of a reward. The slave traders. The forest. Downstairs. My stomach churned at the thought of having to face those people in the dining hall at lunch. I wanted to dissolve into the air, to fly out the window and never have to set foot in the same room with those people again. I caught a strand of my honey-blonde hair and twirled it between my fingertips. I could stay in my room for lunch and compose myself before I endured my music and dance lessons. Or, I could take the rest of the day off and suffer the consequences of my actions later.

A proper princess would go down to lunch, endure the muffled giggles and stares with a smile, and continue on with her day as usual. But I wasn't a proper princess. While I tried like heck to be Princess Victoria, to be what they want me to be, deep down I was just Tori.

I inhaled in a deep, fortifying breath and sat up. It was almost like I was forgetting who I was before this dream. Fear snaked around my spine and cinched tight. What happened if I completely forgot who I was? Would I be trapped here forever?

I slid off the bed and hit the floor running. I threw open the door, raced down the hall, down the stairs, through the great hall and burst out the front doors. My feet crunched on the pea-gravel road as I ran, following the same path I took yesterday when I escaped the castle.

My heart lurched when I neared the gate and drawbridge, both open, beckoning me to make my escape. This time no guards stood watch. I hefted my skirts higher and raced out the gate. My feet pounded against the wooden drawbridge as I dashed for the other side of the river. *Almost there.*

Something rumbled across the drawbridge behind me. I didn't look back. I didn't want to see who was coming after me to take me back to my elaborate prison. I couldn't do it anymore. I just couldn't. I couldn't fit myself into their mold. I couldn't be who they wanted me to be. I was a round peg trying to fit into a square hole. The more they pounded, the more the wood splintered from my peg. Soon I'd be nothing more than a pile of slivered wood.

I clamored up the grassy hill where I first saw that fated castle what felt like ages ago. The scent of grass and sunshine overwhelmed me like it had on the day I woke up in the orchard. It smelled like freedom.

The orchard! That was the one constant thing since I woke up in this dream. It was where it all truly started, where I met Claire for the first time. Maybe if I could get into the orchard, I'd wake up. In the distance the climbing rose-covered arch invited me into the orchard. I could make it!

"Victoria! Wait!"

My stomach churned at Brandon's frantic voice in the distance. I seriously didn't want to see him right now. Not with the taste of Darien's kiss still fresh on my lips.

His voice spurred me to run faster and I ducked under the arch into the orchard. A ladder rested against a tree. But it wasn't the tree I'd fallen from. My gaze darted around the orchard as the sound of horse hooves approached. About halfway down the line of trees, one stood out in a ray of dusty sunshine. It was like an omen or something. I grabbed the ladder and took off for the tree.

Smacking my head into the back of the seat in front of me was what made me end up in this place, maybe something similar would wake me from this dream. I propped the ladder against the tree and scampered up.

Brandon ducked under the arch. "Victoria! What on earth?"

"Leave me alone! I'm done with this dream!" My hands landed on the top rung of the ladder. *Should I jump or simply fall backwards? What happened if I didn't wake up? Did they have emergency rooms in this time? Would I crack my head open and die? What happened if you died in a dream?*

A perfect, ruby-hued apple glittered before my face, distracting my rambling train of thought. It was the prettiest thing I'd ever seen. I reached for it, but was too far away. My mouth watered to take a bite of it. I reached again, leaning out a bit further from the tree, one hand barely holding on to the ladder.

My center of gravity shifted as the ladder tipped away from the tree. Somewhere in the back of my mind I heard Brandon's terrified cry as the air rushed past me. A smile spread across my face as the ground rushed toward it. I was going finally going to wake up, finally be able to go home.

Instead of connecting with the hard ground, a pair of strong arms caught me. The air whooshed from my lungs when I collided with his rock-hard chest. Dazed, I gazed up at him.

Brandon's furious eyes searched mine. "Are you mad?"

I blinked. "What?"

He shook me, as if trying to shake the sense into me. "Are you trying to kill yourself?"

Was I crazy? "Huh? Of course not. I was just trying to wake up."

"You have to cease this. 'Tis is not a dream. You could've died!" The rage was barely restrained in his voice. His body trembled and he clutched me to his chest.

"It is a dream. I know it, I just have to try—"

"Nay! I cannot listen to any more of this!" He put me down and grabbed my chin roughly with his fingertips. "This is real!"

My heart clenched at the ferocity in his words, the intensity of his gaze as he lowered his lips towards mine. Before I could think, his lips crushed mine with the same ferocity I felt in his words.

"What is going on here?" Darien's voice shot ice water through my veins. I turned away from Brandon's lips and looked towards the entrance to the orchard, where Darien stood panting. His eyes shot daggers at Brandon.

"None of your concern," Brandon growled.

"Maybe the lady can answer." Darien raised an eyebrow.

"I..." I stopped. I wasn't sure what to say. My emotions roiled inside of me like a storm-tossed sea. I didn't know what I wanted. Who I wanted.

"I said, 'tis none of your concern. Go back to your post as Marcilena's lap dog," Brandon snarled and heaved up off the ground.

I didn't see them reach for their weapons, but the scraping of metal on metal echoed in my ears as they simultaneously unsheathed their swords.

Darien cocked his head to the side. "She is not yours."

"Not yet." Brandon swung towards Darien, his thin sword arcing through the air and the clank of metal hitting metal filled the orchard.

"Not ever." Darien countered with both words and a swing of his own.

"Stop this!" I shrieked, but my voice sounded ragged and puny beneath the clattering of swords.

They danced across the uneven ground, the sunlight reflecting off their swords, sending ricochets of light flashing across the orchard like lighting. They dodged between the trees, narrowly missing each other's blades. They were playing for keeps. Someone was going to die.

Brandon's heel caught a root sticking up out of the soil and tumbled onto the soft earth, his sword bouncing across the ground a few feet away from him. He scrambled for it but stopped short when Darien's blade pressed against his neck.

"STOP!" I screamed.

Darien's coppery eyes locked with mine. My stomach clenched at the intense desire that rushed through my body at the thought of how his eyes smoldered when he kissed me.

"Please," I whispered.

A twinge of something crossed his face and he turned back to Brandon. "No one owns her. Ever." He sheathed his sword.

His eyes caught mine as he passed. "No one owns you. Remember who you are."

My breath caught in my throat at his words and a warmth of realization trickled through me.

In one movement, Brandon hauled himself up, snatched his blade from the ground and lunged at Darien's back.

I didn't have time to think, only to act. I dove for Darien's sword, unsheathed it and brought it up behind him just in time to connect with Brandon's blade.

Brandon's vibrant green eyes widened when he saw me holding the sword against his.

"It's over," I commanded.

His face fell in defeat and he sheathed his sword.

I handed Darien's sword back to him. His eyes flashed with pride as he took the weapon. "Thank you," he murmured and slid his blade back into its sheath.

I nodded.

He shot me a half-smile and disappeared behind the climbing-rose archway.

I turned back to Brandon. "I'm sorry."

"Nay, don't be." His jaw clenched as he watched Darien's retreating form.

"It's not a contest, you know."

His eyes shot back to me, studying my face, as if he didn't recognize me for a second. "You are wrong, Victoria. And I, apparently, am losing." Without giving me a chance to respond, he marched out of the orchard.

12

Chapter Twelve

Brandon's slumped shoulders disappeared around the corner of the orchard wall. Why did things have to be so complicated?

I scrubbed my face in frustration and paused. On the ground before me, in a glowing ray of sunlight, sat the perfect, shimmering apple. I picked up the fruit and studied it, turning it over and over in my hand. It was the apple from the tree, right before I fell.

I raised it to my lips, closed my eyes and sunk my teeth into its ripe flesh.

I wasn't sure what I expected to happen when I took that bite, maybe for the world to spin as I collapsed to the floor like Snow White? I didn't know. But other than the intense flavor of unadulterated apple and the clear, sticky juice running down my chin, nothing happened. I took another bite and munched thoughtfully.

Well, the orchard thing hadn't worked in helping me wake up. My heart twisted as my sister's freckled face flashed before my eyes. I had to figure out a way to get back to my family. But how?

Darien's words echoed through my head as I meandered back towards the castle and contemplated how to escape from this dream. "Remember who you are." I had to hold onto those words. But first, I had to deal with the heap of trouble I'd be in for missing my afternoon classes. That was a given. Just how much trouble I was in was a frightening thought.

Obviously I couldn't wake up, at least not using the same method in which I ended up in this dream. And apples, apparently, were out too. So what did I have to do to wake up from this dream?

My stomach churned when I approached the drawbridge and found Antonio leaning against the pylon. Again.

"You know, in my world, that's called stalking."

Confusion flitted across his scarred face for a moment before he recovered. "The queen is waiting for you."

"I would imagine she is." I marched past him.

He caught my arm and tugged me to him. His breath was hot on my ear. "Caution, little Princess."

"I don't know what you're talking about." I shrugged out of his grasp. "Don't touch me."

"I think you do." He held up his hands in a defensive gesture. "She is in her sitting room."

I didn't respond and stomped across the weathered wooden bridge into the castle.

With each step, a blood cell in my body turned to an ice cube. My heartbeat was so loud by the time I reached the sitting room I couldn't hear my hand connect with the wooden door when I knocked.

"Enter."

My stomach dropped to the floor. I was going to throw up. Each time she'd used that saccharine, sickeningly sweet tone of voice, I'd ended up in *serious* trouble.

I pushed the door open and entered into the room. It was like stepping onto the set of a renaissance period movie. Gold and crystals dripped from every surface that wasn't covered with an expensive, deeply hued tapestry.

Marcilena sat on a golden couch and raised her chin slightly at my approach. Her black eyes stared unblinking at me.

I curtseyed low before her. "You wished to see me, your highness?" I tried to inject my voice with the same artificial sweetness she was trademark for. You can't catch flies with vinegar, Mom always said.

Her eyes narrowed slightly. "You missed your lessons today."

I flinched, but didn't get up. "Yes, highness."

"Why?" She actually made it sound like she didn't know, but wanted to.

"I was too ashamed to show my face before your highness's grace." I swallowed the bitter taste that filled my mouth as the lie fell from my lips.

She paused. She actually paused. "I see."

I could feel her eyes on me, as if she was trying to decide how best to punish me. Her nasally voice broke the silence. "Very well."

My gaze shot to hers. After everything that had happened, I expected house arrest, or boiling in hot oil, or the racks or something. Maybe shove me down that garbage chute. But not "Very well." I eyed her skeptically.

Her face softened slightly and her saccharine-sweet voice was back. "I have planned a ball. In three weeks."

"Your highness?" I started to ask why, but I knew she wouldn't tell me.

An innocent smile played across her icy features. It looked artificial, like those mannequins in the windows at the mall, their faces permanently frozen in a weird smile-grimace. "Come now. You are practically a daughter to me, and I have not had a chance to properly debut you at court."

I blinked. "Um, thank you, your highness."

"'Tis all." She nodded towards the door.

I bowed my head and hauled myself off the floor, stifling the urge to run as I glided from the room.

"Oh and Princess Victoria?" she called out.

My hand stilled on the door handle.

"Next time you try, you better plan on succeeding."

The air sucked from my lungs as her words hit me flat in the chest. I closed the door behind me.

##

Danielle gaped at me as we strolled arm and arm through the meticulously manicured garden. Mistress Elandir was ill and so our class had been canceled. I felt bad for being happy she was sick, but the chance to talk to Danielle out of the earshot of the walls was a relief. "Wait, explain to me again how you managed to kiss *both* men on the same day."

"I didn't mean to. It just sort-of happened. I'm *so* confused." Since the day I made out with Darien on my bed and Brandon and Darien's swordfight in the orchard, my emotions had churned over and over until I was a frothy, confused, irritable bitch. For that reason, I pointedly avoided both guys at all cost. I had to get myself in a better frame of mind, make some decisions about who I wanted to be with more, before I faced either of them again.

Danielle nudged me. "Why did you not tell me about this sooner?" Her hazel eyes flashed as she studied my face. There was something under the surface, something I couldn't quite put my finger on. But something was off.

"Because the walls in that castle have ears, and this is the first chance I've had to get you alone."

"Oh." Danielle resumed her ambling pace down the freshly shorn grass path, her curvy hips swaying with each step.

"What's wrong?" I matched my pace with hers.

"Nothing." She didn't meet my gaze. "I understand how you would be confused, having both throw themselves at you like that."

I blinked at the slight tinge of venom in her words. *Was she jealous?*

She finally brought her gaze to mine. "Which one do you prefer?" Her eyes were slightly bloodshot, like she'd been fighting off tears.

"I'm not sure." I sighed. "It doesn't really matter though. At some point I'm going to wake up and this whole crazy dream will be over."

Danielle sighed and rolled her eyes. "You really should cease speaking in that way, or they are going to lock you up for being bewitched. 'Tis already muttering amongst the hags about you being a witch."

I nodded. "Hags" was the term we coined for Bianca and the ladies in our classes. Apparently, they were my ladies in waiting, but they never waited on me. It was more like they wanted to take my place. Each was wicked in their own way, constantly teasing Danielle for being overweight, or making snide comments toward me about being the 'favorite'.

At one point, Bianca called me out in the middle of dance class, saying I bewitched the men with some sort of spell. Bitch-slapping her for calling me a witch earned me an entire day of chamber-arrest. But it was *so* worth it.

"Well, you know Bianca desires Brandon. 'Tis why she is so horrid to you. She would do anything to see you fail so she could step up and take your place."

I snorted. "I know. There are a lot of people here who would like to see me fail."

Danielle skidded to a stop and spun to face me. Her eyes locked with mine. "Not I."

"I know." I smiled and wrapped my arms around her, squeezing her tight. "You're one of the few true friends I have here."

"Well I am sure if you would cease saying this 'tis a dream, less people would avoid you."

A strangled chuckle escaped my lips. "I kind-of like people avoiding me."

"Well, then, by all means, continue!" Danielle laughed and tucked her arm in mine again.

I sighed. I'd come to love the friendship I'd developed with Danielle and Claire, and they filled the void in my life Casey left behind. I'd miss that once I woke up.

My chest clenched at the thought of my sister. This place could make me forget I was dreaming, but one thought of Casey brought reality crashing down on me. Tears burned my eyes and my stomach soured.

Danielle must have sensed my change of mood because she took my hand and pulled me through the garden. "Come, let us play a game of garden chess."

I blinked back the tears and let her lead me through the garden to the giant chessboard. Twelve-inch stone squares were strategically placed in a checkerboard pattern across the grass. Giant chess pieces carved out of some lightweight stone were set up before us, white and black.

I smiled at the familiar set-up. Finally, one game I could succeed at here. "I'll take white."

"Very well." Danielle exaggerated a sigh and took her place behind the black line. "White goes first."

I eyed the board, then Danielle, trying to decide on strategy.

"Well, well, look what we have here, a battle of wits between two beautiful ladies," Brandon murmured from behind me.

My eyes widened and I glanced at Danielle. She hadn't even warned me of his approach. There was something in the way she was staring at him, the blush that crept to her cheeks as she watched him. Something close to jealousy seized my stomach.

"Better than a battle of wits between a man and a woman, for surely the man would be a sore loser." I marched to my pawn in the center of the board and moved it up one space.

"Oh, really." He crossed the garden and stopped beside Danielle. "Might I take this round?" He gestured towards the rows of black chess pieces.

Her cheeks flamed and she curtsied. "Not at all, sire."

I chewed my lip at the charming smile he shot at her, the way his eyes lingered too long on her. I cleared my throat. "Excuse me, can we play please?"

Brandon laughed, his eyes twinkling. "Allow me to ponder my move, fair lady." Rather than moving one of his pawns, he brought out the big guns, moving his knight out over the top of the pawns.

He raised his eyebrow and nodded towards the giant board. "Your turn."

I narrowed my eyes and calculated the next moves. I hefted up another pawn and moved it right in line to capture his knight if he didn't move it. I smiled slyly and nodded to the board.

He smiled and moved the knight, easily snaring my pawn in the process, but leaving himself open to lose it. I smiled triumphantly and captured the knight.

"You haven't seen anything yet," he murmured, and over the next several moves took many of my high-powered pieces.

I glared at the board and mentally calculated the possibilities of my next move. It appeared I was losing. I couldn't lose. Not to him. Not when my pride was on the line.

I closed my eyes and pictured my dad's fingers on the ivory chess set in our living room. What would he have done?

I could hear his deep, smooth voice in my head. "This is casting. It's the only time you can move two pieces on the board, and can be a very powerful move if used correctly."

I pushed aside the twinge of homesickness, opened my eyes and studied my remaining pieces. It was perfect. I grabbed the rook and moved it three places over.

Brandon grunted.

"I'm not done yet." I went back to the king and moved him three places over, to the other side of the rook. "Checkmate."

His eyes widened as he examined the board, trying to figure out a way out of the checkmate. A frustrated smile stretched across his face. "Where did you learn that?"

I smiled triumphantly. "My father."

He bowed in defeat. "Well, then, I must ask the king for some chess lessons before I take you on again."

My heart sank. "Not the king," I snapped. He still didn't believe me. No one believed me.

His brow furrowed in confusion. "What do you mean?"

"You know exactly what I mean!" With that I marched past a bewildered Danielle and out of the garden.

13

Chapter Thirteen

My heart thumped to the beat of hooves on the wooden drawbridge as our horses ambled across them. It was the sound of freedom. Well, sort-of. I glanced back at Darien, who had been given the task of escorting Danielle and me on our journey to Danielle's house, a half-day's ride from the castle through the Eastern woods.

Somehow Marcilena missed the fact that he'd helped me release the slaves and it was his sword that had actually sent the slave traders packing. I wondered what the consequences would have been had she found out. I shuddered at the thought.

"You *cannot* be cold already. 'Tis barely fall!" Danielle gasped.

I shook my head. "I'm fine." I didn't mention the fact that back home in Phoenix, anything below seventy-six degrees was considered cold. I was sick to death of the "she must be crazy" looks I got from everyone.

"Good. I cannot wait for you to meet my parents and my brothers. This will be so much fun!" A secretive chuckle escaped her lips. She leaned over and whispered into my ear. "And without battle axe Marcilena supervising your every move."

It was my turn to chuckle. I quickly glanced back at Darien, and sure enough, he'd caught the entire exchange.

I sighed. "Not entirely free of supervision, though, I'm afraid."

Danielle lifted her chin towards Darien. "Oh, him? He's harmless."

"How so?"

"Did he inform on you about the slaves?"

I shook my head. "But he was involved. He couldn't do that without hurting himself."

"He could have. But did not. Do not worry so much. Look at him. I would be willing to wager you could strip naked right here and ride in the buff and he'd not tell a soul. Would you, Darien?" Danielle batted her eyes flirtatiously at him.

The metallic taste of jealousy filled my mouth. My eyes widened at the realization and my cheeks warmed as I turned to glance at Darien, whose cheeks were a nice shade of pink. *Was he blushing?*

He nodded his head reverently. "Your secrets are safe with me, m'lady."

"I bet she told you to say that." I spun back in my seat to hide my flaming cheeks from the thought of riding naked before him.

"I may be bound to serve Marcilena, but my honor knows no master."

I nodded, but didn't turn to face him again. Bound. He was bound to serve her. My stomach soured a little as I turned scenario after scenario in my head. Ultimately, nice guy or not, he was bound to Marcilena.

We passed through the small village I'd seen from the hill my first day in Aislin. Tiny thatched roof cottages dotted the green hills. Sheep, goats and cows grazed freely on the abundant grass, their stomachs bloated from overindulgence.

The same could not be said about the peasants living beside them. Most scurried inside at the sound of riders on horseback, but those that stayed to watch us were little more than skin and bone. Children barely old enough to walk teetered on too-skinny legs, their threadbare clothes hanging from their skinny bodies.

Danielle held her head high, her eyes locked on the forest before her. I wondered if she even noticed the poverty around her, if she didn't care, or if she felt helpless to do anything about it. I glanced at Darien from the corner of my eye. His pouch was in his lap and his hand worked quickly to fling coins from it as he passed. My hand caught my own pouch at my side. I slipped the cord free and flung the entire bag to a family with too many undernourished children to count.

"Bless you, m'lady!"

I blinked the tears away and nodded at the woman. Even with my new knowledge of the slave trading that happened within the walls of Aislin castle, I had no clue of the severity of the poverty inflicted on these poor people. My heart ached. I was so preoccupied trying to find out what happened to my family that I never noticed the horror of life for the peasants under Marcilena's rule. While finding them was still at the forefront of my thoughts, now I also felt the overwhelming desire to somehow help the people of Aislin.

We left the village behind and entered the dense forest, dodging thick-trunked evergreen trees as we ambled towards Danielle's home. I tried to push the mental picture of the starving peasants from my head as we picked our way through the forest since I couldn't do anything for them at the moment.

Before long, the trees thinned and Danielle's family manor came into view. Between a pair of manicured lawns separated by a huge pond, a two-story manor rose up to meet us. The horse's hooves crunched on the pea gravel road that led to the building. We slid from our horses and handed their reins off to a stable hand who came out as we approached. The house doors flung open and dogs and people came pouring out.

"Danielle!" a female voice called through the chaos and I turned to see a plump woman about my mom's age gather Danielle into her arms. My heart wrenched. What I wouldn't give to feel my mom's arms around me right now.

"And this must be Princess Victoria." Danielle's mom turned her hazel eyes on me. The love and kindness in their depths made my heart ache, desperate for just a taste of maternal comfort in all this craziness. "Come here, child," she murmured and pulled me into her plump arms, enveloping me in the warmth of her love for just a moment. I closed my eyes and imagined it was my own mother hugging me. I lost myself in the feeling and tears of longing filled my eyes.

I stumbled back and mumbled an apology.

Her dimples deepened with her smile. "Do not be sorry. With a stepmother like yours, I assumed you were in need of a good motherly hug."

I blinked. Was I that easy to read?

Danielle laughed and caught my hand. "And this, Princess Victoria, is my father."

Danielle's father looked like the red-headed version of Santa Claus, complete with the red beard and the bowl full of jelly belly. Even his chuckle had a bit of the ho-ho-ho quality. I smiled and wondered if he had a bag full of presents somewhere with a pair of ruby slippers for me. Maybe I could triple click my heels to get home...

I curtsied. "Nice to meet you, sir."

He bowed slightly, as much as his belly would allow. A smile, as warm as Danielle's mom's, stretched across his rosy face. "My Danielle here tells me that you abolished the slave trading in Aislin."

My stomach lurched. Was Danielle's family involved in the slave trade? "Yes, sir?" I said tentatively.

He laughed and pulled me into his arms and squeezed me tight. "I am so glad of it! Someone is finally willing to stand up to that evil witch."

Danielle's mom gasped "Harold! Hush!" She glanced around the courtyard as if the bushes had ears.

He released me from his hold and eyed his wife. "Oh, Bessie. Don't tell me to hush. These are my lands. Her henchmen aren't welcome here."

Bessie inconspicuously shifted her eyes in Darien's direction. "Of course you were just jesting."

Harold choked and cleared his throat "Of course, all in jest."

I glanced at Darien, who stood a few feet back from the group. His features remained stoic as he nodded his acknowledgement of Harold's misstep.

"No fear," he said and bent to pet the dog sniffing his boot.

Harold coughed and pulled my hand into the crook of his arm. "Come, I want you to meet my sons."

I tore my gaze from Darien and studied Harold's face for a moment. "Of course." I allowed him to usher me towards a group talking amongst themselves.

Danielle launched herself into the group and laughter echoed through the courtyard. I smiled even as homesickness twisted my gut. If only I knew what happened to my family...

"Princess Victoria, I would like for you to meet my sons. Arden, my eldest." He pointed to the oldest, who had to be at least twenty-six, if not older. He bowed, his red-brown hair falling into his dark eyes as he bent.

"Ethan, the next eldest." He nodded to the flaming red haired man next to Arden, whose vibrant green eyes reminded me of Brandon's. But his features were out of proportion, his freckled nose being a little too big for his face. He gave a slight inclination of his head to acknowledge me.

"Mason." He nodded to the brother with his arm slung around Danielle's shoulders. He had deep burgundy hair and eyes an exact copy of Danielle's. His cheeks reddened a bit as he nodded to me.

Harold reached out and ruffled the littlest brother's copper hair. "And this little hellion is Aiden." Aiden's cheeks reddened and he swatted at his father's hand.

"Can I go now father?" he whined.

I forced myself to smile over the lump in my throat. Aiden had to be the same age as Casey. Even his whiney tone reminded me of Casey's before we got on the plane. A twinge of guilt twisted my stomach. If only I had been nicer to her. If I really was dead...

"Wait!" I gasped and knelt before Aiden. "Have you recently met a little girl who kind-of looks like me, but she's your age and has chestnut hair and brown eyes?"

The fear in the little boy's face had me back-tracking. His eyes flitted from Danielle to Harold and back. Danielle bent over and whispered something into his ear. He shot her an incredulous look and shook his head. "Nay, m'lady."

I glanced at Danielle but she was avoiding my gaze. Had she told him to tell me no, when he *had* seen Casey? Or that I was crazy and to ignore my rants? Doubt swirled in my mind like fog, thickening until I could barely see the ground in front of me.

Harold patted my hand. "Come, now. Let us go have our midday meal, shall we?"

I inhaled a few deep breaths and my surroundings came back into focus, the panic subsiding a bit. I nodded and looked at Darien. His brows furrowed with concern as he studied me.

Before I could blush, Harold and Bessie ushered us into their great hall, which was already set up for the midday meal. I smiled and murmured my thanks to the servant who held my chair for me. His face wasn't sunken like the peasants living outside of Aislin's walls were. It was obvious that Harold and Bessie treated their servants a lot better than Marcilena treated hers.

Darien sat beside me and Danielle took her seat across from me, her four brothers taking up the rest of the chairs. Danielle's parents took their positions at the head and foot of the long table.

My mouth watered as the servants brought out plate after plate of meat and cheese and vegetables. I took a few pieces, but my appetite diminished as guilt tingled through me at the thought of the starving peasants outside of Aislin. I put my dagger down and put my glass to my lips.

"Not hungry?" Harold asked.

I shook my head. "It's hard for me to stomach eating like royalty when there is so much suffering in Aislin."

Harold nodded and set his own dagger down, pushing his plate away from him. "You really are your mother's daughter."

"Harold!" Bessie gasped.

Harold's eyes shot to Darien, who nodded along with him.

"I agree with you, sire," Darien murmured. "Aislin has seen nothing but pain and suffering since Marcilena took the throne."

I studied Darien's face. Up until this moment I thought I knew where his allegiance lay. Now I wasn't so sure. He could've been instructed to say what he had to in order to pull information out from us. Or he could be sincere.

Harold nodded. "That be the truth. Regardless of where *your* allegiance lies, a person would have to be blind to not see what is there in front of them, and an idiot to not acknowledge it."

The gauntlet had been thrown.

Darien nodded and stood. Bessie stuttered an apology, but Darien silenced her with his hand. "Nay, hear me. I shall allow you to enjoy your feast without fear of persecution. Speak of what you may. I will leave you. And fear not. Nothing I have heard thus far shall ever leave my lips."

He turned to me, caught my hand and raised it to his soft lips. His words were spoken against my hand. "Stay as long as you wish. Summon me when you are ready to leave and 'twould be my honor to escort you back to Aislin."

"Please don't go," I whispered.

He pulled his lips from my hand and a half-smile stretched across his face. "Summon me when you are ready."

And with a quiet click from the door he was gone.

Chaos erupted in the following silence.

"Harold!" Bessie snapped. "What have you done?"

Chairs toppled backwards and clattered to the floor as Danielle's brothers shot up from their seats. Their shouts drowned each other's out until it was merely a chorus of angry male voices in the background.

Danielle's shrill shriek silenced everyone. Six pairs of astonished eyes turned to the mild-mannered Danielle where she stood perched on her chair.

"Enough! Nothing was said that Darien could take back to the queen, even if he wanted to!" One of her brothers, Arden, I think, helped her down from the chair. "Listen. Every soul in the kingdom knows that things are worse since Marcilena took the throne. Her lackeys included." She paced to stand behind her mother, who she encouraged to sit back down.

She continued her tour of the room, easing each person back into their seats. "Now, Darien seems like a person of honorable intentions. I have never, ever, witnessed him do anything that would betray that opinion of him. And besides, he even saved Princess Victoria when she tried to stand up to the slave traders alone, and he did not inform on her to Marcilena about the incident." Her hand landed on my shoulder.

Harold cleared his throat and his hazel eyes locked with mine. "You single-handedly stood up to the slave traders?"

Blood heated my cheeks and I dropped my gaze to study the food cooling on the trencher before me. "I couldn't stand for children, or anyone for that matter, being sold as slaves. I even tried to see the King, but she wouldn't let me."

He smiled. "Your mother's daughter, I say. But no one sees the King these days. That evil witch has him under lock and key. Under a spell, me thinks."

"Harold!" Bessie gasped, yet again.

"Tis true, and you know it Bessie! You remember the ways of the old world, before Queen Katherine passed, God rest her soul."

My breath caught at the mention of the previous queen. Katherine. My mom's name... Was she really dead? Cold fingers of dread tingled along my skin at the possibility.

Bessie made the sign of the cross over her chest. "But you *do* recall that *she* banned us from speaking of *certain things*, punishable by death?" Her eyes implored him to see the meaning behind her words. Her eyes flicked to me for a moment.

I flinched, the dread turning to suspicion. "What *certain things* do you speak of, Bessie?" I asked.

"Magic. Fae. Dragons!" Aiden spoke up from his place beside me, his face glowing with ten-year-old excitement. "Mama always said to stay out of the North forest because of them. If you go in you never come back!"

"Hush, Aiden!" Bessie snapped.

Simultaneously with Bessie's words, Harold's fist landed on the heavy wooden table with a resounding thud. My hand flew to my throat to slow my heart beat. "Enough!" he bellowed.

My fingertips tingled with cold as my gaze flitted between Danielle's parents. Bessie sighed and threw her hands into the air before marching from the room.

I leaned over and whispered in Aiden's ear. "What was that all about?"

He turned and smiled. "Mama d'na want us to talk about the fae. The evil queen forbids us from talking about the time before she ruled."

I nodded. "Dragons?"

He nodded, a wide smile stretching his little face.

Harold's deep voice echoed across the room. "There be no such thing as dragons, right, Aiden?"

Aiden dropped his head and studied his hands in his lap. "Aye, Papa."

The rest of lunch was eaten in relative silence, with Danielle's mom conspicuously absent. I sighed and pushed the peas around in my trencher with my dagger. It was just like the arguments between Mom and Dad at home. But instead of Casey, Dad and I at the dinner table, I was surrounded by Danielle, her brothers, and her brooding father.

At that moment, I'd have given anything to be at home, sitting around the dinner table, throwing peas at Casey while my parents weren't looking. The homesickness and guilt built in my body until I was drowning in it. Tears welled in my eyes. I cleared my throat and stood up. "I should be getting back." I had to get out of this house, away from these people who made me miss my own family with a ferocity that I didn't think possible.

Aiden caught my hand. I knelt down and gave him a big hug, squeezing him harder than was probably necessary. But he was the closest thing I had to my sister at that moment, so he'd have to do.

His breath brushed across my ear as he whispered into it. "Dragons *do* exist."

14

Chapter Fourteen

The wet sucking sound of the horse's hooves in mud was almost nauseating. I pulled my hood closer to my face as we rode toward Aislin. Aiden's little voice echoed in my head over the rain pattering off my cloak.

"We should turn back," Darien said from beside me. His hood was pulled well over his face, but I could still see the strong line of his nose and the foggy air puffing from his mouth.

I shook my head. I had to get back to Aislin. I had to get back to trying to find my way out of this crazy dream and find my family. Besides, the warden had only given me a day pass. Who knows how much trouble I would have been in if I had decided to make it a slumber party. I didn't want to find out. At least Danielle had the sense to stay behind and wait out the storm. Then again, she didn't have to be back under the hawk-like eye of her evil stepmother. *I* did.

The memory of Bessie's love-filled face, even in the face of an argument, warmed me and left me cold at the same time. God, how I missed my family. The cold, horrible excuse for a family I had in this dream had to be some sort of punishment for something I did wrong. But I had to make it right.

My frigid hands tightened on the reins, which slipped a little more from my numb grasp. The freak storm had chilled the air to the point that I could see my breath puffing before me. My hands were bright red from being beaten by the rain and wind. It was almost as if someone had conjured up the brutal weather just to spite us for taking the trip.

The late afternoon light was quickly fading due to the overcast skies, turning the forest around us from watery golds and greens to grays and blues. My eyes scanned the forest to my left, the Northern forest, or the forbidden forest as Aiden had called it. The light disappeared in the dense trees, only the first two or three rows of trees were visible. Beyond that an inky black forest lurked. Goosebumps pricked my skin and my breathing quickened.

"That's the North forest?" I asked.

Darien nodded.

"Can we go that way?"

His concerned gaze shot to mine, and he studied my face intently. "Nay."

I studied his face. "Why?"

"No one who enters that forest e'er returns."

I snorted. I didn't want him to know that I already knew a little something about the forest. Especially not from Danielle's family. I didn't want to get them in trouble. "What's so dangerous about a forest?"

He shrugged. "Rumors say magical creatures live in that forest, enslaving anyone who dares to enter."

I cocked a brow. "Magical?"

"Fae."

I grunted. I hadn't really expected him to tell me the truth. Especially so blatantly with no qualifiers or any sort of warnings. "You don't actually believe in that kind of stuff, do you?"

He nodded. "From my infancy I have been taught to stay out of that forest."

"Where exactly is Kovanic?"

"On the other side of the Northern forest."

I snorted. "So if no one ever returns from the Northern forest, how come you live beyond it but yet are here now?"

A chuckle escaped his lips. "I went around."

Well, duh, I guess. My cheeks warmed, a welcome feeling from the tingling numbness from being so cold. "Oh. Why did you come to Aislin?"

The rain picked up and pounded against my cloak. My poor horse whinnied in protest at the chilling bath she was getting.

He paused, as if contemplating how to explain. "The Queen summoned me."

I frowned. "What do you mean?"

Darien inhaled in a great breath and blew it out slowly. "Her highness came to visit Kovanic when I was just a babe. She saved my mother's life, and thus my parents were indebted to her. They agreed to give me up in service at age eighteen for four years. Then I am free. On my eighteenth birthday, I received a summon to serve her. I had no choice but accept."

I nodded along, but could tell he was lying to me. First of all, Marcilena saving someone's life? Highly doubtful. She definitely had a black thumb in the nurturing and caring department. Now, if he'd said Marcilena had attempted to slaughter his entire family, *that* I would have believed.

"I know you d'na believe me. I would'na either." He pulled back his hood a bit, his sculpted features misted with rain. His eyes searched the Northern forest.

"But you expect me to believe you?"

He shook his head and whispered quickly. "I expect you to seek out the truth. About everything."

Well, *that* was unexpected.

I blew out a long breath, the heated puff of air curling in tendrils before disappearing in the fading light. "Then tell me the truth. Do you know what happened to my sister?"

He sighed. "So the rumors *are* true."

I bristled. "What rumors?" But he hadn't answered my question.

"That you believe that you're not really from Aislin. Not really Princess Victoria. And that you have a missing sister."

"Oh, that."

His eyes searched my face, as if trying to discern the truth in the rumors. "Where do you hail from, then, if not from Aislin?"

"Reality."

A smile stretched across his face. "This is reality."

I shook my head. "You, Aislin, everything, is all in my head. It's all just a dream."

He reined his horse in and caught my reins as well. We stopped beneath a grove of evergreens, their thick foliage effectively shielding us from most of the rain pouring down in sheets from above. In the distance, Aislin castle peeked out above the tree line. We were almost back.

I glanced at Darien, who was studying me closely. My cheeks warmed under his scrutiny, and I dropped my gaze to my hands folded in my lap. "What?"

"You dream of me?"

That brought my gaze to meet his. "I'm saying all *this* is a dream. Everything." I waved my hands around in an ineffective gesture to encompass everything around me. I bowed my head at the realization that up until that moment, Darien had been the only person who didn't look at me like I was crazy. Now that I'd admitted to the rumors, he'd probably look at me that way too. And I hated the thought of seeing that look on his handsome face.

He brought one hand to my hood and pushed it to the side, removing the barrier I was hiding behind.

"If this is all a dream, why not just awaken?" He leaned forward slightly, trying to get his face into my line of vision.

I shrugged. "I've tried. But I don't know how."

"What have you tried?"

My eyes shot to his. "You name it, I've tried it, such as attempting to throw myself from a ladder in the orchard, eating an apple, pinching myself, stabbing myself with a needle. Nothing works." I heaved a great sigh, as if that action could somehow fix everything.

"Hmm." He tapped a long, tanned finger against the cleft in his chin. A slight smile quirked the corner of his mouth, but didn't touch his eyes. "Well, then maybe 'tis not a dream, right? You can wake yourself up from dreams. So maybe 'tis not one after all?"

I couldn't fight the smile that sprung to my lips. It was sweet that he was trying to reason that I wasn't crazy, just a bit confused. "Maybe." I conceded.

We stared at each other while the rain pounded against our shelter of pine branches. The scent of wet pine needles and mud permeated my senses. The chill from the damp air bit at my face.

Darien's gaze dropped to my lips. Then he leaned toward me across the small distance between our horses.

"Darien, I think..." I started.

His warm finger touched my lips, silencing me. "For once in your life, dream or not, d'na think. Just be."

He slid his finger from my lips, cupped my cheek and leaned in a little more. Our breaths mingled and heated the air between our lips. My lips ached for the feeling of his lips on mine, the second time since we met. But this was like our first kiss, all over again. My stomach fluttered in anticipation.

"Darien! 'Tis about time! You d'na meet us at the location we had agreed upon." My blood chilled as Antonio's voice called out of the darkness of the edge of the Northern forest. He appeared astride a huge midnight horse, reminding me of a ring wraith.

I shrugged from Darien's grasp. "Location you agreed upon?"

"Tori, I..." He held his hands up in a helpless gesture and his face twisted with misery.

Antonio eyed Darien with suspicion as he nudged his horse between us. "I shall escort you the rest of the way to the castle, Princess."

"Of course you will. I'm surprised that the warden allowed the shackles off this long as it was." I yanked my hood over my head and spurred my horse to a hard gallop towards Aislin. The pounding of wet earth close behind me qualified my statement. I might have held the title of Princess in Aislin, but I was little more than a prisoner in a gilded cage.

15

Chapter Fifteen

I tugged at the bodice of the spaghetti strap dress Claire squeezed me into for the feast. If I were honest with myself, I'd admit it was the most gorgeous thing I'd ever seen. The sheer burgundy fabric was cinched up into rose-like twists over the fairytale-like ball gown. If my five-year-old self could see me now...

Claire slapped my hand away. "Please cease fidgeting, m'lady." She pulled another lock of hair and twirled it, shaping it into a swirl that mimicked the ones on my dress and secured it in place with a crystal-tipped pin. I'd lost count of the number of pins she used. I'd no doubt sleep on a few tonight.

With a satisfied smile, Claire stepped back. "There. Perfect."

I glanced in the mirror and gasped. "Wow." The little gems in my hair twinkled in the firelight, mirroring the babies-breath like crystalline necklace draped around my neck. I was getting used to the sight of my chest practically popping out of my gown, but tonight the dress laid perfectly against it, like it was made just for me. I practically beamed as I turned to face her.

My happy little bubble deflated at the sight of tears glistening in her eyes. "What?"

She scrubbed her eyes with her fists. "Nothing, m'lady. Got something in my eye, I did."

I made her sit beside me on the bed. "Tell me."

"'Tis nothing, m'lady. You be looking like your –"

A sharp knock on the door brought our heads up.

"One moment!" I called.

Claire shook her head, the tears in her eyes replaced with fear.

"Her highness requested that I escort the princess to the feast." Antonio's deep voice echoed through the heavy wooden door. My skin crawled.

"Coming, sir." Claire hurried to the door and opened it. "She is ready."

I crossed the room and shrugged away from Antonio's grasp before he could get a hold of my arm. "I'm perfectly able to find the hall. Thank you." I marched towards the stairs.

Heavy boot steps followed close behind. The next instant, a hand clamped on to my arm and my back was against the wall. Antonio's hot breath puffed against my face, his lips a breath away from mine. I tried not to breathe, but my chest heaved at the tight bodice of my dress. I twisted to escape from his grasp, but his body only pressed harder against me as a result. The hilt of his sword jutted into my hip.

His dark eyes surveyed my body before settling on my eyes. "Auch, Princess Victoria, how your chest heaves for me! I knew you wanted me." A satisfied smile pulled on his scarred mouth.

"Get off me," I hissed and tried to knee him in the groin.

Anticipating my move, he caught my knee and hiked it up over his hip, shifting so he pressed harder against me.

"See? You should heed her highness' wishes. One word from her and I shall be your permanent, *personal* guard. Oh, how I would relish the opportunity to know you better..."

Acid rose in my throat at the mental picture his words conjured. "Touch me again and you're a dead man."

"Oh, I shall touch you again. And you shall beg me for it..." His lips descended towards mine. I choked at the heavy scent of alcohol on his breath.

I shoved against his immovable body. "No!"

A chuckle rumbled in his throat and he lowered his lips towards mine again. I turned my head at the last second and his lips connected with my jaw. He planted a series of slobbery kisses along my cheek and neck.

My stomach roiled. I was going to throw up.

A deep voice echoed in the hall behind Antonio's back. "I believe the lady said nay."

As quickly as Antonio threw me up against the wall, the weight of his body left me. I drew in a shaky breath and glanced at my rescuer.

Antonio was against the opposite wall, with the point of Darien's sword at his throat.

Darien's copper eyes flashed with rage. "You are a miserable excuse for a man."

"She wanted it." Antonio seethed. His eyes widened and he inhaled sharply as a tiny drop of blood beaded at the spot where Darien's sword pushed into his skin.

"Doubtful." Darien glanced at me. "Are you all right?"

I nodded and smoothed my dress down. I cringed at the thought of what he must've seen before he intervened.

Darien's eyes locked with mine. "Say the word and he is dead."

A morbid tingle of excitement coursed through me at the thought he would kill a man simply because I asked him to. Even with everything that had happened between us.

I crossed the hall and confronted Antonio, my face inches from his. "The next time you touch me, I will kill you. Don't think for a second I need Darien to do it for me."

Antonio's eyes flashed and then he hissed in pain as the tip of Darien's sword pushed a little deeper into his neck. "Never again m'lady," he stammered.

I nodded and Darien yanked his sword away from Antonio's neck. He crumpled to the floor and gasped for breath.

"The queen shall hear of this!" Antonio shouted as Darien and I descended the main stairs.

I glared at him over my shoulder. "Make sure she does."

We paused outside of the banquet hall and Darien held out his hand. I stared at his long, lean fingers, tanned by the sun. On one hand I wanted to trust him, since he had just saved me from Antonio's unwanted advances. But he was bound to Marcilena, and I couldn't stop thinking about what happened in the forest the week before on our ride back to Aislin. The rain pouring around us as he leaned in, his lips so close to mine, when Antonio ruined everything by breaking down the trust I had started to have in him.

"Tori?" he asked, a confused look twisting his handsome features.

I blinked and took his offered hand instinctively. He smiled a wary smile, tucked my hand in the crook of his arm and escorted me into the banquet hall.

The scents of the feast overwhelmed me, a heady mixture of alcohol, roasted meat and spices. My mouth watered.

A hushed silence fell over the crowd.

I glanced at Darien. "Did I do something wrong again?"

A wide smile crossed his face and his copper eyes twinkled in the torchlight. "Nay, they stare because angels pale in comparison to your beauty."

My face flamed. In the flickering glow of candlelight, every set of eyes *was* on me. Even Bianca, who usually shot me death glares, stared at me with her mouth gaping.

When my gaze made it to the head table, rather than the scathing glare of hatred I usually got from Marcilena, a smug smile stretched across her face. It was the first time I'd ever seen her smile. It was about the creepiest thing I'd ever seen in my life. But she wasn't looking at me. She was looking at Darien. Suspicion tingled across my stomach when I glanced at Darien and found his gaze locked with hers. His jaw clenched slightly.

I glanced back to the head table, where the king, a grizzled man with scraggly hair and a thick mustache and beard covering most of his face, sat slumped in his chair. It was the first time I'd ever seen him, but something was oddly familiar about him.

I could feel someone's eyes burning into me. My gaze moved to Brandon, whose green eyes blazed as he stared at me. His jaw clenched and his hands were balled into fists on the table.

I smiled slightly and nodded my head in his direction.

Darien's arm tightened around mine. I glanced up at him to find his gaze locked on Brandon.

I cleared my throat quietly. "Is there something I should know?"

Darien turned his dazed gaze to mine. "Nay, of course not. Come." He led me to my seat at the head table. He bowed and his warm lips brushed my knuckles. "M'lady." His eyes twinkled.

"I didn't get a chance to thank you properly," I whispered.

He winked. "Later."

My cheeks burned as I settled into my seat. What did he mean by that? I watched as he crossed the dais and slid into his chair beside Marcilena. She smiled sweetly and whispered something into his ear. His slight smile faded and the color drained from his face.

My stomach jolted when his eyes met mine. I spun and studied the dancers before us, who were twisting and twirling in what looked like a very complex dance.

"You seem to be enjoying yourself." There was an edge to Brandon's voice I hadn't heard before.

"Darien helped me take care of an unwanted situation. Enjoying is a bit of an exaggeration." I shot a glare at Antonio, who had a small bandage on his throat from where Darien's blade had pierced his skin.

"Oh." Brandon turned and stabbed a strawberry with his dagger with so much force the blade sunk into the trencher.

I put my hand on his on the knife. "What's wrong with you?"

Brandon shook his head, his blonde hair falling into his eyes. "It does'na matter."

"Please?"

He abruptly kicked his chair back and held out a hand to me. "May I have this dance?"

My cheeks warmed and I shook my head. "I'm horrible. Ask Danielle."

He winked. "Trust me." He leaned forward and grabbed my hand, pulling me up and out of my seat.

My face was going to spontaneously combust. I was a horrible dancer, and the dances I'd witnessed so far tonight were way too complex for me to stumble my way through.

I reluctantly followed him as the men lined up on one side, the ladies on the other. My eyes widened as the music started, slow and serene. The ladies stepped forward, and I followed their lead. One hand up. The men stepped forward. Brandon put his hand against mine. I kept my gaze lowered, studying the footwork as we began to circle.

"Look at me, Victoria," Brandon whispered.

I lifted my gaze to meet his. His sexy half-smile spread across his face as we switched hands and circled the other way.

The music increased in tempo and my heart pounded in sync with the beat. I was going to screw up. Maybe fall on someone. Either way it would be sheer humiliation.

We separated back into our lines, opposite partners crossing over and spinning before replacing the person on the opposite side of the line. Brandon moved further and further down the line. Each man who I passed eyed me in the same way – something like curiosity and the unmistakable stare of desire.

The lines broke into smaller groups of mismatched partners, spinning in circles, boy, girl, boy, girl. My head spun from all the twirling. I had no clue where Brandon went, or if I was even supposed to get back to him. So I followed along, stumbling through the dance steps, allowing myself to get passed along from man to man. One more twirl and somehow we ended up back in our original lines.

The music slowed to the original melancholy tones and we started again with the hands and spinning. Brandon's lips brushed my ear as he passed. "You look absolutely beautiful."

I smiled, trying to focus on his face. "Thanks. You do too." I cringed.

On his next pass his eyes flashed defiantly. "Tell me, is Darien your new guard?"

I grit my teeth. "I don't need a guard. I can take care of myself."

His face softened. "Obviously."

I glared at him.

He put his hand up to mine and led me down the center of the two lines. The other partners stopped and split at the end of the line. When we got to the end of the line he pulled me with him towards the side door to the gardens. "Hurry!" He led me out into the darkness.

The scent of night-blooming jasmine on the cool night breeze caressed my skin.

"What...?"

"Shh!" He whispered and pulled me through the moonlit garden.

We took a sharp right and again I found my back to stone. But this time, rather than brute force, he gently pushed me against the wall.

"Finally," he growled. "I swear Marcilena has been plotting to keep you away from me." He brushed a stray lock of hair off my shoulder.

"You want me alone?" I mentally kicked myself for how that must've sounded.

"Always." His warm breath caressed my face as he lowered his lips towards mine.

My eyes fluttered closed, but popped open at the mental picture of the possessive look on Brandon's face when I walked into the banquet hall with Darien. I pushed against his chest and stared up into his eyes. "Is this because you're jealous of seeing me on Darien's arm tonight?"

A twinge of hurt flitted over his handsome features as he pulled away. "Nay... And aye. I admit I was beyond rage when I saw him escort you to the ball. But I should have been the one to rescue you, not him. When I saw Antonio disappear, I realized too late what he had planned. The Queen had me distracted with some mundane conversation when he slipped away. By the time I arrived, Darien already had things under control. Almost like he had it all planned..."

"Oh," I whispered. The thought that Darien arrived just in the nick of time was planned never crossed my mind. Until now.

"I am relieved you are well. If anything had happened to you, I would..."

"Shh." I put my finger to his lips to silence him. "I'm fine. Next time I'll be ready for him."

Brandon's jaw clenched. "There shall not be a next time if I have anything to say about it."

"I appreciate your concern, but I can take care of myself."

His body pressed a little harder into mine. The cold stone at my back contrasted with his hot body pressing against mine. "Oh, can you now?"

I nodded and swallowed the nervous lump that built in my throat. My body hummed at the sensation of his body pressed against mine.

"So if I were to kiss you, you would be able to stop me if you wanted to right?"

I nodded.

"Like this?" His lips descended slowly towards mine, our breaths mingling against my lips.

I nodded again.

He slid one hand over my arm, raising goose bumps along my skin in response. His other arm braced against the wall for support. "Do you want this, Victoria?"

My body trembled when his lips barely brushed mine. "I don't know." I whispered. I was so confused. My heart told me one thing. My body told me something else. And my brain – well don't even get me started about my brain.

"Tell me to cease and I will." His lips brushed against mine, once, twice, waiting for me to tell him no.

It's just a dream...

I sighed and parted my lips slightly, lifting my chin just enough so our lips met.

A growl rumbled through his chest and he devoured my lips with his. His arms slid around me, one hand cupping the back of my head, the other on my lower back, pulling me against his hard body.

Kissing him was exactly the opposite of kissing Darien. Sweet, gentle, perfect. Exactly how I envisioned Prince Charming kissing Cinderella. I gasped as his tongue delved inside my mouth. Okay, not *exactly* like Prince Charming kissing Cinderella, because I'd never envisioned them frenching. He tasted like wine and strawberries.

"Princess Victoria!" Marcilena's angry shriek echoed through the garden, effectively ending my kiss with Brandon. Again. *The bitch.*

Brandon sighed and pulled away, straightening his coat and smoothing my dress quickly. He held one finger to his lips and motioned for me to go. He turned and ran deeper into the garden.

I watched him disappear into the darkness. When he was out of sight I straightened my dress and hair as much as I could.

"Princess Victoria!" Marcilena's voice was closer. "Where has that evil little brat gone?" Footsteps echoed on the stone path leading to me.

I stepped out from behind the wall. "I'm here. I just needed some fresh air."

"I see," Marcilena said. The light from the ballroom spilled out into the garden from the open doorway. "You are needed inside at once for the announcement. Come."

I crossed the garden and tentatively put my hand in hers. Her claw-like fingers clamped down on my hand as she drug me into the ballroom. Every eye in the room was fixed on me as she paraded me back to the main table. Out of the corner of my eye, Brandon entered the hall and slid into his seat. No one seemed to notice.

Marcilena sent a scathing glare at Brandon when we reached the table, but we didn't climb the dais and sit down. Instead, she motioned for Darien to join us where we stood before the king.

Darien's coppery eyes darkened as he moved to stand beside me.

"Ladies and gentlemen, may I have your attention please?" Marcilena called out in her nasally voice. "I have an announcement."

A quiet hush fell over the room. Whispering here and there punctuated the silence.

The debilitated king grumbled something under his breath, but I couldn't make it out.

"After much consideration, the king and I are pleased to announce the betrothal of our daughter, Princess Victoria, to Darien of Kovanic." Gasps and murmurs erupted throughout the room. Something crashed into the table behind me. The blood rushed to my head. I had to have heard wrong. Betrothal meant marriage. Like till death do we part marriage. I glanced at Darien. His face was drawn, sad even. But not surprised. *Had he planned this all along?*

My heart lurched. Not two minutes ago I was making out with Brandon in the garden. Now I had a fiancé. Again. While I liked Darien, I wasn't ready to marry a guy I didn't necessarily trust. Especially when it gave Marcilena such pleasure.

"No," I whispered.

Marcilena turned her scathing black glare on me. "You shall do as we bid. You are our daughter and it is your responsibility to do as we see fit. 'Tis a good match."

The king grumbled again, this time louder behind me.

"I won't," I said, this time with conviction.

"You d'na have a say in this *Victoria*." My name coming from her mouth sounded more like a curse.

"I will not marry Darien, or anyone else, for that matter."

"You shall not defy me, little girl, or I shall see to it you pay dearly." Marcilena seethed between clenched teeth, a fake smile plastered on her ruby lips.

"*I will not*!" I shouted. Silence fell over the banquet hall and every pair of eyes fixed on me. "I've tried to do everything you expect from me and still you loathe me. I draw the line here. I *will not* marry Darien."

"*You shall not defy me!*" Marcilena screamed, a shrill cry that made my brain rattle. She snatched my wrist, her nails biting into my skin as she yanked me behind her, out of the banquet hall, up the stairs and all the way to my room.

The air gushed from my chest as she threw me to the floor with more force than I would have expected from such a slight woman.

"You will stay in this room until you have learned your place. You *will* marry Darien or you shall grow old within these four walls!" Marcilena shrieked and slammed the door.

I hauled myself off the floor and rushed at the door. My hand closed over the handle as the metallic sound of a lock slid into place. Tears pooled in my eyes as I slid down the wall and wrapped my arms around my knees.

16

Chapter Sixteen

A gentle knock sounded at the door, but I continued to stare out the window. The grayish-blue light of the impending darkness filtered on to the garden below my window. The hedges swayed against the sheets of rain and wind that pelted them. I'd lost all track of time since being locked in my chamber. I was like Rapunzel sitting in her tower, wishing for someone to come rescue her. How long had it been? Weeks? Months?

A knock rattled the door again, this time more insistent.

"Enter," I snapped. The door creaked open behind me. I didn't turn to see who entered. The only people Marcilena allowed to see me were Claire and Antonio. If it were the first, she knew my sadness. If it were the second, he could go to hell.

My eyes searched the gardens below my window for any sign of life, anything to watch besides the tapestry-covered walls of my prison. But with a storm like what was blowing outside, it was hopeless. No one would be braving this weather.

Some days I'd catch the ladies on their walks through the garden. I longed to talk to Danielle, who seemed to be out of sorts with the other ladies, walking a few paces behind, her head bowed. Every once in a while she'd glance up at my window with a timid smile before running to catch up with the others. At least she hadn't completely forgotten about me.

Other days, servants trimmed the hedges into manicured circles and squares. I smiled at the thought of the day I caught sight of Claire sneaking into the garden with Charles. My stomach clenched when he pushed her up against the wall as Brandon had done to me that fateful night.

I sighed as my eyes traveled over the garden, to the tall walls surrounding them and finally settled on the cloud-shrouded mountains towering in the North.

"Princess Victoria," Marcilena's voice filled the room.

My shoulders stiffened, but I didn't turn.

Her voice was sweeter than usual. "I have decided that you have served your sentence. Tomorrow you may attend your lessons."

"And the betrothal?"

"Still stands." Her delicate footsteps crossed the room and stopped behind me. "You should know that Prince Brandon returned to Crell the day after your betrothal was announced."

I spun around and glared at her.

Her face softened. "Men can be so fickle. He could have fought for you, could have gone to the king and demanded the betrothal be canceled."

My heart sank and tears threatened to well up in my eyes. The closest thing I had to a knight in shining armor fled at the first sign of conflict.

Marcilena caught a lock of my hair in her fingers and inspected it. "But why would a prince want *you* when he has so many other breathtaking beauties to choose from, ones who would not embarrass him at every turn? Besides your father's crown anyway..."

I snatched my hair from her hand. "You don't know anything."

A wicked chuckle escaped her lips. "You would be surprised what I *know*." Her black eyes flashed before she composed herself into her trademark 'sweet smile while I stab you in the back' look. "You shall be on time to your lessons and be on your best behavior or I will have you confined to your chamber until your wedding day. Is that understood?"

I glared at her.

In an instant her hand wrapped around my neck and her claw-like fingers dug into my neck. My eyes bulged and I gasped for breath.

She punctuated each word as she repeated her question. "Is that understood?"

Light flashed before my eyes. I nodded.

Her fingers released their death grip and I crumpled to the floor, sucking in deep breaths of stale air. The blood rushed to my face and my head throbbed.

"You shall learn your place, or else your next jail cell will be a little less... comfortable."

I cringed when the door slammed shut.

The door creaked open again. "M'lady!" Claire rushed to me. "What happened?"

"Marcilena," I said between heaving gasps. *How could one tiny woman have so much strength?*

Claire nodded and helped me off the floor. She settled me into a chair beside the fire and stoked the flames with a poker.

I watched the back of her dishwater-blonde head as she stoked the fire. "Why didn't you tell me Brandon left?"

Claire glanced at me before resuming her prodding of the logs. "Her highness forbade us from telling you."

"So you wouldn't ruin her little surprise?"

She nodded.

I slumped back and stared at the fire.

Claire knelt before me and took my hand in hers. She glanced around the room, as if eavesdroppers were hiding in the shadows. "Brandon did'na leave on his own free will." She whispered. A log popped in the fireplace and she nearly jumped out of her skin.

I stared down at her, my eyes wide. She motioned for me to come closer and I leaned in.

Her breath was hot against my ear as her words raced from her lips. "Marcilena took him prisoner. She does'na know I saw. Antonio shackled him and threw him over the back of a horse. I heard them mention the abandoned castle at Rostellan in the Northern forest and removing temptation from distracting you from your duty."

My skin tingled. "Do you know where this castle is?" I whispered.

Claire nodded. "If you want to help him, I can help you get out of the castle without anyone knowing. Get you a horse too. But you must leave at once. The storm is the perfect diversion. No one will hear your escape." Her round eyes flickered in the firelight as they searched mine.

"Let's go." I shoved off the chair and dashed to the wardrobe.

Claire came up behind me. "What are you looking for?"

"A bag for supplies." I pawed at the clothes, not knowing exactly what I had that could help me.

"Like this?" She yanked an overstuffed satchel from the back of the wardrobe.

I gaped at her.

She winked. "Come. Let us get you changed." She rifled through the closet until she came up with a lightweight dress of black, grey and blue fabric. In her other arm was a black hooded cloak. "This should be perfect."

She quickly unlaced the golden cords crisscrossing my stomach. At least being confined to my room meant I didn't have to be paraded around in miles of satin and velvet, so it took no time to get out of my dress. I pulled on the thin blue blouse then stepped into the skirt. She quickly cinched the laces around my hips before turning to the corset over the blouse. The laces crossed just over my chest and cinched tight, reminding me of a bra. Nothing squeezed my stomach for once.

"Why didn't you tell me about this dress earlier? It's heavenly." I pulled the ends of the blouse apart, exposing my midriff to the firelight.

Claire chuckled. "Because her highness would have had my head if she saw you wearing it. 'Twas your mother's, given to her by the Gypsies."

I glanced down at the dress. It totally looked like a gypsy dress, with its handkerchief points and large expanses of exposed skin. Why couldn't I have dreamt of a gypsy camp instead?

Claire strapped a beaded pouch around my hips and pushed nudged me to sit on the bench. She pulled my hair up into a half-ponytail and a few stray ringlets fell about my face and glistened in the firelight. She'd grown as bored as I had under chamber arrest and insisted on curling my hair just to have something to do.

I stood and flung the cloak over my shoulders and settled the hood over my hair. "Well?"

Claire smiled. "No one will recognize you."

"Let's count on that. Okay, so how do we get out of here without getting caught?"

"Follow me." Claire opened the door, peeked out and motioned for me to follow. We tiptoed out into the hallway, the soft soles of our leather slippers silent on the stone floor. The torchlight cast long shadows along the wall behind the suits of armor as we passed. I half expected one of them to jump out at me. I tugged my hood around my face and followed Claire down the hall.

My pulse leapt when metal clattered at the end of the passageway. We dashed into the shadows and plastered our backs against the cold stone in the darkness. My hands trembled. If I was caught sneaking out of the castle, I had no doubt Marcilena's punishment would be brutal.

I stifled a gasp as footsteps echoed down the hall, closing in on our hiding spot. I scooted behind the suit of armor next to a column and prayed whoever was about to pass didn't peer too long into the shadows.

"This way," Antonio's muffled voice sounded.

Four pairs of heavy footsteps tromped past us. I peered between the armor and the column, trying to see who else was with him without revealing my hiding place. Claire shifted to stand behind the other suit of armor.

Antonio paused directly in front of me, the torchlight reflecting off his scar, casting eerie shadows across his face, making him look even more sinister than usual.

A hand clamped onto Antonio's shoulder, turning him roughly around. "I will not force her to do something she does not want to do." My blood ran cold when I heard Darien's deeply accented voice.

Antonio grabbed Darien's shirt with both hands and pulled him so their faces were inches from each other. "'Tis the Queen's declaration. Follow her command, you will, as will Princess Victoria." He shoved Darien away roughly. "I am sick of babysitting the lot of you. If it was up to me, she would already know her place..."

Metal scraped against metal as Darien unsheathed his sword and pointed it at Antonio. "Might I remind you what happened last time?"

Antonio's dark eyes flashed. "I recall. And so does the queen. You are already on thin ice with her. What do you think defying her about the marriage would do?" Antonio spat.

Darien's shoulders fell and he sheathed his sword. "At least let me talk to her first."

"Fine. But be quick. The Queen wants to see you at once." Antonio nodded to my chamber door. "Good luck," he sneered.

My breath caught in my throat. I was about to be found out and I wasn't thirty feet from my room. Some escape...

The three men marched ahead and disappeared around the corner. Darien approached my door, but stopped. He mouthed something over and over again.

Claire's breath brushed my cheek. "M'lady, we must hurry. 'Tis our only chance."

Darien paced back and forth in front of my door, as if he was rehearsing what he was about to say to me. His face was drawn in despair.

"'Tis now or never!" Claire hissed.

Darien glanced in our direction. His eyes searched the darkness, but didn't lock in on us.

He returned to his pacing, and while his back was turned, Claire pulled me away from the column. We dodged from one shadow to the next until we were at the end of the hallway.

In the shadows, Claire reached behind a column and stuck her hand into a small opening in the stone. Something clicked and the wall turned in. I gaped at the doorway that magically appeared.

"Come m'lady, quickly, before Darien discovers you are missing!" Claire pulled me inside the opening and shoved the wall shut behind us, effectively plummeting us into complete darkness. The air was stale and stunk of mildew.

"I can't see a thing." I cursed when I stubbed my toe.

Something flickered. Claire lit a candle and handed it to me. "Have you used flint before?"

I shook my head.

"Should have been teaching you survival skills instead of how to be a lady, methinks." She quickly showed me how to use the flint to light another candle.

She hefted my overstuffed bag on one shoulder and held the candle out before her as we descended the circular staircase.

We reached the bottom and Claire cautiously pushed the wall before her. It swung open and wet, frigid air swirled about us and extinguished our candles. I tugged the hood around my face again and followed her out into the storm.

We raced across the courtyard and ducked behind a hedge as the wet clopping of horse hooves approached. Huge wooden wheels squished in the mud as a carriage rattled by. Once it turned the corner, we dashed toward the barn and ducked into a doorway.

I pulled back my hood when we stepped into the barn. The scent of wet hay and horse manure assaulted my nose. A torch flickered at the end of the barn and horse stalls lined either side of the long building.

"Come." Claire pulled me toward the light. A young boy with mousy brown hair and round eyes waited in the last stall. "Connor's my little brother." Claire waved her hand towards the slight boy. "Connor, this is Princess Victoria."

"I know who she be. I used to watch her when she went on walks through the garden with Prince Brandon." His pale face turned beet red from the tips of his ears to his hairline. "Prettier close up, you are."

My blush must have matched his. "Thanks. I have a little sister about your age."

He cocked his head to the side and shot Claire a confused look.

"Oh, right. Well, I did. Oh, never mind," I rambled. A twinge of guilt hit me. Now Claire had gotten him involved in the scheme too.

Connor smiled and disappeared inside the stall, returning a moment later leading a massive black horse. His sleek coat glistened blue in the torchlight and his black eyes had swirls of gold. He snorted and pushed against Connor towards me.

I smiled and closed the distance between us, holding my hand out tentatively for him to sniff. He held one nostril over my hand for a moment, his hot breath puffing against my skin. He shifted his lips over my hand and mouthed at it with his gushy lips.

I giggled and smoothed my hand over his long face. "He's sweet."

"His name is Dorcha." Claire threw a blanket and a saddle onto him and pulled the straps tight.

She fastened my pack behind the saddle and her chocolate brown eyes met mine. "You can do this, m'lady. I have faith in you."

"Thank you for helping me." I grabbed her hand and squeezed it. "If there is anything I can ever do to repay you..."

Her cherub-like face and round eyes contrasted with the venom in her voice. "Bring the queen to her knees."

I nodded. A lump built in my throat. *How the hell was I supposed to bring down an evil queen?*

She held Dorcha's reins as I mounted him and then led him to the door. "See those mountains?" I followed her finger to the mountains I'd studied from my prison window. The Northern mountains, the ones Danielle's family warned me from going in to. The ones that no one ever returns from.

I nodded.

"The castle is on the other side of those mountains, at the top of a mountain in the valley on the other side. Be careful. No one has ever come back from that valley."

Fear sizzled through my veins. "Thank you. Get back inside before someone sees you."

Claire nodded and pulled Connor back inside. I was plunged into darkness when they extinguished the torch.

I pulled my hood over my head and nudged Dorcha. Apparently he didn't like being wet any more than I did, because he took off at a full gallop out of the stable. Rain pelted my cloak, but somehow nothing seeped in. I clung to the reins as Dorcha shot through the open gate, across the drawbridge, across the open grass and into the cover of the forest.

My heart lodged in my throat when a muffled scream cut through the drenched air.

"Claire!" I pulled hard on the reins and Dorcha skidded to a stop, prancing back and forth across the soaked earth. *Should I go back?* I shook my head. I had already made it out. And I was too late. Maybe it wasn't even her. Going back could get her into more trouble. Besides, I had to find Brandon if I had any hope of bringing Marcilena down.

I spent another few seconds debating the pros and cons of going back when the metallic rattle of the chains filled the night air. The drawbridge pulled up as the river overflowed its banks.

The river made my decision for me.

17

Chapter Seventeen

A shiver raced over my skin as Dorcha dashed through the forest, dodging between trees and jumping over fallen logs. Lightning flashed overhead and cast shadows resembling people hiding among the trees. I clung to my dark horse, grateful for the warmth that radiated from his slick coat.

After what felt like an eternity trudging through the roaring storm, the clouds receded and the rain thinned to a trickle. I pulled back my hood and studied the thick woods surrounding us. Moonbeams filtered through the branches overhead, casting the woods in an eerie blue light.

For a forbidden forest, it was surprisingly peaceful. And, for the first time since I woke in Aislin, I was alone. Completely and utterly alone. The serenity that settled over me was surprising. I'd almost forgotten what being alone felt like. The metallic taste of fear tingled on my tongue, but I ignored it. I could handle this. I didn't need someone to protect me.

I straightened a little in the saddle, the thought strengthening my resolve to push forward, to save Brandon from whatever horrors Marcilena had planned for him because of me.

A branch snapped behind me. My eyes strained against the darkness. Nothing moved. I let out a relieved breath and turned back around, but my grip was a little tighter on Dorcha's reins.

Another snap, then another. I searched the forest but again there was nothing. The skin tightened on the back of my head and fear trickled through my veins.

"Hurry Dorcha," I whispered. I could see my breath in the chilled air. I squeezed his flanks with my knees, urging him to a trot.

The black trunks whizzed by us as we raced through the forest. I relaxed a little when the trees thinned and we found ourselves in a grassy meadow. The breeze rustled the wet grass that swayed around Dorcha's knees as he waded through it. Twice I had to pull on his reins to remind him we were trying to escape, not stop for a snack. But, at least out in the open there was nowhere for someone to hide.

No quicker than I had the thought, something flew out of the grass before us. Dorcha whinnied and reared back. I rolled from the saddle and the breath left my lungs in one gush when I landed flat on my back on the ground.

Fear pricked my skin as the pounding of Dorcha's hooves on the wet earth faded in the distance. Everything I had to help me on my journey was on the back of that horse. I sat frozen on the damp ground and scanned the darkness for movement.

My heart leapt into my throat when a human-shaped figure stood up where Dorcha had startled. Then another, and another. There were at least ten of them in the field.

"Did the rider fall?" a grizzled male voice with a Greek-sounding accent asked from behind me.

I flattened down in to the grass, praying the he didn't trip over me.

"The rider wore a dark cloak. Could'na see."

"Me either," the other voices chimed in.

A thread of hope wound around my heart. They didn't know I was here.

"Let's get the horse..." the voice behind me approached.

I couldn't stifle the startled scream of pain when something hard connected with my ribs.

"Guess she did fall off..." He grabbed me by the back of my cloak and hefted me to my feet.

Someone lit a torch and brought it over. I kept my head lowered so my hood blocked most of my face. All I could see was their feet and the rags they wore as pants.

The man who held me yanked back my hood. "What do we have here?"

A shocked gasp erupted from the group.

"Get your hands off me!" I shrugged out of his grasp. I spun in a circle and took in the faces of the people surrounding me. Each had dark hair, eyes and skin, and gold hoop earrings. Even the men. The women had handkerchief-hem dresses with white puffy shirts barely concealing huge boobs, bare midriffs, and bandanas tied around their heads.

Gypsies.

A curly-haired woman about my mom's age tentatively approached me, eyeing me like I was a ghost. "Queen Katherine! It's Queen Katherine!"

The bottom of my stomach dropped out. "I'm not Katherine. My name is Victoria."

The woman chuckled. "I should'a known. You look exactly like your mother." She turned to face the mob. How had I managed to miss a small town worth of people hiding in the trees? "'Tis our beloved Queen Katherine's daughter, Victoria. Princess Victoria!" Her dark eyes flashed and a great smile spread across her face as she knelt before me.

I watched in awe as the entire group knelt around me. Whispers carrying my name filtered around the group.

"Please, don't do that. Get up." I pleaded.

The woman smiled and got up from the ground. She took my hand and kissed it. The scent of patchouli and spices rose from her hair. "Please forgive us. We've waited for this day for almost ten years."

I cocked my head to the side. "Ten years?"

"The day Queen Katherine died. The world as we knew it ended that day." She let out a wistful sigh. "Come. Let's not discuss this here. You look frozen solid." She pulled me through the darkened woods.

The soft footfalls of the crowd followed behind me, and muffled conversations in an exotic language filtered along the breeze.

The silence was painful. I had so many questions. "What's your name?"

"Nadya. Shh. We'll be at the camp soon when I promise I'll answer all your questions."

She led me deeper into the forest and eventually we came to a circle of tents. A large wagon sat at one end, the light spilling out of its open doors onto the mossy ground. Crystals and dried herbs hung from ropes strung across the small windows.

"You're gypsies."

The woman chuckled, her huge chest bouncing. "Aye, that we are. You fit right in wearing that dress." She pointed to a blanket on the ground before the largest tent. "Sit," she commanded.

I sunk down on to the thick fabric. She picked up a blanket from beside the fire and draped it over my shoulders. A young boy handed me a steaming mug of something that smelled vaguely like apple cider. I took a sip of the spiced fruity liquid and sighed in contentment as the warmth seeped into my body. The heat of my blush warmed my frozen cheeks. "Claire told me this dress was my mothers, given to her by the gypsies."

"Aye, that it is. I gave that dress to your mother at her coronation celebration. It was such a grand party. I remember it like 'twas yesterday." She plopped down beside me and draped a blanket over herself. Soon the entire group gathered around the fire, all intently watching and listening.

Nadya stared into the fire and the flames reflected in her dark eyes, making them look like they were on fire. "Sometimes 'tis hard to remember there was a time before the dark queen ruled."

A breathless cackle echoed in the night air. I glanced up to find an ancient woman climbing out of the wagon with the help of a boy about my age. "Nadya. Don't bore zee poor little girl with stories of how tings were." Her foot dragged as she shuffled towards the fire. "It won't change anything. Look at her. Zere's no way she can restore peace to our troubled kingdom. Too puny. No backbone."

I bristled and glared at the haggard old woman, who looked like a shriveled raisin with beady black eyes and three teeth jutting from her sneering mouth.

She leaned over Nadya and studied my face, her black eyes squinting to slits. "Oh! Perhaps she does have zee spirit."

Nadya rolled her eyes and shot me an apologetic look over the old woman's stringy gray hair. "Ach, Vadoma. Watch your mouth. D'na you see who this is?"

"I see who she appears to be. We shall see if she is truly Queen Katherine's heir soon enough." Vadoma's gnarled hand snatched a lock of my hair and the firelight glinted off something metal in her other hand as it arced over her head towards me.

"No!" I shrieked and flung myself away from her.

The crazy old woman cackled and sniffed the lock of hair she'd sheared from my head.

I glared at her. "You could have just asked, you know."

"Vadoma." Nadya's tone scolded, but she couldn't conceal the laughter in her eyes.

The old woman muttered to herself and put the hair on a platter by the fire. She rifled through her pockets and pouches, grumbling and patting like my dad did when he lost his glasses. I bit my lip when a satisfied smile stretched her wrinkled face and showed off her three remaining teeth. She held up a vial of an amber-hued liquid. The muffled conversation of the group fell silent as everyone watched her movements. She rattled off something in a language I didn't understand and deposited three drops of the orange liquid onto the lock of my hair.

Oddly, the lock hissed like a snake and writhed on the platter. I watched wide-eyed as she sprinkled various powders and dropped other liquids onto the hair. With each addition, the hair undulated and hissed. Vadoma's chanting reached its peak, and she threw a pinch of something powdered onto the hair. It shot up into the air like a rocket and exploded like fireworks in the sky above us. Glittering ash fluttered down on to the fire, where it sparked and sizzled.

"Well? Is she?" Nadya asked.

Vadoma sighed and shook her head. "Zee spirits could'na answer. But she is our only hope – zee first hope we've had in years."

Angry grunts of disappointment erupted from the group as they wandered off to their tents.

I sighed. "I'm sorry I'm not who you need me to be. I'm just a seventeen-year-old girl. And this is just a dream."

Nadya smiled warmly. "But you are Katherine's heir. Even if Vadoma and her 'spirits' d'na see that, I can. I see Katherine's spirit in you." She winked. "You've got her fire."

"Tell me about the time before Marcilena. And about Queen Katherine." I leaned back against the blanket.

"Your mother was a kind and just queen. The kingdom of Aislin was beautiful. Everyone worked together for the greater good. Everyone always had enough to eat, someplace warm to sleep, and was treated with respect. It was like Heaven on earth."

My heart jolted. It *was* like Heaven when Queen Katherine reigned. Maybe I was dead...

"When the king and queen had you, there was a great feast to celebrate the birth of an heir. The faeries came to the feast and blessed you with beauty, talent, kindness and joy. The kingdom was overjoyed to see the reign of your family would continue. When your mother gave birth to your sister, there was another feast. The faeries came again to bless the child with their gifts. But one of the faeries seemed to be ill. When she came to bless your sister, she uttered a curse over the child. Your mother threw herself over her and the faerie cursed her as well. Queen Katherine collapsed, limp on the floor. Dead."

My skin tingled. Nadya was the first person to admit I had a sister. "The faerie killed Queen Katherine and my sister? Why?"

She nodded. "No one knows. On the day of the funeral, the bodies were stolen from their crypt. Your father ne'er got a proper burial for either of them. Shortly after the memorial the king descended into madness."

Tears pooled in my eyes and rolled down my cheeks. A lump grew in my throat. Finally someone had admitted that I had a sister. But that she was dead. And my mother was dead too.

Nadya cleared her throat and continued. "Marcilena came to Aislin to visit the king from somewhere beyond the mountains. No one knows where. Within a few days the king announced his engagement to her." Her eyes narrowed.

"So the reign of terror began. The gypsies were run out of the castle, as Marcilena accused us of being witches and plotting against her. People were forced to live in poverty, except for the hand-selected elite. The king grew more and more resigned. Soon he stopped leaving his chambers. Rumor has it Marcilena is a witch and cast a spell over the king to get him to marry her."

"A witch..." I turned the word over and over in my mind.

"Strangely, no one e'er told us what happened to you, Princess Victoria. How is it you d'na remember all of this?"

"You wouldn't believe it if I told you."

"I bet I would. It was rumored that Marcilena locked you in a tower somewhere. But here you are." Nadya patted my knee reassuringly.

"Now what?" I asked more to myself than her.

"'Tis up to you." Nadya winked as she hauled herself off the blankets and headed for her tent.

I stared into the fire, watching the white-orange flames dance across the logs. "Now what?" I whispered. The fire blurred as my eyes slid shut.

18

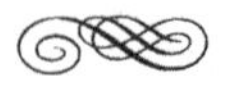

Chapter Eighteen

My eyes fluttered open to the golden rays filtering through the canopy of leaves. Something soft and warm nudged my neck, its hot breath puffing against my skin. I squealed and jumped up, practically tripping over the stones that lined the smoldering ashes from the fire.

Dorcha stood before me, eyeing me like I'd lost my mind. If horses had eyebrows to raise, he'd have done that too. I snickered and stroked his long face.

"Thanks for deserting me last night, buddy. Some stud you are."

He whinnied and nuzzled my hand. I breathed a sigh of relief when I saw the bag of supplies was still fastened in place behind his saddle.

I glanced around to see if the gypsies were awake yet and my heart sunk. I was alone. The only evidence they were real was smoldering ash in the fire pit and the blanket I slept on.

Dorcha nudged me again.

"Hungry?" I rifled through the bag on his back and found a sack of some sort of grain. One sniff and regardless of who Claire intended the grain for, there was no way in hell I was eating something that smelled like the boys' locker room.

I folded the edges of the canvas bag into a makeshift bucket and set it on the ground. Dorcha sniffed it, whinnied and pranced as he dug in.

After ensuring the fire was sufficiently extinguished, I grabbed the blanket and shook the leaves from it. An object sailed out of the thick fabric and hit the ground with a thud.

My footsteps crunched in the leaves as I searched the ground for whatever it was. Out of my peripheral vision something glittered. I picked up the metal disc and brushed the dirt from it. The silver disc was a little bigger than a quarter with a hole in the center and a ridge around the outside. My face reflected in the highly polished metal as I studied the words in some foreign language etched into the rim.

I shrugged and tucked the disc into the pouch at my waist and folded the blanket. At least I'd have a little extra warmth tonight, even if I *was* all alone.

My chest constricted as a wave of panic washed over me. I was really on my own. Again. I glanced around the empty forest, searching for signs of the gypsies, which way they went, anything. But nothing stood out. Not a twig was broken. Save the ring of stones around the fire, it was like they were never there.

I stuck my hand in my pouch and rubbed the metal disc. They had been there. The disc proved it.

Dorcha's hooves crunched behind me, warning me of his approach a moment before his soft mouth nuzzled my cheek, puffing hot air against my ear and hair.

I turned and stroked his long face, my finger tracing over the little white diamond between his eyes. "You're right. I'm not alone am I? I have you."

Dorcha snorted and ducked his head, positioning my hand behind his ear and nudged, like he wanted me to scratch.

I laughed, the sound instantly relaxing my chest and slowing my racing heart. "You know exactly what you want and how to get it, huh?" I gave him a good scratch behind the ears and then tied the blanket above my pack on his back. The rumbling in my stomach demanded attention, so I rifled around until I found something that looked like a really dry biscuit. I took a tiny bite and was surprised to discover it tasted pretty good. That or I was so hungry an old sweaty sock would be good right now.

I clenched the biscuit between my teeth and swung up into the saddle. I smiled and sat straighter, the confidence returning to my body. "Come Dorcha. To Rostellan." I nudged him to walk.

##

I shifted in the hard leather saddle and winced as I tried to find a comfortable position perched on Dorcha's back. My butt hurt. Come to think of it, everything hurt. We'd ridden for hours, but it felt like days. I now completely understood the term 'saddle sore'.

The forest had progressively grown thicker as we ambled up the mountain, and by the shift in the light from golden rays filtering down through the branches to a more muted grayish blue, my guess was it was nearing evening. The trees were a bit more gnarled here, and the air was thick with mist and the scent of decaying vegetation. Moss covered the ground and climbed halfway up the twisted trunks around us.

Dorcha whinnied and took off at a run through the trees.

"Dorcha! Stop!" I pulled back on the reins, but he was determined to make it to wherever he was going.

I clung to him as he ducked around bushes and leapt over fallen trees covered with moss. They reminded me of fallen soldiers, forever frozen beneath a blanket of moss.

We broke through the trees and found a small spring-fed stream surrounded by tall grass. It was so out of place in the middle of what had become a very eerie forest. I practically tumbled over his head when Dorcha skidded to a stop and leaned forward to drink.

"Thanks buddy," I chuckled and slid from his back. I guess I deserved it. I kind-of assumed horses knew where the water was and would find it when they needed it. While I was queen of extracurricular activities, horsemanship was never on my list. That wouldn't help me get into medical school.

I stroked his withers as I grabbed the water skin from my pack. I squished it and sighed when I found it was almost dry. What the heck was I doing out here? Some rescuer I turned out to be. I was going to end up dying of starvation or dehydration, or some other –tion I hadn't thought of yet. It was a good thing Dorcha was a better wilderness explorer than I was.

I chugged the rest of the water and knelt down to refill it in the stream. I watched the skin expand as it filled. I sighed. How could I be almost out of food and water and be only a little more than a day's ride from the castle?

A fly buzzed my face as I pulled the skin from the stream and jammed the stopper back in. A day's ride from the castle. Enough time in which Marcilena had, no doubt, been alerted to my disappearance.

The picture of Claire and her brother, hand in hand, watching me as I raced for the drawbridge in the rain flashed before my eyes. And memory of the strangled scream that cut through the air brought a new wave of goose bumps racing across my skin.

Like a whisper on the wind, Claire's words filled my head "Bring the queen down."

"I promise you Claire, I'll bring the queen down." Without realizing it, I said the words aloud. For Claire. For Casey. For my parents. For Brandon. For every man, woman and child who suffered under Marcilena's reign. An overwhelming sensation of hopelessness tingled along my skin. I was just one teenager. Marcilena was a powerful, potentially magically inclined queen.

The annoying fly buzzed my nose again. I swiped at it, but hit only air. I put the skin on the grass beside me and leaned over the edge to fill my hands with the cool, clear water. I brought a handful to my lips and drank deeply. It was sweet, not like the artificially sweetened stuff I used to drink at home, but fresh and clean, like water with essences of mint and blueberries. It was ridiculous, but I could feel the bubbles in the water burst on my tongue in little explosions of flavor.

I glanced at Dorcha, who munched the lush grass on the edge of the stream as I drank. "This stuff tastes almost like carbonated flavored water!"

Dorcha snuffed and resumed his munching.

I swatted at another fly that this time buzzed my ear as I surveyed the clearing around the odd little stream. My stomach growled when I caught sight of a plant closely resembling the strawberry plant my mom had growing in a pot on our patio.

My fingers traced over the broad three-leaf pattern. From beneath the leaves, stems shot out tipped with pretty white flowers, each one with the beginnings of a berry. And hanging down towards the stream, were luscious, bright red berries. I plucked one from its stem and turned it around between my fingers. It looked exactly like a strawberry. I sniffed it and my mouth watered. It smelled exactly how I remembered strawberries tasted when I was a kid, but once I got older I could never find that fresh, perfect flavor. Commercial berries always tasted like dirt, and the manufactured strawberry flavor, while it smelled real, tasted like plastic.

"What do you think? Is it safe?" I called back to Dorcha, who had moved on to munch something that looked similar to the shoots from green onions.

Dorcha snorted and ambled a little closer, finding a small berry plant of his own and dug in.

"Well if you're eating it, Mr. Wilderness Explorer..." I popped the berry into my mouth. The flavor exploded on my tongue. It tasted exactly like I remembered strawberries were supposed to taste. Fresh and sweet and strawberry. I was in Heaven.

The annoying fly buzzed my nose again, thwacking into me before I could swat it away.

A voice chimed beside my ear, tiny and high-pitched like a little bell. "'Tis stealing, you know."

I jumped and almost fell into the stream. My gaze flitted around the small clearing, but it was just me and Dorcha.

"Who said that?"

Four voices, all tiny and high-pitched, chimed together like a song. "We did."

I scrambled to my feet and looked around wildly. "Where are you?"

"We are everywhere," their voices echoed on the wind.

What the heck was in that water? Was I hallucinating? I glanced at Dorcha, who was still happily munching away on the strawberry plants. He seemed fine, and didn't seem to notice the voices.

"What do you want?" I spun in a circle, searching the clearing and the woods beyond for any sign of movement.

"To know if what you said is true," they spoke in unison, their voices a melodic harmony.

"What I said?" I frowned. What *had* I said?

"You promised someone named Claire you would bring the queen down." Still no one emerged from the forest to claim the voices.

My stomach churned. I'd inadvertently incriminated myself by assuming I was alone with Dorcha in these woods. Who knew if these women, or spirits, or whatever they were, worked for the queen?

"Enough games. I won't answer until you show yourselves."

That darn fly buzzed me again. I swatted at it and actually managed to catch it in my hand. It wriggled inside my fist as I pulled my hand away from my face to look at it. I slowly peeled my fingers back one at a time, so the bug wouldn't escape until I had a look at it first.

"What the hell was in that water?" I gaped down at the thing in my hand.

19

Chapter Nineteen

The little winged creature sat on my palm, its legs folded beneath itself, its gossamer wings spread out like a butterfly's.

I laughed. "You're a faerie!"

The little red-haired faerie tentatively fluttered her wings and smoothed them with her hands. "And *you* practically killed me!" She shot an angry glare in my direction.

"You were the one pretending to be a fly! What'd you expect?"

"To annoy you until you went away. 'Tis what flies do."

A sarcastic laugh escaped my lips. "I have an evil queen for a stepmother. A little fly annoyance isn't going to make me leave."

Her little green eyes widened as she stared up at me. "So 'tis true then?"

"How do I know you don't work for her?"

This time the sarcastic laugh came from her. "Because we have been waiting for you for a very long time." She flew up out of my hand and hovered before my face.

"I don't think I am who you think I am, but yeah, my goal is to rescue the prince and hopefully bring the queen down in the process."

Another voice chimed by my ear. "We know who you are. Even if you do not."

Of course I get the smart-ass faeries.

"Come." The little redhead darted towards the stream, leaving a glittering red trail of light behind her. Purple, yellow and white streaks shot past me and swirled with the red faerie's trail. It was like watching a laser light show, the light patterns swirling and zigzagging across the moonlit meadow. Then they shot towards each other and collided, causing an explosion of light and glitter like a tiny firework.

I ran to where they exploded and scanned the ground, fully expecting to find tiny body parts scattered on the grass from the explosion.

"Sit," a melodic female voice called out from the trees. It wasn't like the tiny high-pitched tinkle of the faeries.

My stomach tightened. I sunk down onto the soft grass and tucked my legs beneath me. The blades tickled my skin.

"Princess Victoria, daughter of Queen Katherine."

I started. I hadn't told any of them my name. "My name is Tori. And I'm not Katherine's daughter. At least not this world's Katherine."

"You are."

I shook my head. "No, really, I'm not. I was in a plane crash and woke up and everyone was gone. Some of them are here, but they aren't themselves. They don't remember. I'm the only one that remembers. They keep telling me I'm a princess, but I'm not. I'm just Tori, and I'm just trying to find my family and get the heck out of this crazy dream."

My mouth fell open when a breathtaking woman wearing a pure white gossamer ball gown with iridescent butterfly wings and blue-white sparkles in her curly blonde hair stepped from what seemed to be thin air. Her vibrant blue eyes searched mine as she floated towards me, her feet a foot off the ground. "Well, Just Tori, if you are na the real Princess Victoria, then where is she? You look like her." She raised a delicately sculpted white eyebrow.

I shrugged. "Maybe she woke up in my body when I woke up in hers?"

"Interesting idea, that. Tell me, Just Tori, do you believe in fate?"

I clenched my fists. "My name is *Tori*. And no, I don't believe in fate. I believe that this is my dream and I'll wake up, eventually, and be back home."

Three more winged women stepped from the forest, their sheer figures becoming more concrete as they came closer. Their voices jumbled as they talked simultaneously.

"What if you never wake up, Tori?" The redheaded faerie, who was now as big as I was, said.

"What if 'tis na a dream?"

"What if that was a dream?"

I covered my ears and shouted. "Stop!" A stunned silence fell over the clearing. Even Dorcha's head shot up and he stared at me with his big dark eyes. I took a moment and studied each of the faeries surrounding me. "Who are you?"

The white faerie spoke. "We are the faeries that blessed you on the day of your birth. We are the keepers of the seasons. We make the plants grow, the seasons change, we keep nature in balance."

"Some balance," I scoffed, but the cold glare she shot me with her ice-blue eyes stopped me dead in my tracks. "Sorry."

Her face softened. "Maybe you are'na the true Princess Victoria. Maybe you are an imposter. The sword of Amaranth will know. Only the true heir to the throne can wield its power."

"The sword of what?"

"Amaranth. 'Twas the king of Aislin centuries ago. A powerful wizard enchanted the sword so only the blood heirs of the king of Aislin could wield its power. The sword gave its bearer the power to break through enchantments and spells, to see the truth behind the lies." She closed the distance between us and took my hand in hers. I flinched at the iciness of her skin but stood.

She chuckled. "'Tis all right. I know my skin is cold. My name is Frost, and I am the winter faerie."

I nodded and followed her to the trunk of a large, gnarled tree at the edge of the clearing. I could feel the eyes of the other faeries on me when she put her long, delicate hand onto the trunk of the tree. Her translucent skin shimmered like a dragonfly's wings against the gray bark of the ancient tree.

Frost closed her eyes and hummed a quiet tune. I gasped when the other three joined in, their voices mingling in a heart-wrenching harmony. The bark glowed beneath her hand and the tree's gnarled trunk shuddered. It writhed like three fat snakes tied together before the individual trunks pulled free of each other and unfurled back like a flower in bloom.

The faerie's voices slowly dwindled until only Frost's voice echoed through the clearing. Her song came to an end and she drew in a deep breath and exhaled, the air swirling with ice crystals as it blew across the spread-open trunk. I shivered as the air around me chilled, and I could see my breath puffing from my gaping mouth. As I watched, a glass case revealed itself in the center of the tree. I could make out the shape of a sword through the frosty glass.

Frost nodded towards the sword. "Get it."

I eyed the tree skeptically. In the back of my mind I could see the Venus flytrap, where as soon as a fly touched the pink mouth of the trap, it snapped shut on the unsuspecting prey.

She gave my frost-bitten hand a reassuring squeeze. "Go."

I inhaled in a frigid breath and stepped inside the gaping tree-blossom. The sword stood on its tip, the glass case around it reminding me of a monolith. I glanced back at Frost. "How?"

"Touch the case."

I tentatively laid my hand on the ice-cold glass. For a moment, nothing happened except for the chill from the glass radiating into my hand. A crack echoed through the air. I watched as the glass shattered beneath my fingers and crumbled into a glittering pile of shards around the sword.

A chorus of cheers erupted from the faeries.

Frost composed herself and caught my eye. "Take the sword, Princess Victoria, daughter of Queen Katherine, champion of Aislin."

My skin tightened at the use of the term 'champion'. I wrapped my fingers around the hilt of the glittering sword. The dim light reflected off its blade as I pulled it from its home in the tree.

"I don't understand." I stared at the sword. The blade was covered in some sort of flowery lettering etched into the metal that looked vaguely familiar. "What does this mean?"

"That's the enchantment, etched into the blade by the wizard, in a language long since forgotten." Frost smiled and helped me from the tree, which, as soon as I was away, wrapped itself back tightly in knots.

I stared at the sword in my hand. It was remarkably light considering how long it was. "What the heck am I supposed to do with this?"

"Slay the dragon, rescue the prince, awaken your mother, and defeat the evil queen."

"Oh, is that all?" My stomach dropped when their wide eyes and even wider smiles proved my sarcasm was lost on them. The chill that seeped into my skin from Frost's icy touch worked its way through my body as I stared at them. They were serious.

"No one said anything about a dragon!" I stomped away, dragging the sword with me through the tall grass. I shouted over my shoulder: "You're serious? You know I'm just a seventeen-year-old kid, right? I barely passed my driving test. How the heck am I supposed to do all that? Isn't that what you have knights and stuff for? Why me?"

The little redhead caught up to me and slipped her hand in to mine. "You underestimate yourself, Tori."

I skidded to a stop and spun to face her. "You overestimate me."

Frost spoke up from a few steps behind. "The sword knows who you are. You just have to remember."

I held my breath. Darien's voice echoed in my head. "Remember who you are."

A sly smile crossed the redhead's freckled features. "Maybe if you complete your destined path, you shall wake up from this dream."

I stopped cold and stared at her. "What did you say?"

She dropped her hand from mine. "I said you must complete your destined path."

I shook my head. "No, the part about the dream."

Her green eyes widened. Their color reminded me of Prince Brandon's. "What part about what dream?"

I shook my head and glared at her. I know what I heard. Why was she denying it now? "What's your name?"

Her face lit up, which made freckles on her face stand out a little more. "I am Summer."

The other faeries stepped up behind her. For the first time, I really looked at them. Each was unique, like the season they protected. Summer, obviously represented summer. The porcelain skinned brunette with the burnt umber wings resembling falling leaves must have been the fall faerie, and I'd bet five bucks her name was Autumn.

I smiled at the fall faerie. "You're Autumn right?"

Her cheeks blushed to match her wings and she nodded.

"So that leaves spring," I turned towards the cheerful blonde faerie with purple flower-like wings. "Who I'm going to take a wild guess is April, right?"

April smiled and her cheeks flushed purple. "How did you know?" Her lavender eyes searched mine.

"It's my dream." I winked. Convinced more than ever this was a dream and I would wake up if I completed the tasks like Summer accidentally spilled, I plopped down on the grass next to where Dorcha was grazing. "So tell me where this dragon is."

Autumn knelt beside me and smiled. "You are truly your mother's daughter. She would have said the same thing."

The story the Gypsies told me of how the queen and her baby were murdered popped into my head. "Why did a faerie kill Queen Katherine and her daughter?"

Frost eased down onto the grass on the other side of me. As soon as she touched it, the blades of grass curled in on themselves and a glittering sheen of ice crystals formed on them. "The faerie did not kill your mother and sister. She cast a spell on them."

I shook my head. "That killed them. The Gypsies told me about it. They were there."

"So were we."

I blinked. They all appeared to be my age, maybe a tiny bit older. They couldn't have been old enough to even remember it, let alone be active participants. "So you were like seven?"

Frost smiled and shook her head. "Faeries d'na age like humans do. Once we reach our season, for each human year, we age a day."

"Oh." I picked a blade of grass and twirled it in my fingers. "Then you know the faerie that cast the spell on them? Why did she do it?" A spell. That meant my mom and Casey could be alive, trapped somewhere in this crazy dream too.

Autumn shrugged. "She was so sick. I did'na think she would cause mischief at the party, so I had pity on her and allowed her to come along. A dying wish, she told me," she sighed. "If only I had known..."

Frost interrupted her. "'Twasn't your fault Autumn. No one knew October was evil until it was too late."

"But she was my sister. I should have known."

Summer plopped down beside Autumn and hugged her. "None of us knew. 'Tis not your fault."

My heart squeezed for the pain in Autumn's face. The pain of losing a sister was horrible. I knew from experience. Finding out a sister was evil had to be unbearable. "So what happened to her after the party? Was she arrested?"

April knelt before me and shook her head. "She disappeared right after it happened. No one has seen or heard from her since."

I glanced at Frost, who watched Autumn with sad eyes. "What happened to the bodies of Queen Katherine and her baby? The Gypsies said everyone thought they were dead, but they disappeared right before the memorial."

Frost seemed a million miles away, her blue gaze fixed on the past. She blinked and then focused her gaze on me. "I know not. But the Gypsies were right, they did disappear. They were stolen."

"But they aren't dead?"

She shook her head.

Stolen. "Okay, so where is this dragon I have to slay?"

Summer perked up. "In the caves beneath Rostellan Castle."

Great. To rescue Brandon, I had to slay the dragon first. "Oh."

"The sword knows what it wants. You just have to have the courage to wield it." My gaze locked with Frost's. The confidence in her icy blue eyes somehow warmed me, even as the icy blades of grass brushed my knee. Her mouth opened as if to speak, but her gaze shot to the trees behind me. Her blue eyes widened. "Someone is coming! You must go. Go now!"

Before I could blink, the four faeries were gone, only a glittering mist fluttered to the ground where they once sat. "Wait! I don't even know where I'm going!"

Four trails of light, each a different color, shot through the forest, practically creating a flashing neon sign that said "this way to Rostellan Castle".

With the sounds of rustling in the forest behind me I dashed for Dorcha and swung up into the saddle. "Hurry!" I whispered and prodded him to run.

We raced through the forest, following the trails of light from the faeries. One by one they flickered out, until it just the white light shot through the darkness before us. Then Frost's light trail shot up into the black sky in the distance and exploded in a tiny blue-white firework. For a moment, the peak of a mountain illuminated in her twinkling explosion of light.

Dorcha snorted.

I leaned down to whisper in his ear. "I see it too. Go!"

He folded his ears back and galloped through the thick forest, dodging trees as we raced for the peak.

20

Chapter Twenty

We ran until the terrain grew too treacherous for Dorcha to run any more. As my mount carefully picked his way through the loose earth, I scanned the darkness behind us, searching for any sign of whoever was following us. My heart lurched when an inky figure dashed between darkened trees. My eyes strained, locked on to the spot where I'm sure I saw the figure. Nothing moved. Nothing breathed. Must just be a trick of the light.

My breath puffed in white clouds around my face as we ascended. The air thinned while the trees thickened, turning the forest landscape from green to gray. I had only escaped from the castle a few days ago, but winter was already setting in. *How long had I been locked up in my elegant prison? Could it really be winter already?*

I shivered and huddled against Dorcha's back for warmth. His breath puffed out in gusts on either side of his long face as he climbed. My stomach growled. I cursed myself for devouring what I had without thinking of the future. It occurred to me too late that Claire probably gave me just enough food that, if I rationed it, would have been sufficient to sustain me for the trip.

At least the brief pit-stop at the faerie spring allowed Dorcha to get his fill of grass and water, and I got to fill my water skin. My mouth watered at the thought of the taste of that perfect strawberry. If only

I'd had enough time to gather more of those before we raced away to avoid whoever was following us.

I shivered when fluffy white flakes drifted down through the canopy like little bits of confetti. They stuck to Dorcha's mane and built in little piles on the ground. I held my hand out and caught a few flakes, which melted the moment they touched my skin.

My cheeks and nose burned from the wind hitting my face. My body felt like one giant Charlie horse, my muscles twinging with each careful step Dorcha took. I led him to an outcropping of rocks where we could camp for the night. If only Claire had thought to pack a tent or sleeping bag. I sighed. Where was a Camping World when you needed one?

I slid off Dorcha's back and let him graze on the bits of grass sticking up through the little piles of snow while I grabbed some sticks. Luckily, the sticks near the base of the trees weren't wet, yet.

The night squeezed in around me as I tromped back to the outcropping with a huge armload of dry twigs. I stashed half of them under a ledge where they would stay dry, and took the rest to build a fire. Thank God Mom forced me to join Scouts when I was little.

"But when will I *ever* need to build a fire?" my whiny ten-year-old self asked.

"You never know when it could come in handy. Besides, it'll be fun," Mom cinched up my scarf and smoothed my dress uniform from behind me. I stared at myself in the mirror. Dimples, round blue eyes, sandy blonde hair and freckles. I was an exact copy of my mom. A miniature, child-like version, but a copy nonetheless.

So, when Casey came along with her chocolate brown eyes and deep chestnut hair, I always teased her that she was adopted. A twinge of guilt twisted my stomach as the memory of my mother and sister flashed in my head. Where were they? Were they all right?

Something rustled in the leaves and shook me from my mental guilt trip. I scanned the darkness behind me. Moonlight sent long, dark shadows through the forest, but nothing was there. I shuddered and got back to work building the fire.

I sat back on my heels and smiled triumphantly when the pile of sticks and logs resembled a teepee. I pulled out the flint from my pack and stared at it, trying to remember how Claire had gotten it to ignite before. Another twinge of guilt turned my stomach at the thought of Claire.

Miraculously, it only took me six tries to get the kindling lit and soon there was a cozy fire roaring before me. I untied my pack from Dorcha's back and pulled out the blanket and wrapped it around my frigid shoulders before tying his reigns to a low branch above a patch of grass.

My gaze traced over Dorcha's glistening coat. "Thanks for being such a great friend." I cringed when I noticed the light sprinkling of snow in his mane. "Sorry I don't have a blanket for you."

He snorted and continued munching on the grass, almost as if saying "No big deal".

I smiled, but it fell from my face when the leaves crunched behind Dorcha. His head shot up and his nostrils flared.

"What is it Dorcha?" My eyes darted around the darkened forest.

Something snapped right behind Dorcha's legs, like a huge branch breaking. He reared back, kicking into the air as he let out an ear-piercing shriek. He landed back on all-fours and fought at his tether.

"Shh, Dorcha," I soothed, but his frantic panting and ears plastered against the sides of his head showed it was useless.

I took a step toward him, intent on soothing him until he calmed down, but a snap in the forest to my right made me freeze. My body trembled and my gaze searched the darkness. I backed up against the outcropping of rocks. The fire and rocks were the most protection I had, so I had to hold my ground.

Leaves crunched and twigs snapped all around me, closer and closer. Something was moving out in the darkness, beyond the light from the fire. My heart lurched with each snap. I clutched the blanket around me and huddled against the rocks. I clenched my eyes and chanted to myself. *This is just a dream. Just a dream.*

As quickly as my eyes flicked open, I wished they hadn't. Firelight reflected off a pair of yellow eyes on the other side of the fire. I strained to see the shape of their owner, but it stayed just out the reach of the firelight. Another pair of eyes appeared, then another and another. I snapped my eyes shut and wrapped my arms around myself, squeezing hard to till my trembling. *It's just a dream. Just a dream.*

I flinched when the first snarl cut through the night. My heart leapt in to my throat when Dorcha's scream followed. His hooves pummeled the ground. I clenched my eyes shut, plugged my ears and rocked back and forth. *It's just a dream. Nothing can hurt me.*

Hot, putrid air puffed against my cheeks. One of my eyes pried itself open almost involuntarily. A breath's distance away from my face was a mangy gray wolf's muzzle, its lips pulled back in a snarl, its razor sharp fangs dripping with saliva. Angry yellow eyes glared at me.

I screamed and scampered backwards until my back slammed against the jagged rock. The wolf reared back and lunged at me.

In the same instant, a huge dark figure flew over the rock and tackled the wolf a moment before its jagged teeth connected with my face. With a strangled yelp it collapsed to the ground. A trickle of blood ran down its matted gray fur.

Darien straightened and surveyed me before turning back to face the wolves, his bloodied sword glistening in the firelight. A huge brown wolf stepped into the circle of light a few feet away from him. Like the first, its lips curled back over yellowed fangs, and a feral snarl reverberated through its body.

They circled each other, but Darien kept himself between me and the wild beast. Its lips quivered and a growl rumbled its chest. I cringed when the beast snapped, each time a little closer to Darien's leg or stomach. And each time he'd lunge out of the way at the last second, only to return to his position between me and the monster.

I choked back a scream when the wolf lunged again and tore a chunk of fabric from his cloak. While it was distracted with the bit of cloth in its mouth, Darien swiped his sword at the wolf and a pained yelp escaped the beast. It limped back into the fight, circling one way then the other. But Darien never relented. Another lunge. Another bit of cloth. Another jab with the sword.

The determined beast regrouped, limping heavily on three legs. It prepared to lunge again. Then, as if sensing it would not win the fight, it turned and limped into the darkness. One by one, the glittering eyes in the darkness beyond the fire disappeared into the night.

Darien panted to catch his breath and cautiously approached Dorcha. He stroked the distraught horse's neck and whispered quietly to him. Instantly he calmed. Then he turned to face me, his coppery gaze unreadable.

The gratitude for saving my life quickly melted into suspicion as he watched me, his face emotionless. "You followed me." It wasn't a question.

He nodded.

My fists dug into my blanket and I winced when my finger nicked the blade of Amaranth's sword. In an instant, I was off the ground, the sword aimed at Darien's throat. My words ground out through clenched teeth. "Did Marcilena send you to follow me?"

Darien dropped his sword and raised his hands defensively. His eyes flicked across the enchanted sword. Surprise crossed his face, but I wasn't going to be fooled that easily.

"Did she?"

He shook his head, a slight movement with my blade so close to his throat.

I searched his face and found no fear in his eyes. "Why did you follow me then?"

His gaze locked with mine. The firelight reflected in his copper eyes, making them look like they too were on fire. "Only to make sure you were safe. I promise you, the queen has no idea of your whereabouts, or your quest."

"Can I trust you?"

"I would die to protect you."

My eyes narrowed as I studied him, searching for any evidence of his lie. But all I saw is the same smoldering look he had when he kissed me. But the word "bound" still rattled around in my head.

"I can take care of myself," I whispered.

I lowered my sword and marched back to my blanket by the fire. I plopped down and wrapped the blanket around my shoulders. The cold had seeped through my clothes and I couldn't stop shaking. *Shaking that had absolutely nothing to do with the wolves almost eating me or the twinge of whatever that was I felt when I saw him*, I told myself.

He raised an eyebrow and gestured to the dead wolf. "I can see that. What exactly were you doing when that wolf almost ate you?"

I shot him my most scathing glare, which only made him chuckle. He gently lifted the dead wolf from the ground and carried it reverently into the darkened forest.

A few minutes later he stepped back into the firelight and pointed to the open ground beside me. "May I?"

I shrugged.

That stupid, sexy smirk crossed his face and he eased himself down beside me. I glared at the fire, watching the way the flames danced across the charred wood. My nose twitched at the pungent scent of smoke as it swirled around us. The heat from Darien's body heated the air between us and I found myself unconsciously leaning towards him, trying to absorb more of his warmth.

His voice broke the silence. "When was the last time you ate?"

I shrugged. "I had a berry earlier today, when we came across the fae –" I cut off mid-sentence. He didn't need to know about the faeries. "When we came across the spring."

"What spring? I didn't see any."

I shrugged again. If he followed me, how could he have missed it?

"A berry?"

I nodded. My mouth watered at the memory of the explosion of flavor fresh on my lips.

He rifled through his pack and handed me something wrapped in cloth. "Here." He smiled and held my gaze for a moment before turning back to the fire. I never noticed how deep his dimples were before. Or the way his skin reminded me of silky, warm caramel. Or the cleft in his chin, but somehow the firelight made them all stand out.

I cleared my throat and shifted my gaze to the package in my hands. "Thanks." I unwrapped the small bundle. A small loaf of bread, a piece of dried meat resembling beef jerky, and some dry cheese.

Even as my stomach growled in protest, I handed the little package back. "I can't accept this. It's too much."

He pushed the package back at me. "I brought this for you, in case I managed to catch up with you. 'Tis more where that came from."

My stomach rumbled again, loudly this time. "Thanks," I muttered and accepted the peace offering.

I ripped off a hunk of bread and handed it to him before ripping off another piece for myself. I caught the surprise in his face when he took it from me. I kept my gaze locked on the fire and took a bite of the bread. My eyes closed in bliss as the flavor melted on my tongue. It was probably because I was beyond starving, but it was by far the best tasting thing I'd ever eaten in my entire life.

"My thanks," he murmured.

I shrugged. "It's your food." I glanced at him in time to catch another sexy half-smile, deepening his dimples in the flickering light and he stared at the fire. My stomach did those crazy somersaults and I tore my gaze from his face to study the flames.

I tried to ignore the tingles that raced over my skin when our knuckles brushed when we reached for another piece of the jerky at the same time. And when his gaze caught mine in the firelight, the fluttering of my heart must have been an after effect of the adrenaline.

Before long, the food sitting on my stomach mingled with the tingling warmth from the fire and lulled me into a daze. I squinted at the flames, trying to bring them into focus. My eyes closed for the briefest second and popped open when Darien laid me back against a thick blanket.

It took me a moment to remember where I was and what was happening. But when his warm fingertips brushed my cheek as he pushed a strand of hair from my face, it all came back to me. I was on my feet instantly.

"Don't touch me!" I snapped. The chill from the night air assaulted me and I stood before him shivering. I clutched my cloak around me and eyed him suspiciously.

He sat motionless beside the warm cocoon I so hastily vacated. "My apologies. I did'na mean to startle you."

"You didn't startle me. You betrayed me." I fought to keep my voice steady.

"I d'na understand." His eyes searched mine.

"How could you? You just went along with the betrothal! You didn't even protest when she announced it. Like you knew what her plans were all along." My voice teetered on the brink of hysteria. I inhaled slowly, desperately trying to calm my pounding heart. "How can I trust you, when you've been lying to me the whole time?"

"I did lie to you, Tori. But I d'na have a choice. Marcilena threatened to kill someone I loved if I even attempted to say no when she announced it. "

I paused. It never occurred to me that he had no choice in the matter either. My teeth chattered from the cold as I spoke. "Why didn't you come to see me after to explain?"

His gaze dropped to the fire, as if he would find the answers in the dancing flames. "I tried. I was going to help you escape. But Antonio found out about my plans. Marcilena had me punished..." He got up off the blanket, turned and pulled his shirt up.

I stifled a horrified gasp with my frigid hands when crisscrossing sets of angry red welts across his wide shoulders came into view. Some of the lash wounds were so deep they had indentations where chunks of flesh had been ripped away.

They matched the scars that peeked out of the top of Claire's bodice at times. Another set of lash wounds that were my fault. Another person punished because of something they did to help me. My stomach lurched at the realization. This was my fault.

Tears burned my eyes. "I'm sorry I caused you pain."

Darien tugged his shirt down and held his hand out to me. He studied me with a guarded expression. "You did'na do this. *She* did. I hope you will believe me now when I say that I would do anything to be free of my tie to Marcilena. But not if it hurt you, in any way. I would bind myself to Marcilena for eternity if it meant keeping you safe."

I studied his eyes in the firelight. He was as much Marcilena's captive as I had been.

"I believe you." I whispered and took his hand and let him lead me back to the blankets. I laid down and he took another blanket and draped it over me, tucking me in like a child.

I rolled on to my side and tucked my frigid hands beneath my cheek. The weight of the day and his confession rested heavily on my consciousness and my eyes fluttered closed within seconds. The world spun out of time and space as I drifted off. It was a refreshing weightlessness, where the hard ground disappeared and the freezing wind blowing around us quieted. I floated on a blissful cloud of nothingness, at peace in my non-dream.

I jerked awake when Darien slid between the blankets behind me. He gently eased one arm under my head and wrapped the other around my torso. I held my breath, feigning sleep when he pulled me against him. Every nerve in my body sparked to life as I lay in his arms, pretending to be asleep. His hard body pressed against me and each ridge of muscle stood out in definition against my back. His hot breath puffed against my neck and ear, causing the delicate hairs to stand on end and goose bumps to prick my skin.

It felt so good, so comforting to be enveloped by the strong warmth of his arms. I stared at his long, tanned fingers pressing against my stomach and watched the firelight dance across his golden skin. Against my will, my skin ached to feel his fingers upon it.

A twinge of guilt fluttered over my stomach. Here I was, on a quest to rescue Brandon from Marcilena's evil plans, while pretending to be asleep in another guy's arms.

God, I was so confused about these two guys. Brandon was everything a Prince Charming should be. And Darien was the opposite in so many ways. But one touch from Darien and my body came alive in ways it never had when Brandon kissed me. With Brandon, I felt every bit the fairy tale princess. With Darien, I felt like a pile of kindling, just waiting for that tiny spark to ignite me into an inferno.

His lips brushed my ear and laid gentle kisses along my hairline. "Are you awake?" he whispered, his breath hot against my neck.

I slowed my breathing, trying to imitate sleep. But I doubted he could miss the thundering of my heart with his body pressed so tightly against mine. I nuzzled my head deeper into his arm and sighed.

A soft growl rumbled in his chest and his hand pressed against my stomach, pulling me tighter against him. His words tumbled from his lips in a half-sigh, half-groan. "Lord, you drive me mad, Tori."

I said nothing, just stared at his hand. His fingers found their way between the thin layers of my blouse, the hot skin of his fingertips tracing circles over my bare torso.

His deep sigh blew a few curls over my face. "If I only I was brave enough to tell you how much you mean to me. Instead, like a coward, I whisper it in your ear while you sleep."

I forced myself to take slow, measured breaths to not clue him in to my being awake. The thrill of hearing his innermost thoughts, those he'd kept hidden from me, made my heart flutter.

"I wish you did not affect me so. 'Twould be so much easier to lie to Marcilena about how little you mean to me if it were not true. But, I think she can see through my lies. You could ask me for the sun and I would throw a rope around it and drag it to earth, if only to bring a smile to your beautiful face." He paused, as if considering how to put his feelings into words. The pounding of my pulse had to be loud enough for him to hear.

My heart galloped at the thought of him lying to Marcilena to protect me. Could it be? Could I really trust him?

"You remind me that there is still unspoiled beauty in the world. Goodness for the sake of being good." Another deep sigh stirred my hair. His next words were pained. "If only I could afford to give you the world. If only I could offer you what that knave Brandon could. Love may be priceless, but love alone c'na provide a princess the lifestyle she's accustomed to."

I stiffened slightly, forgetting I was supposed to be pretending to sleep. His fingers resumed their soothing circles against my stomach, dipping into my navel slightly on each pass. Rather than soothing, goose bumps raised along my skin.

He buried his face in my hair, his fingers digging into my stomach slightly. My hair muffled his words. "If only love were enough."

My breath caught in my throat. Had he really confessed his love for me while he thought I slept? I shifted in his arms so I was facing him. His gaze traveled down to my exposed navel.

"So beautiful." Still unaware I was awake, he gently ran his fingers over my bare stomach. He raised his eyes to study my face and froze when he saw me watching him. He trembled slightly against me. "You are awake." His cheeks flamed, which was one of the sexiest things I'd ever seen in my life.

"Maybe love is enough," I murmured. At least for tonight, his love would be enough. We'd deal with tomorrow when it came.

His copper eyes flashed. He opened his mouth to say something, but I covered it with mine. The intensity of the emotions running through me crested like a wave crashing against the rocks and I poured everything I was into that kiss. The feelings I had for Brandon were like a childhood crush compared to the emotions his confession and his kiss awoke in me. It was like my heart had been locked away in a chest and Darien was the only one with a key.

His tongue traced across my lips, and I touched his tongue with my own. He wrapped his arms around me and crushed me against him, pressing every inch of my body against his. His hands traced up and down my back, my shoulders, my arms, tracing each finger before entwining his own through mine.

"Tori," he murmured, a warning and a question in his tone at the same time.

My skin flamed everywhere he touched me, begging for him to touch me again. I smiled and pulled him back to my lips, this time sliding my hands under the hem of his shirt, tracing each ridge of his six pack, working my way up his chest, his shirt shirring up with my hands. He shifted and I yanked it over his head in one quick move.

He pulled the pile of blankets over us and lowered his lips to mine, his fingers pushing the hem of my dress away from my torso. His hand trailed down my thigh and caught it, hitching it over his hip as he deepened the kiss.

His hands drove me crazy, skirting along my hips, cupping my butt and pulling me against him, trailing over my shoulder and the side of my breasts. It was like he was doing everything in his power to not touch me inappropriately.

I pulled away a little and untangled my hands from his thick hair. Disappointment flashed across his features, but was replaced ten-fold when my fingers found the leather lacing to my bodice. I blushed and slowly tugged, loosening the knot.

His burnt-umber eyes flamed as I tentatively pulled my bodice away from my breasts, leaving them open and exposed to the frigid night air, which made them to tighten almost painfully.

My name was a groan on his lips when he leaned in and cupped my chest in his hands and crushed my lips with his. An ache built deep within me as he kneaded my breasts. No one had ever touched me this way before. If only it were real. I sighed and gave myself over to the incredible feelings building in my body.

He shifted over me, keeping the blankets pulled over our heads, the light from the fire barely filtering through the thick fabric enough for us to see each other.

"Tell me to cease and I will," Darien murmured, his gaze locked with mine, his features flushed with desire. His jaw clenched as if he were fighting a losing battle.

"I want this." I spread my legs to accommodate him.

"Thank God," he groaned. He unlaced his breeches and shoved them around his knees. I couldn't see much of him in the darkness of our makeshift blanket-tent, but I could feel his hardness against my thigh as he shoved my skirt higher.

A thrill rushed through me at the gasp that escaped his throat when his fingers brushed across me. While I was forced to wear corsets and other instruments of torture for the world to see, there was no way I was going to wear those frilly, horrendous granny panty things Claire laid out for me each day. So I went commando, privately protesting in my own non-confrontational way. Besides, this dress didn't work well with underwear anyway. I blushed when he raised his astonished gaze to mine.

My name was on his lips as he eased his weight onto me and brought himself inside. I gasped at the searing pain, but it quickly receded. *Who would have thought that a virgin in real life would be a virgin in her dreams too?*

He froze at my slight whimper. "Am I hurting you?" he whispered against my ear.

"Not anymore." I ran my nails down his side, a little harder than I meant to as he started to move.

He didn't even notice. The heat within our little cocoon built as the ache inside me did. I bit my lip to keep from crying out when the tension in my body peaked and exploded, the fireworks before my eyes so bright I was temporarily blinded.

Darien collapsed on top of me and pulled me with him as he rolled to his side. He stroked my hair away from my face with one hand.

When he caught his breath he spoke. "I am sorry I lost control." He caught my chin and lifted, making me raise my eyes to meet to his. "Did I hurt you?"

I shook my head and buried my face in his damp chest.

"You are a terrible liar, a ghrá."

I furrowed my brow. "What does 'a ghrá' mean?"

He blushed again, this time all the way to the tips of his ears. "It means 'my love'."

The words came to my lips, but I was terrified to let them out. Instead I smiled.

The hurt flashed in his eyes, and seeing that hurt felt like someone had stabbed me in the heart. God, how I wanted him to be real. But it was just a dream. He might look like the Darien I went to school with, but I knew now that he wasn't. Why let myself fall in love with a guy who doesn't really exist?

Something inside me died a little when he nodded, as if resigning to the fact that I couldn't, or wouldn't verbalize my feelings for him. He reached down and wrestled his pants back up, smoothed my skirt down and pulled his shirt on before pulling me against him.

I fumbled with the ties on my bodice and miraculously managed to fasten it again. I wanted nothing more than to tell him I loved him, to tell him that my soul was his for eternity. But what good would that do me once I woke up, to pledge my undying love to a figment of my imagination? I'd end up comparing every guy I met to him. The one guy who looked like him had said less than two words to me since the day we met. Provided he had survived the crash, there was *no* chance the real-life version Darien would be interested in me, and no one else would come close. I'd die miserable and alone because no man could measure up to the perfect guy I'd dreamed up.

It was for the best. For both of us.

21

Chapter Twenty-one

What felt like a few minutes after I closed them, my eyes fluttered open to the golden sunlight filtering down through the thick cover of trees, illuminating the crystalline flakes of snow as they fluttered to the ground. I shivered and rolled over, tucking my blanket over my head. It was so toasty under the pile of thick blankets and cloaks, nestled against Darien's warm chest. *I must still be dreaming.*

"Wake up, a ghrá," Darien murmured and kissed my forehead. He ran gentle circles over my back with his free hand.

I froze. The blissful feeling of sleep left my body as reality set in. I was wrapped tightly in Darien's arms. I shifted slightly and gasped at the ache that twinged between my legs. It wasn't a dream. I'd really slept with Darien last night.

The blood rushed to my cheeks as I raised my dazed gaze to meet his clear, coppery one. "Did we really...?" My mouth went dry and I couldn't force the words from my lips.

He nodded, his sexy half-smile crossing his face as he leaned in and pressed his lips to mine. It took one half-second before I lost myself in his kiss, so tender, so gentle, so tentative. Like he wasn't sure how I'd react to waking up in his arms. Like he thought I might disappear.

My body tightened with pleasure when he pulled me against him, one of his thighs slipping between mine, his kiss shifting from tentative to frantic, almost desperate. I sighed and parted my lips, welcoming his tongue into my mouth.

He nudged me from beneath his clothes and my body ached to welcome him again. Just as the thought crossed my mind, a damp, hot whoosh puffed against the back of my head.

I pulled away and cold air hit my face. I squinted at Dorcha, who'd managed to untie himself from the tree and was nosing through our blankets trying to find me.

"Morning, Dorcha," I grumbled and sat up, shoving my tangled hair from my face. He nudged my hand towards my pack. I smiled. "Hungry?" Without leaving my warm cocoon, I pulled the pack open and rifled around until I found another sack of stinky grain. I folded the top down and set it on the ground beside me.

A chuckle rumbled in Darien's chest when I plopped down and pulled the covers over my head, my teeth chattering.

"We really should depart," he said almost apologetically.

I frowned for a moment and studied his face in the darkness under the blankets. It took me a second to remember why I was sleeping on the ground in the first place. I shot up and grabbed my cloak. "Brandon!" I gasped.

A flash of hurt flitted across his features, but he ducked his head and made with folding the blankets. I knelt before him and cupped his cheeks in my hands, pulling him gently to face me. His eyes searched mine, the pain evident in their depths.

"I'm sorry." I kissed him gently on the lips.

He shook his head, his dark waves falling into his eyes. "'Twas ridiculous for me to hope you would want me over him. He can give you so much more than I could ever dream of. You shall be happy with him. D'na worry about me." His words tumbled from his lips like he had practiced them all night. A part of me wondered if he had.

Tears burned my eyes at the resignation in his eyes. I brushed his hair from his forehead and kissed the exposed skin. "I'm not interested in what he could give me," I whispered against his skin. I pulled back and gazed into his eyes. "It isn't fair to you, or to me, to pretend that this is real. When I wake up, I'll be heartbroken to find out you don't exist."

The tears that burned my eyes rolled unchecked down my cheeks. I blinked them away and turned away with a sob.

This time it was his turn to catch my chin with his fingers and turn me to face him. "You have said that since the moment I met you -- that this is all a dream. Do you truly believe that?"

I nodded.

His eyes smoldered as he leaned towards me. "I d'na feel like I am not real."

"But you are," I whispered. "I can't bear to think that when I wake up you won't be there."

"Then never wake up." He covered my lips with his. I shuddered, the tears falling faster down my cheeks. The salt from my tears mingled with the sweetness of his lips as he kissed me senseless.

As much as I wanted to spend forever in his arms, the image of Brandon shackled to a wall in some dungeon lingered on the edges of my mind.

I drew in a ragged breath and pulled away. "We have to help Brandon. He doesn't deserve this."

He nodded but didn't say a thing. The set of his jaw made me wonder if he misunderstood what I meant. Before I could say any more, he hauled himself off the ground and snatched up the roll of blankets and our packs.

I sighed and shoved up from my knees. The scent of damp leaves and ashes swirled around me as I kicked piles of dirt on the smoldering embers until they were completely extinguished. Dorcha's hooves crunched in the snow to my left. I opened my mouth to ask Darien if he was ready to go, but my breath rushed from my chest when Darien leaned down and hoisted me into the saddle before him. My body flared to life again at the feeling of his body pressed against mine.

I expected to see another horse, but only trees surrounded us. "How did you manage to catch up with me without a horse?"

"She ran away last night at the first snarl from the wolves. I imagine we'll probably come across her on the way back from rescuing your Prince."

I glared at the trees in our path. "He's not my Prince."

He leaned forward slightly, pressing his body against mine, his breath hot against my ear as he spoke. "Peace, Princess, I was teasing. A ghrá."

I fought the tingle that raced over my body at his proximity. "And don't call me that."

He stiffened and pulled away. "A ghrá? Very well." He sighed deeply and spurred Dorcha to a brisk walk.

I leaned back against his chest, savoring the way the ridges of his muscles fit perfectly against my body. "No, don't call me Princess."

A chuckle rumbled through his chest. He wrapped one arm around my torso and held me against him. "A ghrá," he murmured against my hair.

The words I so wanted to say sprung to my lips, but common sense pushed them back down.

The sound of Dorcha's hooves on the snow thumped along with my pulse until I couldn't stand it. The words swirled over my tongue until it was everything I could do but bite the tip of my tongue off. Instead I decided to change the subject. "Tell me about your home."

A warm chuckle rumbled in his chest. "Kovanic?"

I nodded.

I could hear his smile in his words. "Think of the meadows outside of Aislin. Now increase that greenness by one-thousand."

"Wow."

"Everything is more potent there. The colors, the scents, the people. The air smells like cinnamon and cloves and pine needles. And so peaceful. I remember when I was a child sitting on my parent's porch and listening to the wind blow through the pine trees."

We simultaneously took a deep breath, as if trying to breathe in that peace.

I sighed. "It sounds like Heaven."

His hand tightened on my stomach. "'Twas. Well, before Marcilena took the throne." His jaw popped beside my ear, like he was clenching his jaw so tight it popped.

"'Twas, at one time, a great metropolis on the rugged edge of the Aislin kingdom. But when Marcilena took the throne, she shoved everyone but her most loyal and discreet subjects into poverty. My family loved Kovanic so much we refused to leave. So now my parents live in the ruins of Kovanic Castle. Little else is there but a few other families that believe in the old ways and pray for things to change."

I tapped my finger on my lips. His words, specifically "Old ways" and "Pray for things to change" wrapped around "Bound" in my head, twisting into an intricate web of confusion. How could he be bound to Marcilena while his family lived in the ruins of a castle that Marcilena herself helped bring to ruin?

"But you're bound to her..." I wasn't sure how to breech the subject without sounding accusatory.

"Aye. But as I said before, my honor knows no master."

I shifted, just enough so I could study his face. "She really saved your mother's life?"

He gazed down at me with his copper eyes clear and full of love. "Saved, spared, in Marcilena's eyes they are the same."

I gasped, a thousand questions rushing through my head and ready to pour from my lips.

Darien raised one finger to my lips to silence me. "I should'na have said that much."

I nodded, wide eyed. He replaced his finger with a gentle kiss.

I melted into him, the relief of his tiny confession flowing through me and into our kiss.

The image of Brandon chained to a wall somewhere in an abandoned castle flitted through my mind again and I tore my lips from Darien's.

"What?"

"I feel so guilty. Brandon is somewhere out there, probably bound and tortured, and here I'm making out with you on the back of a horse."

Darien sighed, wrapped his arms around my torso and nuzzled my neck. "I know how confused you are."

I shook my head. "Not confused any more. I know what I want." I leaned my head back on his shoulder. "I just feel so guilty about being so happy while he's trapped somewhere waiting for us to come and rescue him."

Darien chuckled. "He shall get over it."

I stiffened. "Hey, now."

He smoothed my hair away from my neck and kissed the tender skin there. I shivered in response. "I jest."

I sighed as the shivers chased over my skin from his touch. "Tell me more about you. What do you like?"

"You mean besides you?" His words were whispered against my neck, making me shiver again.

I nodded.

"I play the lute, and paint, although I'm not very good at with a brush, I enjoy it nonetheless." He planted another kiss on my neck and short-circuited my train of thought. "Perhaps you would allow me to paint you, someday," he murmured suggestively against my neck.

My skin hummed at the mental picture of me naked, sprawled across a couch while he painted me. I blushed from head to toe at the thought of being so prominently exposed to his gaze. "I'd like that," I squeaked.

The chuckle that rumbled through his chest made me wonder if my blush had traveled to the tips of my ears.

The terrain leveled out, and I found it hard to breathe as I gazed down at the castle that rose up out of the fog, like it was floating above the clouds, an abandoned castle in the sky.

My skin pricked with sweat at the thought of what lurked below the fog. My thoughts turned to the sword the faeries gave me, tucked securely in my pack. *Would one terrified girl with an enchanted sword really be enough to slay a dragon?*

22

Chapter Twenty-two

The terrain steepened as we picked our way down to the bridge that stretched across the valley to the castle. Dorcha snuffed and pawed at the ground. Darien tried to nudge him on, but he dug his heels into the rich earth.

"Looks like we go on foot from here." I slid to the ground and pulled my sword from my pack. Darien slid down beside me.

His gaze traveled over my blade. "'Tis an interesting sword. Where did you get it?"

"You wouldn't believe me if I told you." I traced the markings with my finger, saying a silent prayer to whoever was listening that the enchantment would work. The scrollwork glowed slightly under my touch. I hooked the scabbard to my pouch on my hip.

"Nothing surprises me. I am just the man you dream about, remember?" He smiled and walked ahead of me towards the bridge.

"Smartass," I called at his retreating form. I brushed my hand across Dorcha's glossy coat. "Thanks for helping me through this. I'll see you when I get back, I hope." I patted him one last time before turning and sprinting to Darien's side.

I slipped my hand into his as our feet touched the stone bridge. We could only see a few feet ahead of us. Beyond that the bridge disappeared into the fog. My free hand clutched the hilt of my enchanted sword. Even as the crisp air bit at my face, my lip pricked with sweat as we slowly made our way across the bridge.

The silence around us was stifling, our ragged breathing the only sound in the still morning air. Step by tentative step, we crossed the bridge. At any second, I expected the mythical dragon to sneak up from behind and turn me into a charred human kabob. Or to pick me up off the ground in his razor-sharp fangs and tear me limb from limb.

I breathed a sigh of relief when my foot connected with the solid ground on the other side of the bridge. The castle courtyard spread out before us, silent and still. Shriveled blood-red roses dotted thorny vines covering practically every vertical surface, weaving in and out of the cracks and crevices in the ancient walls.

A frozen fountain stood in the courtyard, with glass-like streams of water shooting up from the center and cascading down into the rock-hard pool below. Tufts of dried grass surrounding the fountain rustled in the slight breeze. I tentatively touched the stream of water, its cold seeping into my fingers on contact. It was as if an ice storm hit the castle, freezing everything instantly.

We passed through a frozen garden filled with statues that looked almost alive in their positioning and location. They gazed down on us with somber faces, lips frozen, unable to tell the tales of the splendor they were once witness to.

I jumped when we turned the corner and a lone black bird screeched into the sky. Its wings beat the air with such ferocity it made me cringe. It was almost painful after enduring the silence of this place.

The crushed stone beneath our feet crunched as we approached the gaping doors to the great hall. Darien dropped my hand and drew his sword, the scraping of metal on metal echoing off the stone walls surrounding us. I followed suit and drew mine.

He raised an eyebrow.

"What?" I grumbled and mimicked the way held his sword.

His white teeth gleamed as a sarcastic smile stretched his face. "Let us hope you will'na need to use that."

"I'm pretty sure I had this very blade to your throat last night. I told you I can take care of myself, remember?"

"Last night was unbelievable—"

"Shut up!" I bumped his shoulder with mine. My cheeks burned from the memories of the previous night.

"Shh." He nodded to the open door.

I gripped the hilt of the sword with both trembling hands and cautiously followed him into the great hall. A quick survey proved that the hall was as empty as the courtyard had been. Our footsteps echoed eerily as we crossed the polished stone floor. In the center of the hall, a massive feast laid untouched, unspoiled across a long table. Chairs were scattered around the room like the occupants had left in a hurry. But the food, the delicious, mouthwatering, beautiful food beckoned me. My stomach grumbled as I picked a perfect, glistening red apple from a pile on a silver tray. If the strawberry at the faerie's stream had tasted that good...

I closed my eyes as I raised the apple to my lips, preparing for the perfect apple flavor to explode on my tongue like the strawberry had.

Darien swatted the apple from my hand like it was poisoned.

My eyes popped open and followed the apple as it sailed from my hand and connected with the floor, shattering into a pile of dust at my feet.

"What—" My brain couldn't wrap around what happened. The apple was heavy in my hand. It felt like a normal apple, its cool, firm flesh filled with juice. How could it be laying on the floor before me, nothing more than a pile of dust?

"'Tis bewitched."

I raised my astonished gaze to meet his, expecting him to tell me more, explain to me what the heck is going on in this strange castle. But he didn't say a word.

He grabbed my hand and pulled me down the closest hallway. "We need to find Brandon and leave, quickly. This place is cursed."

I dug my heels in and pulled my hand from his. "What do you mean cursed?"

Darien stalked back to me and cupped my face with his hands. "Someone cast a spell on this castle and froze it in time. Made all of its occupants disappear. No one e'er returns from the Northern forest. Rosteallan appears to be the reason why."

I frowned. Nothing made sense to me. Castles didn't just freeze. But, then again, I thought faeries and dragons didn't exist either.

"Come, let's find Brandon and get out of here." This time when Darien took my hand and pulled me down the darkened hallway, I followed.

We searched room after room. Each was the same as the main hall, perfectly frozen in time. Not a single book, or tapestry, or anything else was out of place.

It was like walking on to the set of a movie, where the director had just yelled cut and all the actors left. The castle still felt lived in, but like its occupants left and couldn't find their way home.

"Anything?" Darien called from the end of yet another dead-end hallway.

I shook my head.

Maybe Claire was wrong. Maybe she misunderstood Marcilena and Antonio's conversation. My head swam with memories of the past few days, from escaping the castle to the Gypsies, the faeries, the sword, Darien saving me from the wolves, giving him my virginity on the ground next to the fire, the frozen castle. I did everything exactly the way I was supposed to. Now I was stuck. How was I supposed to complete my destined path when the path was a dead-end? I slumped against the wall and rubbed my temples, trying to ease the mounting headache.

Something clicked behind the tapestry that hung on the wall behind me. I pulled it aside and gaped at the door-like opening in the stonework.

"Darien!"

"Aye?"

I bit back a smile at the fear in his tone as he rushed to my side. "I think I've found the tower." It was hard to keep the proud smile off my face, but I gave it my best effort.

"You are brilliant." He pressed his lips against mine.

I kissed him back for a moment before my conscience screamed at me about how inappropriate it was when Brandon was imprisoned somewhere in the castle. I tore my lips away from his and peered into the hidden passageway. His deep sigh ruffled my hair. He pulled away and his footsteps echoed from somewhere behind me as he walked away.

My eyes strained against the darkness and the little hairs on the back of my arms stood at attention. "What I wouldn't give for a flashlight right now."

"A what?" A flickering light from behind me sent my long shadow down the hallway.

I turned and smiled at the torch he commandeered. *Well, I guess considering this is sometime in the dark ages, a medieval flashlight will do.*

He raised an eyebrow in question.

I smirked and ducked into the tunnel. The pressure of his hand on my shoulder forced me to pause.

"I shall go first, if you d'na mind."

"What happened to "Ladies first"?"

"That only applies when said lady is not potentially in mortal danger."

I held my ground. But when he didn't budge, only stared at me intently with his soul-piercing copper eyes, I sighed.

"Sometimes I forget you're living in the dark ages here."

He snorted and stepped into the passageway.

The air was different, stagnant in the long, dark hallway. Not a single door or window dotted the wall. It felt like we'd walked the entire length of the castle before we finally hit a staircase. I sucked in a deep breath as we ascended the spiral steps to the tower, preparing myself for the worst.

When we finally reached the top, a heavy oak door barred our way. Darien jostled the handle, but it was locked. From the outside.

He sheathed his sword and handed the torch to me. Like something out of a movie, he kicked at the handle of the door. I rolled my eyes. That crap only worked in bad cop movies. Kick the door, the jamb goes splintering and viola!

He huffed with each kick, and eventually gave up. Next he tried man-shouldering the door, punctuating each collision of shoulder against ancient wood with a loud grunt. Still the lock held.

On what must have been the tenth try, he stopped and rubbed his shoulder and his face fell in defeat.

"Don't be disappointed, it always works in the movies..."

He leaned against the wall to catch his breath and looked at me quizically. "The what?"

I shook my head. My sarcasm was completely lost on these people. I opened my mouth to remind him that figments of my subconscious should have better senses of humor when a current of electricity zapped the hand resting on the hilt of my sword.

Frost's chilly voice echoed in my head. "The sword knows what it wants. You just have to have the courage to wield it."

The blade scraped on its scabbard as I unsheathed it. The scrollwork across the blade glowed slightly and faded.

Darien took the torch. "You shall only damage your blade if you try to break it with—" his voice cut off as my sword connected with the lock.

A sharp crack resonated down the staircase, followed by the tinkling of sand as the lock crumbled into dust.

"Huh," Darien grunted.

My breath caught in my throat as the door groaned open.

23

Chapter Twenty-three

Cold, stale air assaulted my senses as the heavy door creaked open on rusted hinges. Dim light filtered through dust-caked stained glass windows, the rays creating long geometric patterns across the dust-covered floors. A rogue rose vine, like the ones surrounding the abandoned castle, had snaked its way through a crack in the wall and wound around the four-poster bed in the center of the room. Gossamer curtains were pulled closed around the bed and swayed slightly in the gentle breeze our movement created.

I crossed the room to the vanity and stared into the polished metal, once gleaming, now tarnished with age and neglect. I picked up the brush and stroked the rough bristles with one hand. I could picture the princess who once lived there, with a servant brushing her hair, like Claire had done for me.

Brandon wasn't here. We'd hit yet another dead-end in a long dead castle. I sighed and slumped down on the stool before the vanity. Maybe Claire was wrong about where they took Brandon. Maybe this was all part of Marcilena's plot to keep me out of the way.

"Now what?" Darien asked from the doorway.

I shrugged and buried my face in my hands. I had no clue. How was I supposed to rescue the prince when I couldn't even find him? At this rate I'd never wake up from this dream.

Darien's footsteps echoed across the floor as he paced. "Wait, weren't there two towers?"

My head shot up and I stared at him in the reflection in the metal. "Two!" There were two towers. When we reached the summit, we looked down onto the castle above the clouds, there were two towers reaching into the sky.

"What if the other tower is also hidden?" Darien's voice was even, but I could feel the excitement in his words. He marched across the room towards the door.

In the mirror, the curtains on the bed swayed, revealing a dark form lying on the bed.

"Darien!" His name was little more than a whisper on my frightened lips.

He followed my gaze to the bed. "What—"

My pulse pounded in my ears as I approached the bed. From behind the curtains, a dark form laid prone on the mattress. I couldn't stop my hand from shaking as I grasped the silky curtain.

"What if it's a trap?" His voice held the slightest tinge of fear.

"What if it is?" I straightened my back and squared my jaw, preparing myself for whatever grisly scene I might see behind the curtains. "If it's Brandon, we have to know what that evil bitch did to him."

I yanked back the curtain.

The air gushed from my chest. "Oh my God! Mom?"

She didn't move. Her hands lay crossed over her stomach, her hair neatly arranged around her still-as-death face. Her eyes were closed, her lips sealed shut. Her face was perfect, not like I remembered her, but like mine, here. My face, but not my face. Everything perfect. Even the little scar she had from when she fell and busted her lip when she was little was gone. Her complexion was life-like, but she wasn't moving. Or breathing.

"Mom!" I shouted and shook her shoulder. No response.

I sunk to my knees beside her and pulled her limp hand into mine and pressed it to my cheek. Her skin was warm. A twinge of hope snuck up my spine and wrapped around my heart as I leaned in to lay my head on her chest.

Silence. I swallowed back the lump building in my throat and pressed her hand to my cheek. Then I heard it.

Ever so faintly, her heart thumped. If I hadn't been pressed so hard against her chest, I would have missed it. Then the gentle whisper of air as she inhaled and exhaled.

"She's alive!" I gasped and sat up. "Mom!" I shook her again. Still limp and unresponsive, but she was breathing.

Darien nodded from where he stood in the center of the room. "She is sleeping."

"Help me!"

He bowed his head reverently. "'Tis nothing we can do."

"What do you mean 'there's nothing we can do'? She's breathing! We have to get her out of here. Take her to one of those witch doctors you guys have at the castle."

He shook his head and looked at me with a helpless expression. "They can'na help her."

Hot rolling waves of rage boiled up inside of me. I'd finally found my mom, and here was the guy I gave my virginity to the night before, and he wasn't even willing to help me save her life! I opened my mouth to scream the scathing insults that were on the tip of my tongue, but his words stopped me.

"She is bewitched."

My mouth snapped shut. His words a few moments ago finally drilled into my brain. *She's sleeping.* "Marcilena." Her name burned like acid on my tongue.

He nodded again, looking almost ashamed. "Cast a spell on her. Made her sleep. For eternity."

"How do you know this?

He paused and studied the floor for a moment before bringing his sad eyes to meet mine. "My mother taught Marcilena the spell."

I was on my feet, my sword out of its sheath and pressed against his throat before I could blink.

He inhaled in a ragged breath but didn't move for his sword. "Trust me. She d'na have a choice. Marcilena was going to kill her child if she did not: me." His copper gaze was steady as he stared at me.

I searched his face for the lie. Only sadness and shame was evident on his face. "Why would Marcilena want me to marry you then?"

"To keep you distracted from trying to find her." He motioned to my mom's sleeping form. "She threatened to kill me should you ever find her."

"Then why didn't you try to stop me?"

He swallowed again, his Adam's apple bobbing under his tanned skin, so alive beneath the razor sharp blade of my sword. "Because I found something worth dying for."

My heart strained against my ribs. It was almost as good as him saying the L word. I sheathed my sword, my gaze locked on the hilt as I blinked away the tears and found my voice. "How do you break the spell?"

"True love's kiss."

My gaze shot to his. "The king?"

He nodded and cleared his throat, rubbing his neck where my blade had been. "But we must rescue the prince first. The king is enchanted. He will'na believe you unless you bring back the prince as proof of Marcilena's deceit."

I knelt beside my mom and kissed her cheek. "I'll be back for you. I promise." My whispered promise brushed across her face and stirred her golden hair.

Resolve raced through my veins as I stood and faced Darien. "Let's go find Brandon."

##

Much to our dismay, the layout of the castle was not symmetrical. This side of the castle was filled with kitchens, and storerooms and other rooms that who knows what they used them for.

After the twentieth storage room filled with food that looked good enough to eat, yet crumbled to dust with the slightest touch, my heart sunk.

"What if he isn't here?" I murmured, more to myself than to the useless storage room I was in.

I jumped when Darien's deep voice filled the room. "He must be."

I turned and my breath caught in my throat. His hair fell into his eyes and the light filtered around him from the dusty window like a halo. My chest tightened and my throat dried. "But where?"

He shrugged, a frustrated smirk stretching his features. *Why was he helping me, when he knew Brandon was his biggest competition?*

I sighed. "There are a few more rooms down this hallway. The entrance to the tower has to be here somewhere." I brushed the potato dust off my hands and marched out the door.

The hallway was flanked by doors on either side, with one at the very end. If experience told me anything, all of the rooms on my left would be useless, like the twenty or so I'd already searched. The ones on my right would probably be servant quarters. This had to be the servant's wing of the castle.

My eyes lingered on the door at the end of the hall once more. Even from this distance, I could make out the shape of a rusted lock on the outside of the door. Could it really be that easy?

"I've got five bucks that says that's the door to the other tower."

Darien raised a perfectly manicured eyebrow. "Five what's?"

Something resembling a growl rumbled from my chest. The sexy smirk that crossed his face at my reaction set my stomach fluttering.

"I shall take your bet. Why would the entrance to one tower be hidden and the other be in plain sight?"

"Because Marcilena didn't want my mother found. She couldn't care less if someone found Brandon... Maybe if Brandon was found so easily, we wouldn't go looking for the other tower?"

Darien closed the distance between us and pulled me into his arms. His breath brushed my lips as he leaned in. "You are brilliant." His mouth barely brushed mine, gently, teasingly. The familiar ache in my body flared to life.

I stifled a moan when he pulled away. This was the last chance I'd get to kiss him before we rescued Brandon, before it wasn't okay to demonstrate the feelings we shared in the open. Before things got really complicated. I wrapped my hands around his neck and pulled him to my lips.

A surprised chuckle escaped him as he complied. Soon his lips were as frantic as my own, like he realized the exact same thing I had. I tried to memorize the way my skin tingled where he touched, how he tasted like strawberries and mint, the way our bodies fit perfectly together.

He sucked in a shaky breath and released me. "I imagine 'tis the last time we get to do that." His eyes narrowed as his gaze settled on the door at the end of the hallway. "Let us go rescue your prince."

The words "your prince" falling from his lips hit me harder than if someone had slapped me in the face.

Like before, the lock disintegrated the moment I whacked it with the hilt of my sword. The door swung open and I gagged when the stench of stale air and mold practically knocked me over.

Water dripped down the slimy walls as we climbed the stairs. I tried not to breathe through my nose, but the air tasted as bad as it smelled. And for some reason, this tower seemed to be much higher than the other.

I wheezed when I got to the landing at the top. Like the other tower, a locked door stood in our way. "What the heck is with you people and towers?" I gasped between breaths.

"Huh?"

I shook my head and drew my sword, quickly smashing the lock. This whole 'enchanted sword' thing was starting to grow on me.

The stench radiating from the room was even worse than the moldy smell in the stairwell. I stifled a shriek when something with greasy fur and a long scaled tail scurried across the room, which was nothing like the queen's chambers in the opposite tower.

This was a jail cell.

The room was sparse, bare stone walls and floor, with a pile of hay in one corner, a pot that I didn't want to know what it was used for, and a small cot. The only light filtering in the room was from the narrow archer slits on the walls. Shafts of icy air drifted into the room, making my already goose bump-covered skin tighten painfully.

"About time someone came to rescue me." Brandon's voice was scratchy and rough, like his scruffy blonde beard that had grown in. His cheeks were sunken, like he hadn't eaten in a long time.

I took an involuntary step back at the venom in his words. "I came as soon as I heard she'd taken you." A quick glance at Darien and I realized Brandon's gaze wasn't locked on me, but on him.

I wriggled away from the protective hand Darien put on my back and glanced at Brandon. Could he tell that Darien and I were more than just friends?

"Missed a lot since I have been away, it appears." While Brandon looked frail and weak, his words were sharp.

"Are you hurt?" I had to change the subject.

He shook his head, but held up his hands, which sported a pair of rusty and painful-looking shackles. The chain attached to the cuffs rattled through a loop on the wall as he lifted his arm.

"That bitch." I couldn't stop the words from falling from my lips. He was here because of me. She brought him here to keep him from distracting me. This was my fault.

"My, my, princess. You have learned quite a vocabulary from this cretin!" Brandon's vibrant green eyes flashed with defiance. They were the only thing on him that I really recognized.

"Please stop." I warned and crossed the room. I knelt before him and inspected his restraints. I glanced around the cell. "Is there a key?"

Brandon shook his head. "Antonio took them with him, just in case." He sighed and leaned his head back against the wall, like he used up all the energy he had just talking.

"Let me try something." I unsheathed my sword. Fear crossed his face at the sight of me brandishing a weapon. "Hold still. I don't want to cut off anything important." I smirked. There was no way he'd get that.

The look in his eyes indicated otherwise. My cheeks warmed, but I ignored the feeling. His frightened "wait" barely registered as I clenched my eyes shut and brought the sword down on the shackles.

My heart lurched at the sharp crack and his gasp of pain. I opened my eyes to survey the damage, and before I realized what was happening, Brandon snatched the sword from my hand and shoved me on to the cot.

The blade sang through the air as he lunged towards Darien. A loud metallic crack echoed off the stone as their swords collided.

"Thought you could have the competition locked away, did you?" Brandon's sword arced through the air and connected with Darien's blade again. Sparks flew when metal hit metal.

"I had nothing to do with your imprisonment." Darien blocked another swing.

"Interesting how your betrothal is announced and suddenly I am carted off." Brandon's eyes narrowed and he lunged, trying to drive the blade of my sword through Darien's chest.

Darien dodged his advance and paused while Brandon regained his footing. He showed such restraint for a guy being attacked. And Brandon had so much strength for someone who'd been locked in a tower for weeks.

Brandon lunged again. Darien parried and knocked him off balance, sending him crashing into a wooden crate, which smashed into splinters upon contact.

"Stop this!" I screamed, but my protest fell on deaf ears.

They danced across the floor, Brandon attacking, Darien deflecting the blows. Each metallic clank rattled me to my bones.

"Are you such a pathetic excuse for a man that you cannot handle a little competition?" Brandon snarled as he advanced.

"I d'na have any competition. She has already decided." Darien's voice was smooth and clear as he laid our relationship on the floor at Brandon's feet.

The air gushed from Brandon's chest, as if Darien had actually struck him. The color drained from his face as he turned to me for a denial.

The flames that ignited on my cheeks raged over my body and threatened to consume me. I hadn't expected Darien to lay it all out there like that. Had I chosen which guy I wanted? The previous night said I had. And my heart, as I stared at the two guys vying for my affections, said the same.

Brandon's eyes pleaded with me to tell him Darien was lying. The look of despair on his face when we entered the chamber paled in comparison to the rejection on his face.

Tears of regret burned my eyes. Not regret from choosing Darien, but from hurting Brandon. I never wanted this to happen. "It's all just a dream..."

"D'na say that," Brandon snarled. My sword slipped from his fingers and clattered onto the dirty floor.

"I'm sorry," I whispered, the words burning my throat as they passed my lips.

His eyes flashed, as if he caught my confusion. "'Tis no reason to be. I am not giving up on you Victoria. I know Darien seduced you. But I shall win your heart. *I* can handle the competition." He scooped his sword off the ground near the door were Antonio had discarded it and shot a glare in Darien's general direction.

Darien nodded, accepting the challenge.

I opened my mouth to reply, but nothing coherent came to mind. I snapped it shut and caught Darien's gaze. His sexy half-grin flashed for a moment before fading to a calm mask. My skin tingled. It was like he enjoyed a challenge!

"Fine. Let us get out of here then." Brandon marched towards the door.

I snatched my sword off the floor where Brandon abandoned it and slid it back into its scabbard. I caught Brandon's arm as he reached for the handle. "My mother's in the other tower."

He turned, his eyes wide with bewilderment. "Your mother?"

I nodded. "She's not dead. Marcilena cast a spell on her. We have to go get the king and bring him here to break the spell."

"A spell." He paused, as if pondering the meaning of the word. "Well, getting the king here might prove harder than it looks. Marcilena has guards around him constantly. That, and he is so far demented, he probably would'na survive the trip here."

A lump built in my throat. With the reality explained so clearly to me, the task seemed insurmountable. Would I be trapped in this dream world forever? "We have to try."

Brandon nodded and wrenched the door open. He took one step into the stairwell when the sound of a train hitting the tower caused it to sway.

24

Chapter Twenty-four

"What was *that*?" Darien and Brandon asked simultaneously.

The tower trembled with each subsequent crash. The hair rose on my neck as I raced for the arrow slit and peered down into the fog encircling the turret. The tower swayed and the sound of crumbling stone clattered beneath the fog.

Then I saw it.

At first, it looked like a giant iridescent iguana scaling the tower. But instead of one ridge of spines down its back, it was covered in spiny scales, with protruding horns on its nose and forehead.

As if sensing me, it looked up and blood-red eyes locked with mine. Long, bat-like wings with claws on the tips spread out behind it. Jagged jaws opened in a terrifying grin, exposing rows of yellowed fangs and a forked tongue. An ear-shattering roar emitted from its mouth, followed by a stream of fire.

Fear froze me as the flames licked up the tower. Hands wrapped around my shoulders and yanked me back as the flames billowed past the little window.

Panic seeped through my veins like liquid fire. I forced myself take deep breaths, but the panic cinched my throat tight. "Dragon," was all I managed to mutter.

"Dragons only exist in fairy tales," Brandon scoffed and poked his head out of the window. His face was death-white when he stepped back.

The tower shuddered again.

"This is *my* fairy tale, Brandon. My dream. They exist here."

Brandon grabbed my shoulders and shook me, shouting into my face, "'Tis. Not. A. Dream!"

Before I could respond, Brandon's body flew across the room.

"If you value your limbs, you shall never touch her again," Darien growled.

I blinked back the tears and rubbed absently at the fingerprints aching on my shoulders.

The tower shuddered again and a stone block dislodged from the ceiling and crashed between us.

"Come on!" Darien grabbed my hand and dragged me down the stairs, with Brandon hot on our heels.

We raced through the deserted castle and out into the frozen gardens. The crashing sound stopped and my skin tingled from the silence.

"Come! We're almost at the bridge." Darien pulled me behind him, our feet pounding the frozen earth as we ran for the bridge.

Sunlight had evaporated the fog hanging over the bridge, and the blue sky above seemed almost too blue as we ran at a break-neck speed toward the other side. Our frantic footsteps echoed across the expanse.

My heart filled with hope when we neared the center. The mountain on the other side of the bridge was so close! Something clattered onto the bridge and I skidded to a stop. It was the metal disk I'd found after I met the gypsies. Something told me I couldn't leave it. I ran back across the bridge, chasing it as it rolled.

"Tori! What are you doing?" Darien shouted when he realized I'd turned back. Brandon practically knocked him over as he skidded to a stop.

"Go! I'm coming!" I stooped to pick up the gypsy's disc when a dark shadow blocked out the sunlight on the bridge before me.

"Tori!" Darien and Brandon's simultaneous screams froze my heart.

As if in slow motion, I straightened from my crouch as the dragon landed on the bridge between the guys and me. It snarled, a strange, lizard smirk crossing its spiny jaws, its red eyes locked on me. My ears rang when it opened its jaws and roared in my face. As if by instinct, I dove to the ground and rolled a second before the fire erupted from its mouth.

The sounds of the guys screaming and attacking the dragon filtered into my ringing ears. I opened my clenched eyes in time to see them launch themselves at the dragon.

Brandon landed on the tail and was whipped violently before it flung him into the mountain above the bridge. His pained cry filled the air when he crumpled to the ground.

"Tori!" Darien screamed and stabbed at the dragon's shin, landing blow after blow. Tiny streams of black blood sprayed from the wounds, but the monster didn't seem to feel it. One swipe of its tail and Darien followed a similar path as Brandon.

"No!" I whispered as I watched Darien's limp body crumple to the ground on the other side of the bridge.

Frost's voice echoed through my head as that same electric current passed from the hilt of my sword into my hip. *"The sword knows what it wants. You just have to have the courage to wield it."*

I drew the sword out of its sheath with a shaky hand. It glowed a vibrant blue. "You've got to be kidding me."

The dragon snapped its head around and flared its nostrils at sight of the glowing sword. Its forked tongue flicked out, tasting the air between us.

"Tori!" Darien's voice drew the dragon's attention away from me and he launched himself onto its back again. A flick of its tail sent him flying back through the trees.

Courage bubbled up through me as I watched his body sail through the air. The sword warmed in my hand, as if in response to my emotions. "No!" I screamed and flung myself onto the giant reptile's back, somehow managing to land between its wings.

It emitted a frustrated roar and flailed its head back, trying to catch me in its razor-sharp jaws. It flicked its tail and flapped its wings. I held firm, the mental picture of everyone I loved lodged at the front of my brain. Casey. My parents. Darien. I'd never get to see any of them again if I didn't finish this.

The bottom of my stomach dropped out when the creature shot into the air, flipping and spinning, trying to dislodge me.

Darien's roar drew my attention to the bridge as he ran out onto it. Within seconds he was tiny as an ant.

I scrambled to dig my fingers underneath the giant reptile scales, desperate to cling to anything to keep it from sending me on a skydive with no parachute.

With one hand, I flailed the sword, trying to poke anything near me. A wing, its neck, the top of its head, anything. One jab of the blade beneath its wing revealed the creature's vulnerability when it swung its head around and blew fire.

I did it again, this time driving it harder and deeper into its shoulder. Black blood sprayed over me and a pained scream ripped from the creature. Its wings tucked in to protect itself from further injury. That's when I realized we were in a free-fall back towards the ground.

The Earth spun up towards us and we shot past the bridge. For a brief second I caught Darien's terrified expression as he watched us fall into the ravine below the castle. His heart-broken scream pierced through the air roaring around me as we disappeared into the fog.

In the second before we hit the ground, the dragon flipped onto its back. I managed to climb onto its chest and brace myself for impact. If I managed to survive, this was going to hurt. Bad.

The sword jolted in my hand. I knew what it wanted me to do. I pulled the sword back and drove it into the dragon's chest.

Light emitted from the wound, blinding me. The creature's death cry deafened me and I was flung into the air. Then I was falling, weightless, into the black abyss below.

The air left my chest and everything went silent when I hit the ground.

25

Chapter Twenty-five

I opened my eyes. Well, at least I think I did. The only way I knew my eyes were open was because they burned from the horrible stench of sulfur and decay. I tentatively tested my arms and legs for injury, stretching and flexing cautiously. A twinge of soreness overall, but nothing felt broken.

My stomach churned from the putrid smell of charred and rotting flesh permeating the darkness. I couldn't control the bile as it rose in my throat and spewed into the abyss. I tried to wipe my mouth, but it did no good. Something thick and slimy covered every inch of my body. I tried to get up but the soft stuff under me shifted and I stumbled back into it. The intense stench of decay rose fresh and strong. I didn't try to fight it when I retched again.

The cold goo under me shifted like Jell-O as I trudged through it in the pitch-black. I tried to breathe through my mouth to keep from puking again from the smell. I froze when something that felt like fingers brushed across my knuckles. I reached out, praying it was someone who came to rescue me. My fingers wrapped around their hand, which was covered in the same slimy stuff I was.

"Thank God!" I pulled, hoping they could pull me out of the putrid pool I fell into.

Only the sound of my ragged breathing echoed in the darkness.

I pulled a little harder and the person fell with me back into the muck. But they made no sound. Not even a gasp as they fell into the sludge. I still clenched their fingers and tentatively traced up their arm, past their elbow, up their bicep to where their shoulder should be. Rather than the curve of a shoulder, my fingers sunk into gooey, ragged flesh. I screamed and dropped the severed arm and stumbled backwards. Things bumped against me and I shuddered. Acid burned my throat and my stomach heaved at the thought of what I waded through.

I forced myself to calm my breathing and think logically. There had to be a way out. I couldn't be trapped forever in this putrid hole of decaying flesh.

Darien's terrified face as I flung past him on the chest of the fallen dragon flashed before my eyes. Maybe if I screamed loud enough he'd hear me and realize I hadn't died from the fall.

I sucked in a deep breath, my eyes stinging as the putrid air burned my lungs. "Hello?" I bellowed up into what I hoped was the sky.

My heart caught in my throat when my name echoed back through the darkness. But it wasn't Darien's voice. It was my sister's.

"Casey?" My voice sounded small and timid even to my own ears.

"Tor?" Casey's voice called back, a little closer this time.

I swear my heart stopped beating in that moment. Casey was the only person who ever called me Tor. Ever.

My heart resumed its erratic pace, and I couldn't contain the hysterical shriek that ripped from my throat. "Oh my God! Casey! Where are you?"

"I can't see anything. Where am I?" Her voice trembled as she spoke.

The fear evident in her voice strengthened my resolve to get out of this alive. To get us both out. "Keep talking. I'll follow your voice."

"I'm scared, Tor." A choked sob echoed through the darkness.

The Jell-O-like goo sloshed as I trudged through it towards the sound of her voice. "I'm coming." I held my hands out before me, searching the darkness for her. My hands closed around her arm. I pulled, but there was no weight behind it and I fell back into the sludge. A shriek partially escaped my lips and flung the dismembered arm away. I grabbed other body parts. My heart pounded in my ears and my hands trembled as I grabbed a severed leg, the spaghetti-stringy hair of a severed head, a foot with its boot still attached. I held my breath and flung body part after body part out of my way as I searched for my sister.

"Casey?" I called.

Nothing. *Was her voice a figment of my imagination?*

"Casey!" I didn't fight the terror from lacing my tone this time.

"I'm here." Casey whispered from behind me.

I spun and pulled Casey into my arms. She was covered in slimy stuff too. "What the heck are you doing here?"

"I opened my eyes and I was here."

"What were you doing before that?"

I felt her shake her head. "I don't remember. It's all black."

I held her in my arms and savored the feeling of my sister alive and well, pressed against me. Tears rolled down my grimy cheeks when I realized I really thought she was dead and this was some twisted version of Heaven. Or purgatory. I stroked her goo-covered hair. She was alive.

She was alive! As the realization hit me, I knew I had to get beyond the nauseating reality of this death trap. I owed it to her to get her out of this.

My hand seemed to find the flint in my hip pouch of its own accord. With one hand, I searched the darkness for something, anything to light with it. My hands closed around something that felt like a barren branch. I grabbed it and shook the goo off. A little more searching came up with a severed arm with what remained of a sleeve. I bit my lip against the burning in my throat as I tore the clothing from the unfortunate victim and wrapped it around the end of the stick.

"Casey." I tried to keep the fear from my voice, but it felt thin and weak in the darkness. "Keep your eyes closed. Don't open them until I tell you it's okay."

"Okay." She clung to my shirt.

I struck the flint against the cloth and it flashed once. Twice. The third time the fabric ignited and illuminated the sea of dismembered human corpses surrounding us. I turned, fighting to keep my empty stomach from heaving and looked at my sister.

She was covered in head-to-toe black dragon blood like me, and for once in her life, she actually listened to me. Her eyes were clenched shut.

My breath caught in my throat at the sight of the exploded carcass of the dragon behind her. My sword still jutted from its chest.

"Can I open my eyes yet?" Casey asked.

"No." I glanced around and found a raised platform against one wall. My heart soared out of the goo-filled pit when I saw the stairs crisscrossing up the wall and disappearing into the dense fog above our heads.

We waded through the sludge and I deposited Casey on the platform.

"Stay here. I'll be right back. Don't open your eyes."

Casey nodded.

I cringed and lowered myself back into the sludge. There was no other way to get my sword. The smell of charred flesh burned my nose as I climbed onto the blackened carcass. I positioned one foot against its chest and yanked on the hilt of the sword. It came free easily and I lost my footing and slid back into the sludge, practically going under.

"Tori?" Casey's terrified shriek echoed through the space.

"I'm okay," I sputtered. I made it to my feet and the dragon's chest was at eye-level. Against my better judgment I glanced at the gaping hole in its chest. Something glittered inside.

I held my breath and reached into the cavity and pulled out the chain. A charm hung from it. It was the faerie charm necklace I gave to Casey for Christmas.

I slipped the necklace into my pouch and waded back to Casey.

It was a long climb back up to the bridge, but Casey didn't whine, which was so unlike her.

When we finally reached the bridge, I took Casey's hand, half afraid she would disappear at any moment, and ran across the bridge toward the mountains. I knew the dragon was dead, but I couldn't help but feel the sticky hairs on the back of my neck try to stand on end, like they were waiting for something to jump out and stop us.

The sound of arguing filtered through the fog, which had rolled back in while I was stuck in the pit.

"Well, how do you suppose we get down there? We d'na have any rope!"

"There is some in the castle. In our search for you we found many storage rooms stocked to the hilt! We can'na leave her there to die!" Darien's voice was strained.

"You think she survived that fall? And even if she did – the dragon had to have eaten her alive."

I bit back a sarcastic smile. Of course Brandon didn't think I could take care of myself. I was, after all, a helpless princess.

Their forms solidified as we approached through the fog. Brandon slumped on the ground, a tourniquet wrapped tightly around his upper thigh, his pants torn and bloodied beneath the knot.

"And besides." Brandon's face twisted into a scowl as he shifted his injured leg on the ground. "I can'na help you."

"I shall go alone." Darien turned and marched in our direction, but froze upon seeing us.

"Darien!" I shouted and ran towards him, dragging my dazed sister behind me.

His sword was out of its sheath before I could blink.

"Wait! It's me, Tori!" I held up my hands defensively, Casey's tiny hand still clenched in mine. I'd never, ever let go of her again.

His face twisted with disgust. "Tori?"

"No, I'm the Easter Bunny. Of course it's me!"

He covered his mouth and nose with a hand, like he'd caught a really ripe fart on the wind. "What are you're covered in?"

Crap. The goo. I'd forgotten all about it. If I looked anything like Casey, who was covered in head-to-toe black goo, we looked like a pair of Orcs straight out of Middle Earth.

"It's dragon blood. And God only knows what else."

"Who is that?" He pointed with his sword to Casey.

I pushed the tip of his sword away. "It's my sister, Casey."

"Your sister?" Brandon and Darien said simultaneously.

I nodded. "Told you I had a sister."

"Did Marcilena put you there too?" Brandon nodded towards the edge of the bridge.

Casey shrugged and looked at me for support.

"She doesn't remember. She woke up and was there."

Darien's coppery brown eyes caught mine for a moment. "Let's get out of here."

After a few tense words between the guys, Brandon conceded to allowing Darien to help him to his feet and shoulder him to Dorcha, who was waiting on the other side of the bridge.

Dorcha whinnied and pranced when he saw me. My heart did the same. When I left him in the woods earlier in the day, I never thought I'd see him again.

"How'd you find him?" I slid my palm over his flank. My hand, completely caked in drying black dragon blood, almost disappeared against his shiny black coat.

Darien shrugged. "He found us. I guess he heard us crash into the trees when the dragon threw us off its back." He lowered his voice. "Brandon did scream quite loud when he hit the ground."

"I did'na." Brandon sulked as Darien helped him into the saddle and settled Casey before him.

"My noble steed," I whispered and stroked his mane.

He flared his nostrils, as if saying: "You stink!"

I chuckled. "You have no idea."

The ride back to Aislin was quiet, each of us lost in our own thoughts, trying to process the events of the day. I trudged on foot beside Darien, a few feet behind Dorcha's lumbering gait. Every so often I'd feel eyes on me and I'd glance up and find Darien studying me.

"What?" I self-consciously scrubbed at the caked-on black goo that coated every inch of my body. What I wouldn't give for a shower right now.

His sexy half-grin stretched across his face as he studied me. "I still c'na comprehend how you slayed the dragon and d'na get killed in the process."

A tingle of defensiveness rushed over my skin. "Is that some suave way of saying "I can't believe a girl slayed a dragon!"?"

His grin fell away and his eyes widened, as if he'd never had the thought. "Nay. I just meant when it took flight with you clinging to its back, I thought for sure it would kill you. Being a lass had nothing to do with it."

"I'd imagine all those bodies down there would agree with you..." I said under my breath.

He caught my arm and spun me around. "The what?"

"Let's just say we weren't the first people who tried to rescue someone from this castle. There was a sea of dismembered bodies down th..." The reality of everything that happened crashed down on me like a tidal wave. The world tilted. I couldn't breathe. The rich brown earth covered with leaves rushed towards my face.

"Whoa, there." Darien caught me before I face-planted the ground.

I breathed in fresh, cool breaths of air. I survived. And got Casey back too. It was over. I opened my eyes and traced every detail of Darien's face. "Thanks," I whispered.

"Hey, if you two love birds back there d'na mind, I thought we would take the shortcut back to the castle." Brandon's voice dripped with sarcasm.

I blushed and cleared my throat as Darien set me back onto my feet. "Wait – what do you mean a shortcut?"

Brandon grinned mischievously, like he had a secret no one else knew. "When those thugs brought me here, they cut through the valley before climbing the mountain. Crossed a river pretty close to here."

My heart leapt. A river! "God yes! Take me to the river!" I rolled my eyes at the corny joke that no one ever got here but me.

Casey shifted in the saddle, a tiny smile on her blackened face.

I wanted to wrap her in my arms and hold her to me. I had my sister back!

##

They always say the first shower, or the first night in your bed at home after being away is always the best. But that's nothing compared to washing dried dragon blood off in the icy river. I couldn't even feel the cold as the black washed away and downstream.

I scrubbed Casey until her freckled cheeks were pink. Her shoulder-length hair returned to its natural deep-chestnut color. Oddly, she didn't seem to have the same 'perfect, fairytale look' the rest of us had. She looked exactly as I remembered her from the accident. Down to her tank top, pink flowered shorts and sparkly shoes she was wearing in the plane when we crashed.

Only one thing was different: a glittery scar in the middle of her chest.

Casey flinched when I traced my finger across the scar. "When did you get this?" I couldn't remember anything that happened to Casey when she was little that would have left such a nasty scar. It reflected in the muted sunlight like tiny scales.

She shrugged. "I don't know."

I studied her face. There were other little changes that at first I didn't notice. Shadows beneath her eyes, slightly sunken cheeks. "Are you sick?"

She shook her head.

"What's wrong?" I asked.

Tears brimmed her deep brown eyes and spilled down her cheeks. "I'm sorry." She sobbed and clung to my chest.

"You have nothing to be sorry for. This is my fault."

She shook her head again, her wet hair flying around her face and spraying me with a tiny stream of water. "I don't remember anything, but somehow I feel like this is all my fault."

The despair in her face silenced my revelation about this all being a dream. "It's not your fault. And I'll get us out of here. I promise."

She sniffled and nodded.

I sighed. At least the hardest part of my quest was over. In comparison to slaying a dragon, it should be easy to convince the king to wake his queen. And then I'd wake up and everything would be fine. Easy.

I wrapped her in a thick blanket Darien left for us before he left to tend to his disgruntled patient. She plopped down on the riverbank and blotted her hair while I stripped from my clothes and submerged in the icy water to finish scrubbing.

When I resurfaced, shivering as the icy water sheeted off my naked, yet sparkling clean skin, a deep gasp echoed through the trees on the other side of the river.

"Hello?" My eyes searched the darkness where I was sure the sound had come from. A dark figure darted from behind a tree to an outcropping of boulders.

"Who's there?" I shouted and scrambled for a blanket to cover myself with. I was just tucking the end in when Darien crashed through the forest behind me, his sword drawn.

"What happened? I heard you shouting!" He surveyed me and Casey. Relief crossed his face when he saw we weren't injured.

"I heard someone gasp and something darted between the trees over there." I pointed to the area where I saw the shape move. It darted again, further down the bank this time. "There!" I pointed towards the dark figure as it retreated. "Do you see it?"

Darien was already trudging across the icy water before he responded. "I do." He made it to the other side of the bank and raced after the retreating figure.

"Casey!" I rushed back to her. "Go back to Brandon. Tell him what happened and tell him we'll be back soon. Here." I pulled out my enchanted sword and handed it to her. "Take this."

"But Tor," she started to whine.

I was already trudging through the water after Darien. "Go! Now!" I called back.

My heart tugged as her little blanket-draped figure disappeared into the trees.

I didn't feel the rocks biting into my bare feet as I raced after Darien. I didn't feel the icy wind blasting at my face and wet hair, or the way my blanket slopped wetly around my legs as I ran. All I felt was my heart slipping further from my body as it stretched between these two people whom I loved, one fictional, the other real. My heart didn't care.

26

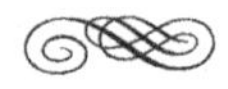

Chapter Twenty-six

Darien ducked into the darkened forest twenty or so feet ahead of me. I opened my mouth to shout for him. Before I could make a sound, the breath left my chest when something slammed into me. My head connected with the rocky riverbank and lights flashed before my eyes. A heavy weight crushed my chest, and I wheezed to catch my breath.

Something sharp and cold pressed against my neck. "Not a sound or 'twill be your last." Antonio's thick accent made every hair on my body stand at attention. "I see you managed to save your prince. Well, he will'na find much use for you when I am finished."

"Please," I squeaked. I gasped for breath but little came.

He shifted slightly off my chest and the icy mountain air rushed into my lungs. My head spun from the lack of oxygen.

"No passing out before the fun starts."

I wanted to warn him that Darien was right on the other side of the forest. He'd be back any second. But "Darien," was all I was able to gasp.

"Is chasing a ghost. One of my men, who will happily keep him occupied so we can enjoy our time together. And you should know I sent a scout to notify the queen of your betrayal. She shall be awaiting your return."

My blood ran cold. Even if we made it through this, Marcilena will kill us at the gate.

"Good. You see the truth in my words." His nose brushed my jaw. "I have wanted to do this since the first time I saw you." His tongue lapped up my cheek before crushing my mouth in a cruel kiss. His tongue pushed at my mouth for entrance, but I clenched my teeth tightly closed and glared at his disfigured face.

He pulled back slightly and studied me. "If you relax, you might enjoy this. At least until I kill you." A wicked grin stretched his scarred features tight.

"Fuck you." If only I hadn't given Casey my sword.

"You will." His grin widened as he folded my blanket back to expose my nakedness. My skin tightened painfully from the exposure to the icy air. "See, you are already ready for me."

I clenched my eyes shut to avoid his leering gaze as it traveled over my exposed skin. With one hand pressing the dagger to my throat, he shifted between my legs, cupped my breast in a vise-like grip and pinched my nipple hard.

I couldn't bite back the pained whimper that escaped my lips. Nausea overwhelmed me at the feel of his hands on me. I'd rather be back in the putrid death filled dragon pit than feel his touch on my skin.

"There, now. I said you'd enjoy it."

My eyes popped open at the confidence in his words. "No."

"Hmm. Now there is a word I hear often, and obey never." His hand left my breast and fumbled with his pants. I tried to kick him off while he was preoccupied, but it only seemed to arouse him more. He caught my ankle as I kicked one well-aimed blow towards his groin.

"Just for that I *am* going to make you scream. Make your lover boy hear you scream as I take you. Then I am going to go kill him when I am done with you."

Hot tears fell unchecked down my cheeks when his naked warmth brushed against my inner thigh as he shifted over me.

"Please, don't," I begged. I strained against his blade and the warmth of my blood trickled down my neck when his dagger pierced the skin.

"At least you shall die happy," he sneered and positioned himself between my legs. I shuddered with disgust as his free hand brushed along my privates, as if testing to see my reaction. I withdrew into myself, trying to disconnect from my body, trying anything to wake up. *Please, for the love of God, wake up!*

A strangled grunt came from his lips, resembling one of pain rather than pleasure. I gasped when his weight crushed me.

"Tori!" Darien's terrified voice called out somewhere overhead.

"Help!" I gasped and flailed my arms around Antonio's heavy body crushing my chest.

He rolled off me and I stifled a scream when I saw the blood running from his mouth and the puncture wound in his chest.

"Are you injured?" Darien's hands were all over me, tracing every inch of flesh, checking for injuries. He carefully inspected the wound on my neck. "'Tis nothing. You should be okay. Here." He ripped a length of cloth from his cloak and wrapped it around my neck. "That should stop the bleeding."

I shivered in the icy air, realizing only then that I was completely naked.

Darien blushed and plucked the blanket off the ground and wrapped it around me.

My teeth chattered as I tried to speak. "H-He tried to rape me."

His coppery eyes darkened, his face twisted into a pained scowl. "I know. I am so sorry." He wrapped me in his arms and rubbed briskly to warm me up. After a few long minutes of silence he asked: "Did he?"

I shook my head. Tears burned my eyes and fell in scorching trails down my cheeks.

"Thank Go,." he sighed and crushed me to his chest.

I couldn't help but sob tears of relief into his chest. After a few minutes of hard crying, I pulled back, hiccupping. "Thank you."

"D'na thank me. I was almost too late. When I realized it was a trap, I circled around and...God, I was almost too late." Despair etched his features.

"But you weren't. And he's dead."

"But the other one got away. Probably on a straight line back to warn Marcilena."

I sighed. "Antonio said he already sent a scout to notify the witch that we succeeded."

"Maybe he lied. If we hurry we might be able to intercept the other one."

"Shh," I murmured and pressed my lips to his. His kiss was tentative and gentle, like he was afraid of hurting me. I reached up and threaded my stiff, frozen fingers through his hair and pulled him harder against me, kissing him with franticness that left us both gasping for breath.

"I love you, Tori," he whispered against my mouth.

My heart jolted at the words as they fell from his lips. My first instinct was to say it back. So I blurted the second thing that came to mind: "Thank you."

He smirked and swung me into his arms.

"I can walk—" I started to argue.

"You have no shoes. And your feet are bleeding." He nodded to the little bloody spots on the stones.

I frowned. "Oh."

His sexy half-grin stretched into a full-face smile. He snuggled me into his chest as he walked across the bank towards where my clothes lay abandoned. "You d'na have to say it, you know."

"Say what?"

"That you love me. I know you do." His chocolaty-caramel eyes gazed into mine.

I blushed. *How did he know I loved him when I wasn't completely sure of it myself?*

"I shall find a way to prove that you can trust me. I promise." His breath ruffled my hair as he nuzzled my neck before lowering me beside my clothes. "I must go check on the others." He briefly pressed his lips against mine before disappearing through the trees.

I sat there, wrapped in the blanket I was almost raped on, and scrubbed my clothes against the rocks. I watched the water turn from black to clear, and wished that my thoughts were so clear.

Brandon had never been the choice for me. Even in this dream world, he'd been the perfect interpretation of Prince Charming from my childhood. Everything I *thought* I ever wanted in a guy.

Darien was the opposite. Dark, dangerous, mysterious. Everything that scared me, but allured me at the same time. But they weren't yin and yang, black and white, right and wrong guy. They each had qualities I loved. And ones I hated.

Yes, I'd given my virginity to Darien. Not because I loved him. But because I wanted to experience that moment in time with him. And it was beautiful. But did I love him? Maybe. Did that mean what I had with Brandon was a lie? I wasn't sure. All I knew was that each embodied something I wanted. But if I had to choose, one or the other, could I do it?

Yes. There it was, somewhere in the back of my head, a tiny whisper of decision. The moment I slept with Darien, I made the decision of who I wanted. And it was the dark, dangerous, mysterious, uncertain, imperfect vision of the future with him that excited me. I felt alive when I was with him, in a way I'd never experienced before.

Even in real life, I'd always gone for the safe choice. I'd never taken a chance, never went for what I truly wanted because of the risk I could get hurt. Now that I'd tasted that bit of freedom, that bit of danger and unknown after taking the chance, taking that blind leap of faith, I knew I wanted more. I wanted Darien.

I slipped back into my clothes, which were still damp. I shivered and wrapped the blanket back around me and dangled my dripping shoes from two fingers. My bare feet picked their way back over the crushed leaf path to our make-shift camp.

"Tor!" Casey shrieked and tackled me.

"Shh." I stroked her chestnut hair, which managed to work its way into a frizzy, puffy mess. I lifted my gaze to the guys, who sat a foot or so apart before the roaring fire and gazed into the flames. Darien's face was serene, bordering on the blissfully happy side. Brandon's, on the other hand, was drawn and forlorn, his gaze a million miles away. Pain etched his features.

"Can we make it back tonight?" I asked over Casey's head. The sun was already setting behind the mountains, sending long shadows across the woods.

Darien shook his head. "There's no way we can make it back tonight. Dorcha needs rest, especially from carrying two riders for such a distance."

"Stupid leg." Brandon muttered and flung a stick onto the fire, which crackled and hissed.

He didn't lift his gaze to meet mine, just stared into the fire. My heart broke for him. It was as if more than his leg was broken. His heart for sure. Maybe even his spirit.

"What about the –" I mouthed the word wolves.

Darien shook his head. "Should be gone after all the ruckus in the woods today."

I nodded.

Darien rifled through his bag and produced a few unappetizing looking biscuits and a hunk of dried meat. "'Tis not much, but I d'na expect to be feeding an army." He handed the rations to me.

"It's great. Thanks." I gave most of mine to Casey. She needed the food. Her coloring wasn't right.

We ate in relative silence until the darkness got to be too much. I kept searching the shadows, waiting for Antonio's corpse to jump out and attack me. The thought of his body rotting down river from us made my stomach churn on what little food I'd eaten. I snuggled down with Casey tucked securely in my arms beneath the blankets.

"Did you want to share heat tonight Brandon?" Darien asked politely.

"I would rather freeze to death," Brandon replied.

I smirked at the venom in his words. Go figure he'd be too macho to allow himself to share body heat with another man.

"Suit yourself," Darien muttered and rolled his blanket out beside mine. I fully expected him to lie down and go to sleep, but instead he rolled out another blanket next to his and hefted a protesting Brandon up off the ground and deposited him on the blanket furthest from me. "You shall not freeze to death tonight. No matter how much you want it." He shoved Brandon back and wrapped him up burrito-like in the blanket.

"Thanks," Brandon said, almost sounding sincere.

"You are welcome." I could hear the smile in Darien's voice as he tossed some huge logs onto the fire. Then he laid down next to me on his blanket and wrapped it over the top of us.

I bit my lip at the desire that flooded through me when every inch of his body pressed against mine, his fingertips tracing tiny circles along my arm, leaving trails of goose bumps in their wake. His hot breath tickled my neck and his lips brushed my skin. I held my breath to keep from reacting audibly to what he was doing to me.

After a few minutes, his breathing matched Casey's. Slow, deep and rhythmic. Even Brandon had fallen asleep, as evidenced by his loud snoring.

But even snugly wedged between my sister and Darien, I couldn't relax. My mind kept replaying the incidents of the day in my head. Finding my mother, enchanted by a spell. Slaying the dragon and ending up in that putrid pit of death. Finding my sister, and then finding her pendant inside the dragon's carcass. Almost getting raped by Antonio.

My mind raced forward to the scene I was sure to encounter when we reached the gates of Aislin. Marcilena would be waiting for us. Probably throw me in a dungeon to be tortured for treason. That's what happened in the movies. Darien would probably end up there too. Maybe even worse for killing Antonio. And Brandon? Heck. Throw him down there too. Couldn't be any worse than what he encountered in that deserted tower. And my sister? What would Marcilena do when she discovered she had two step-daughters instead of one? If her treatment of me was any indication, it wouldn't be pretty.

I had to protect Casey from her scheming at all costs. I had to get us out. Which meant I had to complete my quest. Rescue the Prince. Slay the dragon. Wake up my mother. Defeat the evil Queen.

Two more tasks. Get the King to wake up my mother and defeat the evil queen. First one, not so hard, theoretically. The second one? Not so much.

With my next breath, I opened my eyes to the muted morning sun filtering down through the cover of pine trees. I shifted in my warm cocoon, snuggled tightly beside Darien with my sister tucked securely in my arms. My heart accelerated. My sister was really here, safe in my arms. I leaned forward and kissed the top of her head.

Casey flopped over and looked up at me, her chocolate eyes filled with tears.

"What's wrong?" I whispered and smoothed her rumpled hair from her face.

"I thought it was all a dream. But I'm still here." She buried her face against me, her shoulders shaking. Her voice was muffled against my chest. "I miss Mom!"

"Shh," I soothed and rubbed her back the way Mom used to do when I was little.

Casey inhaled in a few shuddering breaths and pulled back and looked at me, her face marred with tears. "It really isn't a dream, is it?"

I half-shrugged. "I don't know, Casey. I thought it was a dream too. But now you're here too, so I don't know what to think." I pulled her tight to me, as if I could somehow infuse some of my strength into her.

The warmth behind me disappeared and was replaced by a cold draft. I grunted and sat up, bringing Casey up with me.

Darien knelt beside Brandon, laid his palm on his forehead and frowned. "He does'na look good. We need to get him to the healer, soon."

Brandon opened his bloodshot eyes and glared at Darien. "I am fine."

Darien shook his head and went to the fire, kicking dirt onto the smoldering ashes. I helped Casey up and we worked together to fold the blankets and tie them securely to Dorcha's back.

With some pained grunting from Brandon, he was soon perched on the saddle, with Casey nestled snugly before him. He wrapped his cloak around both of them, so just their heads poked out the top. I smiled reassuringly at Casey. Her cheeks flamed. If I didn't know her better, I'd think she had a little crush on him.

The rest of the journey back to Aislin was uneventful, but as we neared the drawbridge, the clatter of horses and shouting filtered out through the open gates. Panic tingled along my spine, but I kept my face stoic.

A guard skirted past us as we led Dorcha towards the stable. No one stopped us. No one even looked our way.

Just as we made it into the stable, a boy ran smack into me.

"Sorry, Miss!" he stammered and tried to duck under my arm.

I caught his shoulder before he could escape. "Connor?"

His flushed, freckled face lit up as he looked at me with his round brown eyes. "M'lady! You are back!"

He reminded me so much of Casey, at least the way she used to look, so alive with youthful exuberance, which used to drive me crazy. Now I just wished I could give it back to her.

I smiled and nodded. "What's going on? Why is everyone in such a rush?"

His eyes widened. "You have not heard?"

I shook my head.

A wide smile stretched across his little face. "The queen disappeared. Her nasty henchmen too! And while looking for her they found this torture chamber..."

It was too good to be true. "What do you mean disappeared?"

"My mother is one of her servants. She went in to wake the queen up and found an empty bed. It's like she just *poof*! Disappeared!" Someone called his name from the other end of the courtyard. "Coming!" he called and shot me an apologetic smile before disappearing out of the stable door.

I turned to Darien, who was helping Brandon down from the horse. "Did you hear that?"

His copper eyes narrowed. "I d'na believe it. She would'na just leave everything she worked so hard to build. 'Tis a trap.

The happy little bubble inflating inside me at the thought that my quest was almost complete popped. I'd never even considered a trap.

I sighed. "What should we do?"

Darien slung Brandon's arm over his shoulder and led him out of the stable. "What we came here to do. Get the king to Rostellan."

I grabbed Casey's hand and we followed them to the main hall. Brandon grunted in pain with each step up the stairs. Sweat beaded his brow and his face was flushed.

I touched his cheek, yanking it away as the heat seared my skin. "He's got an infection. We have to get him to the doctor. Now."

"Some rescue..." Brandon muttered before passing out. Darien wavered beneath his dead weight and I nudged underneath his other shoulder so we carried his weight equally.

"M'lady!" Claire's voice echoed through the hall as she rushed to my side. "You are alive!"

"I could say the same about you." I stumbled as I tried to help Darien carry Brandon across the hall.

Claire shot Darien a confused look and waved over a couple of frantic guards.

"Princess Victoria!" Danielle's voice echoed across the cavernous hall. I spun in time to catch Danielle's ample chest in my face. She wrapped her arms around me and squeezed. "Worried about you, we were! The castle was in an uproar when they found you were missing. Marcilena said the gypsies kidnapped you and sent her guard to find you!" Her words came out in one breath as she squeezed mine from my lungs. "What happened? How did you escape?"

I squeaked out an inaudible response, which clued her in to my inability to breathe. Her grip on my rib cage relaxed and I sucked in a huge breath. "I was rescuing Brandon. Marcilena locked him in a tower."

A pained groan from behind me drew her gaze from my face. "Oh my God, Brandon!" She shoved me aside and crouched beside the unconscious Brandon.

She stroked his sweaty hair from his face. "What happened to him?"

Darien answered for me. "A dragon threw him into a tree." He pulled her to her feet. "We must get him to the healer now, before it is too late."

"Of course." Danielle pulled her arm away, but her gaze didn't leave Brandon's sweaty face.

We followed closely behind the guards as they hauled Brandon's unconscious body to the healer, the seed of doubt that this could be a trap sprouting firmly in my head. I gripped Casey's little hand, my other hand firmly wrapped around the hilt of my sword. If anyone tried anything funny...

The guard kicked the door open, sending it slamming into the wall. The healer, an elderly man who reminded me more of a wizard than a doctor with his flowing white beard and long robes, leaped from his seat. "What's the meaning of this?"

I stepped forward and the guards unceremoniously dumped Brandon onto the cot in the corner of the room. He groaned in pain but didn't open his eyes.

"He broke his leg when he was thrown into a tree. I think it's infected." I watched Danielle kneel beside him and wipe the sweat away from his face with the sleeve of her dress.

"You are a healer?" the old man muttered and ushered me out of the way to inspected Brandon's leg.

"No, but before I ended up here I planned on going to med school."

His bushy white eyebrows knitted together. "Excuse me?"

I shook my head. It didn't matter.

He poked around in the wound, causing Brandon's eyes to pop open and a string of curses flying from his mouth. Danielle cringed but held her position crouched beside him.

"We must amputate immediately before the infection can reach his heart."

My stomach lurched. "Don't you even want to try antibiotics?"

Again, his almost colorless glare caught mine. "Anti-what?"

"Antibiotics. You know, stuff to fight the infection."

He hefted himself off the floor and crossed the room to rifle in his wardrobe. "My usual preparations are'na strong enough to deal with this. What do you know of this anyway?" He pulled out a wooden box that reminded me of a treasure chest. The latches flipped and he pulled out a vial of some liquid, a narrow wooden rod, some strips of white fabric and a long saw-like thing.

My legs went weak at the sight of the saw. Darien tried to pull me from the room, but I dug my heels in. "You *are not* sawing off his leg," I shouted.

Darien cupped my face and forced me to look at him. "Brandon will die if he does'na do it. The infection will kill him."

I shook my head. "No." I twisted from Darien's arms and shoved the old quack out of the way. I leveled my gaze with his. "If I can get the infection to subside, can you fix him?"

The old man's papery features paled for a moment, but I could see the gears working in his ancient brain. One - I was a child. Two - I was a female. And three - I was a princess who shouldn't know anything about medicine.

I grabbed his frail hand and squeezed it. "Trust me. Please."

He studied me for a moment, then nodded.

I closed my eyes and tried to remember the herbs commonly used to fight infection from my medicinal plant book. Mom had given it to me for Christmas after learning I was applying for the Naturopathic Doctor of Medicine program after graduation.

I flipped through the pages in my head. There was something that doctors used in World War I to remove infection. Something edible... I gasped. "Get me a ton of garlic, snapdragons, yarrow, houseleek, boiling water and some thick bandages. Now."

The ancient man paused for a second, as if he was contemplating the efficacy of my request. A wise smile spread across his face, practically ripping his paper-thin skin. "I shall be back in a moment. It might help, but don't expect a miracle..." He disappeared out a side door.

My gaze shot to Claire, who had Casey wrapped in her arms like she was her own long-lost sister. "Claire, take Casey up to my room okay? I'll be there in a few. Don't leave her side."

"Aye, m'lady. Not take my eyes off her, I will."

Casey caught my gaze, a sheen of tears in her eyes, a brave smile plastered to her face. "It's okay, Tor. I'll be okay. I'm not a little kid anymore."

That confession was enough to have me across the room, pulling her into my arms for a tight hug. This was the second time I'd been forced to leave Casey alone since I'd found her. I'd already broken my promise to her to never leave her side again. This made it twice.

"I'll be there as soon as I can okay? I promise."

"Okay." Casey wriggled from my death-grip to follow Claire down the hall.

She was probably safer with Claire anyway. Marcilena didn't even know who she was. Claire could pawn her off as one of her own sisters. She'd be all right.

Darien's voice brought my attention back to Brandon's side. "Tori, 'tis not something to trifle with. Are you sure you know what you are doing?" His voice was cautious as he stared at Brandon's bloody wound.

"I'm trying to save Brandon's leg."

He raised his gaze to meet mine, concern furrowing his brow into a deep V. "How do you know those herbs will work?"

I knelt beside Brandon and brushed his stringy blonde hair from his face. Danielle stiffened next to me. "When Casey was little, she had so many ear infections the doctors threatened to put tubes in her ears to help with the ear infections. Poor thing was miserable. Then my mom met this naturopathic doctor, one that used herbs rather than drugs, to heal people. We took Casey to her and within a few days she was better. Right then I decided I wanted to be a naturopath too. My mom got me this medicinal herb book last Christmas when I told her I was applying for naturopath school after graduation."

His frown deepened as he tried to process my explanation. "There is so much of that I d'na understand."

I sighed. "Let's just say I was studying to be a healer before I woke up here, okay?"

He nodded. "If 'tis not a dream, if you d'na wake up, what will you do? Would you be able to live the rest of your life here? Would you be happy?"

He, in a round-about way, just asked me if I would be willing to live happily ever after in my fairy tale should it prove not to be a dream.

The side door creaked open before I could reply.

A parade of servants came in with baskets full of the various plants and herbs I requested followed by an out of breath healer. Following my directions, he set Danielle and the servants to work preparing the herbs, grinding the garlic into a paste, boiling the rest in water.

I winced at Brandon's hiss of pain when I pressed the warm, pungent mixture on to the open wound. "Sorry," I murmured and gently continued applying the compress.

After a few tense minutes when I thought he might actually levitate off the cot, he relaxed and his breathing slowed. The old healer roused him slightly to get him to drink the broth of boiled herbs.

He pressed his wrinkled hand against Brandon's forehead and his colorless gaze caught mine. "His skin already feels cooler. Where did you learn to use herbs like that?"

I smiled at the fresh look of wonder and awe on the ancient man's etched face. "From a book."

"But women d'na read," he started to argue.

"This woman does." I got up from my knees and nudged Darien, who'd fallen asleep slumped against the wall. I glared at the healer. "Promise me you won't cut his leg off while I'm gone."

Danielle slumped to the ground beside Brandon, exhausted from the labor of grinding so much garlic into a fine paste for his compress. "He would have to get through me first."

The old man chuckled. "I d'na need to now. Go. I can take it from here, Princess." He nodded humbly. "Thank you."

"You're welcome."

27

Chapter Twenty-seven

After grabbing some much-needed food, a quick change of clothes and checking in on Casey and Claire -- who were camped out on my bed playing a game of chess -- we raced across the castle to the king's chambers. No one guarded the door, which had never happened before. On the few occasions I tried to gain a private audience with the king, I had been firmly deterred by a pair of burly guards.

I knocked gently on the door, which creaked open upon contact.

A muffled grunt came from somewhere near the fire.

I glanced at Darien. He nodded and stood guard outside the door.

"Your highness?" I asked tentatively and came around a large chair in front of the fire.

I stifled a gasp. It had been a while since I saw him on the night of the ball, maybe a month or more, but I was unprepared for the sight before me.

His sandy blonde hair was streaked with gray and fell around his shoulders in a tangled rat's nest, mingling with his long beard and mustache into one big dreadlock. He watched me with heavy-lidded light-blue eyes, the color setting off a twinge of homesickness. They were the exact color of my dad's.

I knelt before him. "Your highness?"

"Hmmph," he grunted. "Hmmphh oomph hrmbaph," he mumbled.

I blinked. He was trying to talk!

"Your highness, my name is Tori. I'm –" Who was I supposed to tell him I was? Tell him the truth, that this was my dream? Or tell him who I was supposed to be? "I'm your daughter."

He mumbled again, this time, a coughing laugh escaping through his yeti-like face.

"Can you talk?"

"Hmph hambaph. Wibach." His eyes were clear as he stared at me, like he was trying to talk to me telepathically. My gaze followed as he raised a shaky hand to his hair and pointed to a side table by the fire. A large pair of shears, not scissors per-say, but like something I'd seen farmers shear sheep with on TV, lay on the table.

My eyes widened. I needed to get him to Rostellan Castle to break the spell holding my mother, and he wanted a haircut. "You want me to cut your hair?"

His eyes flashed with excitement and his lips twisted into a smile as he slowly nodded.

I picked up the shears and stood beside him. "After I do this, I need your help."

Another slow nod and an unintelligible mumble.

I tentatively started snipping away at the base of the massive rat's nest. I chewed my lip as I worked, and before I knew it the debilitated king sat surrounded by huge piles of tangled graying blonde locks.

I jumped and dropped the shears when the king spoke.

"Thank you, Princess Victoria," his words were clear as day.

My heart clenched when the king turned to face me. Like Katherine, he looked like a perfected version of my dad. Laugh lines etched the corners of his light blue eyes, the color of the sky on a hot summer day. Just a hint of dimples on either side of his thin-lipped mouth. His strong chin with a deep cleft in the center was shaded with the remains of his beard. Just like my dad. "Dad?" My heart pounded in my ears.

He smiled and pulled me into his arms. He smelled exactly like my real dad, like aftershave and chocolate. But he called me Princess Victoria. The tears streamed down my cheeks and I hugged him, pretending for a moment he was my real dad.

After a moment of crying into this familiar stranger's chest, I pulled back and looked up at him, sniffling and wiping my eyes self-consciously. "What happened to you?"

He sighed. "The witch cast a spell on me, forced me to marry her. 'Twas like I was trapped in my own body. I could watch but could not do anything to stop her."

"Then you know what she did to your wife?"

"Katherine? A faerie killed your mother and sister long ago." His eyes were distant as he spoke the words.

I shook my head. "She's alive. And my sister is too."

He drew in a ragged breath. "How?"

"The faerie cast a spell on her, made her sleep. I accidentally found her when I rescued Prince Brandon from Rostellan Castle."

A growl rumbled through his chest. It was the sound my dad used to make when he was frustrated too. "Rostellan... How did you manage to get into the castle, let alone rescue the prince, without being killed by the dragon?"

My stomach churned at the thought of the dragon. "I slayed it."

His bellowing laugh filled the room. "You slayed the dragon and rescued the prince? Nay, I d'na believe it."

I scowled. "It's true. The faeries in the forest gave me this enchanted sword to slay it with." I pulled my sword from the scabbard and held it before him. The etching across the blade glowed.

He took the sword and inspected it by the light of the fire. "The sword of Amaranth." He handed the sword back to me. "The folklore is true then." He slumped down into the chair and stroked his stubbly chin.

"Please believe me. I found her. She's in the tower at Rostellan Castle. Darien said the spell could be broken by true love's kiss. Please, come with me to see her?" My voice was on the verge of panic.

"Darien? Marcilena's pet?" He snapped. "D'na believe a word he says! Who knows if she cast a spell on him to do her bidding too."

My stomach flip-flopped at the venom in his words. I trusted Darien with my life. I knew he wasn't under her control. Didn't I? I glanced at the door, and could see Darien's profile through the opening. He couldn't be a traitor. I couldn't love a traitor.

"Please, your highness. Come with me to Rostellan. Let's set things right." I held my hand out. *Let's complete my destined path so I can wake up.*

His big hand wrapped around mine and he stood.

We made the ride back to Rostellan castle in record time, using the shortcut Brandon showed us to shorten our travel time to a half-day. If we hadn't had Claire and Casey riding with us, we might have been able to cut it even shorter. But there was no way I was leaving Casey behind when I didn't know where Marcilena was. And the king, upon learning Casey was his long lost daughter, wouldn't allow her to be left behind either. He couldn't take his eyes off her.

Brandon was still with the healer, who had set the bone and sewn up the wound. Miraculously, his fever broke shortly after the herb compress. The healer had high hopes he would have use of his leg again once healed.

Our horses thundered across the bridge, past two pairs of dried black footprints on the bleached stone. My skin tingled. Had it really only been yesterday we escaped from the castle? We left the guards with Claire and Casey in the frozen garden and cautiously entered the silent castle.

"This way." With Darien by my side, I led the king to the hidden tower.

I pushed the door open and stepped aside to allow him to enter the chamber. He rushed to the Queen's bedside, a choked sob ripping from his chest. Tears streamed down his cheeks. He knelt beside the bed and took her limp hand into his. "You said she lived!"

I crossed the room and put a gentle hand on his shoulder. "She does. She's asleep."

He raised his tear-streaked face and stared at her chest. My heart skipped a beat, my gaze locked on her still chest.

"No!" I cried. "She was alive when I left her!" Even though she wasn't really my mother, it was like I had just lost mine.

"Wait." The king's blue eyes were intense, his eyes locked on his wife. "She breathes."

I glanced up and caught the faintest movement of her chest. "Oh, thank God."

My chest burned and Darien pulled me into his arms. I breathed in the sweet smell of him, a heady mixture of cinnamon and cloves. Just being in his arms calmed my frantic heart. She was alive. And the king would break the spell. Leaving one more step until I woke up. A bittersweet twinge of sadness clenched my heart. One step closer to leaving Darien forever.

"Shh," he murmured and stroked my hair.

I closed my eyes and savored the feeling of being wrapped in his arms. I would miss this. So much. It was like home. But this wasn't my home. And this wasn't real. I had to wake up.

The heartbroken voice of the king filtered into my thoughts as he spoke to his sleeping wife, who he hadn't seen in ten years. His voice broke as he apologized to her for believing the lies that she and their daughter were dead, for being incapacitated by the evil witch and unable to discover the truth for himself.

I turned to face them and my breath caught in my throat as he leaned in to kiss her. Instinct told me to look away, that it was gross to watch one's parents make out, but the beauty of the moment, a man finding his long lost love, waking her from her spell-induced slumber, outweighed all that.

His lips touched hers, tentatively at first, and then with the passion of ten long years of thinking his beloved wife was dead.

He pulled away and stared at her face. She was still as death, the only indication she was alive was the rhythmic rise and fall of her chest, which barely registered unless you were looking for it.

I turned to Darien. "You said true love's kiss would break the spell!"

Confusion washed over his handsome features. His mouth opened and closed as he stammered to figure out what happened. "I d'na understand. My mother always said 'twas how you broke the sleeping spell."

I let out a sigh of frustration. "Well, it didn't work."

"We can go see my mother in Kovanic. We can bring her here to wake her. She will know what to do."

The king turned slightly but didn't raise his gaze from his wife's slumbering form. "We will not rest until she is awakened."

A wicked cackle filled the room and brought the hairs on the back of my neck to attention. We turned in unison to find Marcilena standing in the doorway. But she was not like I remembered her, the almost-white skin, unnaturally tiny waist, soulless black eyes, her hair pulled back into a severe bun.

The creature who stood before us was Marcilena in her true, faerie form. She reminded me of Autumn, with her wings resembling fall foliage. But where Autumn's wings were lacy burnt-umber leaves, Marcilena's were ragged, withered brown leaves, cracked and torn in places, with big bug-eaten holes in others. She studied us with her black, soulless eyes. At least some things hadn't changed. Her black hair flowed around her bleached skin, her flowing dresses replaced by a simple ragged black frock.

"Evil witch. You shall pay for your treachery!" The king reached for his sword.

Marcilena flicked her long, thin blade towards him. "Do not even think about it." Her eyes flicked back to me. She smirked, revealing sharp, almost canine-looking teeth. "Did you really think true love's kiss would wake her? What do you think this is, a fairytale? The only way to awaken her is with the spilled blood of her offspring. Which I would be happy to spill today."

Before I could blink, Darien lunged at Marcilena. She flicked a hand at him, uttering words in an ancient language. He crumpled to the floor, his eyes glazed over and stared unseeing at the ceiling. His chest wasn't moving.

Rage and sorrow threatened to overwhelm me as my eyes locked on Darien's still form. In the blink of an eye, she'd killed him. I didn't even get a chance to say goodbye. Or that I loved him.

Marcilena turned to face me again, her sword poised before me. "Now, let's see about waking dear old Mommy up."

"Over my dead body," the king growled. His sword sung from his scabbard.

I put a staying hand on his shoulder. He glanced at me with a confused look and I shook my head. "This is my battle. Let me fight it," I whispered.

His eyes locked with mine, and from the set of his jaw, I worried for the briefest second he might not consent.vHe nodded and stepped back.

I unsheathed my enchanted sword.

Marcilena's shriek ricocheted off the stone. "Where did you get that?"

I raised an eyebrow and took a step closer to her. She stepped back. Ahh, she knew the sword. Hopefully the sword knew her too. "Some friends I made on my way to save the prince you kidnapped and imprisoned."

She smiled, but fear was evident in her black eyes. "I should have killed those mosquitoes when I had the chance. Nasty little pests."

"They say the same about you."

"How is my twin, Autumn? I have not seen her since the day I cursed your mother and sister."

I blanched. "Twin?"

"Oh, she did not tell you?"

I shook my head. "It doesn't matter."

"You are right. It does not matter." She circled, her bare feet barely touching the floor, her ragged wings flapping.

I backed away, circling in the other direction, my sword raised and ready to defend myself. But first I had to know why. "Why did you do this?"

A manic cackle escaped her lips. My skin crawled at the similarity to the mentally ill patients I'd volunteered to read to over the summer at the hospital.

Her sword made little circles in the air as she spoke. "Because I wanted to be eternally beautiful." I matched her footsteps as she circled me. "You see, a faerie's beauty comes and goes with the seasons. We shrivel up like flowers when it is not our season. But I am an oddity. Stuck between fall and winter, my season never came."

She gestured to Darien's body. "I discovered a spell that would steal beauty. But there were side effects. When you stole their beauty, the beauty would fail when the person died. I came across Darien's mother in the forest and she inadvertently revealed she knew a spell to keep it eternally. So, I threatened to kill her firstborn son if she did not tell me the spell. And, of course, I chose the most beautiful woman in the kingdom – your mother."

"And that's why you planned to have me marry him?"

"Nay. The betrothal was to keep both of you under my control. Him from telling anyone what had happened to your mother, and you from finding her." She nodded to Queen Katherine's sleeping form in the bed. "But apparently I failed on both accounts. Well, 'tis easily remedied."

Marcilena lunged, her feet barely touching the ground, her ragged wings flapping, her black eyes and blade glittering in the light filtering in through the stained glass window. I deflected the blow and lunged out of the way from a second wave attack. We fenced across the chamber and ended up back by the door.

"Mom!" My heart lurched at the sight of Casey, defenseless, standing in the doorway next to Marcilena, with her eyes locked on Queen Katherine's form.

"Casey! No!" My voice mingled with the king's cry.

It was too late. Marcilena's blade was already sinking into Casey's stomach. A deep crimson stain spread across Casey's pale blue dress. Shock and pain twisted her face and she collapsed to the ground.

A heart-broken scream tore from my throat. I lunged at Marcilena and a sickening crunch filled my ears as I drove my blade deep into her black heart. My eyes locked with hers, which widened in shock. Black tar seeped from the wound. She gurgled on the black blood that filled her mouth and collapsed onto the floor.

The evil witch's blood-curdling scream echoing through the room barely registered in my head as her body shriveled like a time-lapse video of a flower in fall. Her corpse crumbled like dust to the floor and scattered in the icy breeze that blew in through the window.

I gathered my sister into my arms as the bloodstain grew on her dress. Tears tore blazing paths down my cheeks.

Casey's eyes were unfocused as she reached a trembling, bloody hand up to cup my cheek.

"You were wrong." Casey whispered.

"About what?" I sniffled.

"This isn't a dream." Her eyes fluttered closed and her hand slipped from my face, leaving a bloody smear across my cheek.

Sobs racked through my body and I buried my face in my sister's limp form. I finally found my sister, and had vowed to keep her safe, but I'd failed. Again.

28

Chapter Twenty-eight

A weak cough from the bed forced me to look up from my sister's still form. A perfect replica of my mom sat up, her unfocused eyes scanning the room until they locked on the king, who knelt beside me, holding Casey's hand.

She cocked her head, confusion flooding her features. "Henry?"

His head shot up and for a moment he was frozen. Waves of emotion washed over his face, first shock, then joy, before returning to sorrow. He laid Casey's limp hand on her chest and stood up before crossing the room. He pulled his wife into his arms and cried.

She stroked his shabbily shorn hair and murmured quietly to him. The lump in my throat grew as I watched these two people who looked so much like my parents embrace, their reunion after so many years apart so bittersweet. Their love for each other was almost tangible, warming the frigid room until the heat was almost too much to bear. In the back of my mind, I hoped to someday feel that kind of irrational, soul-consuming love.

My gaze lowered to Darien's body. I had experienced that kind of love. And Marcilena took it away with a flick of her wrist. Anger seared through me at the havoc one mentally ill faerie had wreaked in my life. Even though this was just a dream, the damage she had done would be with me always.

"Oh Darien," I murmured and clutched my sister's cooling body to my chest.

The moment his name crossed my lips, he took a great breath into his lungs. He scrambled from the floor and raised his sword, his eyes darting around the room, searching for any threat.

His eyes fell on me and his sword clattered to the ground. He was by my side in an instant. Agony twisted his features. "What happened?"

"Marcilena." I choked on a sob.

He stroked Casey's cheek with one finger. "I am so sorry, little one."

A gentle hand touched my shoulder and Queen Katherine knelt beside me. "My daughters. My daughters." She pulled us into her arms and her tears splashed against my cheek. "I am so sorry I could not protect you. My little girls."

Through her tears I recognized the mother I missed, the mother who never had a chance to watch her children grow up. My heart shattered at the thought of my mom. I'd been so bitchy to her just because I wanted a little freedom. God, I really was the spoiled rotten princess everyone in this dream tried to convince me I was.

"I'm so sorry." The words came from my very soul.

The queen pulled back and gazed at me with her stormy blue eyes, identical copies of my own. "'Tis over now. I have awakened and the evil witch is gone forever. Thank you, my daughter, for saving us all."

My breath caught in my throat as her words registered. It was over. I clutched Casey's limp body. It was over. I glanced at Darien, the panic rising like a tidal wave. My blood pounded in my ears. How long did I have before I woke up? Minutes? Seconds?

"Darien, I..." I had to tell him. Before I woke up and lost him forever.

A solemn smile stretched his lips, but didn't touch his sad eyes. He nodded and pulled Casey's limp body from my arms. "We must leave if we wish to get to Aislin by nightfall." He nestled her head into his shoulder like he would have done if she was sleeping. The picture of him cradling my dead sister so tenderly in his arms burned itself into my brain.

"Wait, that's not what I—"

King Henry stepped forward and helped his wife to her feet. "The boy is right. And we must start preparations for the funeral immediately."

Tears stung my eyes as Queen Katherine slipped her hand into mine and pulled me from the floor. Her arms encompassed me in a motherly hug, just like my mom did when I was little. For a moment, I almost forgot she wasn't really my mother and this wasn't real.

##

I shouldn't be here. I shouldn't have to walk down that snow-covered path, following behind the horse-drawn cart carrying my sister's coffin. I completed my destined path. I should have woken up.

But here I was, standing before the window in my room, still as a statue, while Claire pulled the gossamer fabric of my mourning gown over my head. I stared out the window at the snow drifting silently to the ground, blanketing the gardens in a thick layer of fluffy white.

Some people say the agony of losing a loved one fades with time, but they're wrong. After waking up here, my every thought was consumed with finding a way to get back to my family, to find out if they were all right. Months passed, and my drive to find them never faded. So when I found Casey, it was like I woke up, if not from the dream, at least my soul woke in my body. Now that she was gone, again, it was as if a part of me died with her. The ragged wound of not knowing what happened to her was replaced with the gaping chasm where my heart used to be, torn from my chest as Casey took her last breath.

"Lovely," Claire murmured and turned me to face her. She lowered the veil over my eyes. For once, I was grateful for corset cinched tight around my torso. The laces held my breath in my body, forcing me to live when all I wanted to do was die with my sister.

"Thanks." A sheen of tears glistened in Claire's eyes. In the brief time she'd known Casey, she'd loved her like a little sister.

"I'm sorry." She sniffled and rushed to the table for a handkerchief.

I didn't respond, just watched her dab her eyes with the cloth.

My stomach lurched at the gentle knock on the door. Panic tightened my scalp.

"'Tis time, m'lady." Claire took my hand and led me to the door. I followed obediently, as if someone else inhabited this body and I was merely a spectator.

The red-haired guard blushed to the roots of his hair when I stepped through the doorway. At one time, he might have been attractive, with his strong jaw, broad shoulders and hazel eyes that flicked to me every few moments. But that was before Darien. Before I found Casey. Before the life I knew here ceased to exist. The fire for life, once burning strong within my soul, had been extinguished.

We descended the staircase into the main hall and found Brandon, looking much like himself again, in a medieval version of a wheel chair, waiting at the bottom of the stairs. Danielle stood behind him with a satisfied smile on her face.

I tried to smile, but could only manage a half-grimace. But it was good to see him out and about. "You look almost like yourself again."

"Thanks to you."

"Thanks to me you almost lost your leg."

"I would still be in that tower if it were not for you."

"With full use of your limbs."

He shrugged. "The outcome was worth the risk." He caught my hand and brought it to his lips. "Princess."

My cheeks warmed and I glanced at Danielle. "Tori." I corrected and pulled my hand away. Danielle pushed his wheelchair behind us as we left the castle and I took my place next to the King and Queen in the courtyard.

My sister's hearse sat before us, a horse-drawn wooden cart laden with every possible flower imaginable. And somewhere beneath the mound of flowers was her body. A lump grew in my throat and tears pooled in my eyes.

As if on cue, the Heavens parted and tiny crystalline flakes of snow fluttered down as the hearse lurched forward. We fell in pace behind the cart, a solemn march to the graveyard in the shadow of the abandoned monastery.

The entire castle had come out to say their goodbyes to the princess they never had the opportunity to know. Every cook, gardener and guard lined the path as the cart passed. Even Mistress Elandir and Mistress Belina were there, the sorrow and regret evident on their faces. A rainbow of flower petals fluttered down, intermingling with the snowflakes as they swirled around Casey's coffin. Every pair of eyes held tears, every face was solemn as we passed.

Frozen tears streamed down my cheeks when Darien stepped beside me and slid his hand into mine. Rather than pulling away, which I'd done since we got back, I allowed him to pull me closer, to borrow some of his strength as my own.

"I'm sorry," I murmured, my gaze locked on Casey's casket.

"As am I. For everything."

I could feel him looking at me, but I couldn't return his gaze. Each time I looked at him, I could only see my sister's death reflected in his eyes. Marcilena had taken more than just my sister from me. When Casey took her last breath, she took my heart with her. I was little more than a shell of the girl I once was.

It wasn't fair to Darien, or to anyone else, to expect them to be happy with a person who wasn't whole. He deserved to be with someone who could look at him with the love and adoration I felt, without reservations. I'd never be able to look at him the same way. I couldn't even look at myself in the mirror. It was too painful of a reminder of what I had lost.

We marched along the road to the Abbey, a place I visited what felt like a lifetime ago. The crowd lining the streets thinned until there was only a group of peasants here and there.

The dark horse pulling Casey's cart whinnied when we approached a group of people on one side of the path. Their exotic dress and exposed midriffs reminded me of the Gypsies I came across in the forest on my way to rescue Brandon.

I gasped when their faces came into focus. Nadya and Vadoma stood at the front of the group, their heads bowed solemnly. I touched the disc on the cord around my neck -- the one I found in the blanket the morning I woke up alone. I'd almost convinced myself they were a figment of my imagination.

"Queen Katherine," Nadya curtsied deeply as we approached. Her eyes caught mine and a slight smile crossed her face.

"Dear Nadya! 'Tis been too long." Katherine broke from the group and caught the Gypsy in a hug.

"She has your spirit." Nadya nodded to me.

"So I have learned." A proud smile crossed Katherine's face as she turned to me.

I stepped forward and pulled the cord over my head. I handed her the disc. "I believe you lost this."

Nadya shook her head and waved her hands. "Nay. We were returning what is yours."

I frowned. I'd never seen the thing before in my life. And the etching was in some language I didn't understand.

"Trust us." Vadoma smiled, her withered face practically disappearing in folds of skin.

Nadya elbowed Vadoma gently. "We are so sorry for your loss."

"Thank you," Queen Katherine murmured. "Please, won't you visit us soon?"

A wide smile crossed Nadya's face. "Of course, your highness."

We returned to our place in the procession and resumed our solemn march to the cemetery. Darien gripped my hand, as if he were afraid I would disappear. When Queen Katherine woke up, I was afraid I would disappear too. But days had passed since I completed my destined path and I hadn't woken up.

What if this wasn't a dream after all? What if I really had dreamt up that other life I remembered? What if this was it, and there was nothing more?

Against my will, my gaze lifted to Darien's face, tracing his strong jaw, deep dimples, high cheekbones and long, straight nose. His eyes were fixed on Casey's coffin, a sheen of tears reflecting in his eyes in the bright morning light. Could I live happily ever after with him? Was that my destiny?

As if he could feel my gaze, lowered his eyes to meet mine.

My breath gushed from my chest and blood pounded in my ears. I was instantly transported to that fateful day, that dusty tower. Marcilena's sword sunk into Casey's chest and the crimson stain covered her shirt. Her eyes fluttered closed as she whispered "This isn't a dream," and went limp in my arms. Darien cradling my sister's lifeless body as we descended the stairs from the tower. He wouldn't let her go the entire ride back to the castle.

I gasped. Casey's words echoed over and over in my head. "This isn't a dream."

I tore my gaze from Darien's and stared at Casey's flower-encrusted coffin. Had I imagined those words from her trembling lips as she took her last breaths?

The ceremony was a blur of lips moving and words buzzing. I didn't hear a thing above the roar of my blood in my ears. My heart skipped a beat when Casey's coffin slowly lowered into the ground. This couldn't be happening. She couldn't really be dead. She had to be wrong. This *was* a dream. It had to be. I clutched at Darien's hand as my breathing accelerated.

Please wake up. Please, please wake up. I pinched my inner arm. Harder and harder until Darien's big hand caught mine and brought it to his lips.

His sad eyes caught mine. "Breathe," he commanded.

My gaze locked with his. I sucked in one slow breath. And another. I closed my eyes and fought the tears that overwhelmed my eyelids.

"Victoria," Queen Katherine put her hand on my shoulder.

I slipped my hand into hers and moved to stand beside her.

She handed a single white rose to me. "'Tis time to say goodbye."

I brought the rose's butter-soft petals to my lips. It smelled fresh and sweet - just like my ten-year-old sister should have smelled. I blinked away the tears that filled my eyes and rolled down my cheeks. I held the flower over her coffin, the stem slipping through my fingers and falling in what felt like slow-motion onto her coffin.

I stared at her final resting place. A million visions of her flashed in my head. Her laughing face, her snuggling with me on the couch as we watched cartoons on Saturday mornings before our parents got up, her twirling in her pretty pink tutu in our parent's study as I played my violin. I fought to swallow past the lump in my throat. She was really gone.

Four streaks of colored light flashed before my eyes and dove into my sister's grave. One by one they touched the rose, leaving a sparkling trail on its white petals.

"Goodbye Casey," I whispered.

29

Chapter Twenty-nine

The wailing was back.

I clutched the covers to my chest, my eyes scanning the darkness. But the sound that woke me wasn't the wailing I'd once heard when I thought I'd seen Casey in my chamber. This was a tortured wail, but more like what I'd heard through the wall of the torture chamber down that horrible corridor. Like someone was having their heart ripped from their chest.

Fire raged in my throat and my eyes burned. Wetness dripped from my nose. I wiped my cheek with my hand, smearing the wetness across my face. I sighed. The wail was from me. Again.

A faint tap on the door was followed by Claire's soft voice. "M'lady, be you all right?" But concern didn't fill her tone. Exhaustion did. How many nights I'd woken her with my screams?

Reality crashed down on me like a tidal wave onto the rocks.

Casey was gone.

She was gone.

A sob wracked my body and I yanked the covers over my head and screamed into my pillow until blackness descended on me.

##

Days came and went, my only knowledge of the time passing was the line of sunlight that traveled across the lush rugs in my room. Even the king and queen, try as they might, couldn't extract me from the depression I'd allowed to encompass me.

"The pain will ease, I promise you," Queen Katherine reassured me before closing my door behind her.

They doted on me, or at least they tried. I wasn't too receptive to their efforts. It sickened me to think that they were trying to fill the void in their lives that by spoiling the one child they had left.

With each day that passed since Casey's death, the chasm in my chest grew. Depression wrapped around me like a blanket, keeping me in a fog of welcome numbness. If I allowed myself to feel even one emotion, I feared all of them would come crashing down on me like a tidal wave and I'd drown in the unfathomable depths of my pain.

Claire shook her head as she stacked the trencher with untouched food onto the tray. "Eat. You're letting y'reself waste away. Your sister wouldn'a have wanted that."

Though I fought the sensation, pain seared through my chest at the mention of my sister. The dam holding back my emotions cracked. For the first time since Casey's funeral, I made eye contact with someone. Anger welled inside of me. Anger was a good emotion. It was stronger than the others and maybe could hold the others at bay.

The glare I sent her could have melted paint. "What would you know of what my sister wanted?"

She glanced at me in shock, as though my speaking took her by surprise. It probably had.

She blinked for a moment before scrambling to respond. "I d'na mean to offend. I know how much you loved her. I just worry about you. Took in your dresses, twice, I have."

I clenched my eyes shut and I pinched the bridge of my nose with two fingers. "It doesn't matter, Claire. None of this is real. And neither are you."

A pained gasp escaped her lips and she scurried from the room with the tray, slamming the door behind her.

I flopped back onto my bed and glared up at the red and gold brocade fabric twisted into a steeple-point above my four-poster bed. I glared at the swirled pattern for so long that after a while they began to move, morph, swirl into new patterns. The emotions I'd locked away behind the veil of numbness overwhelmed me.

Nothing mattered anymore.

Nothing.

My sister was dead.

And it was my fault.

I fought the memories from surfacing, but the air in my lungs chilled as the memory replayed itself on the cieling. Darien collapsing to the floor, lifeless. Casey's surprised shriek from the doorway followed by the sound of blade sinking into soft flesh. The satisfying feeling of sinking my blade into Marcilena's chest and watching the life fade from her eyes for a moment before collecting my sister into my arms.

I'd kill the bitch all over again if I had half the chance.

The blood stain spread over Casey's chest, the red spreading until my memory was nothing but red.

Her words echoed in the air. "It's not a dream."

I'd pondered that phrase so many times over the hours, days, weeks since her death. Was this really all there was? Panic constricted my chest. It couldn't be. Because if it was, I'd have to admit that Casey was really, truly dead. And letting go of that tiny spark of hope that she was still alive somewhere was the only thing keeping me from taking the sword of Amaranth, the one given to me by the fairies to help me complete my destined path, stashed under my mattress to my breast.

I snorted. "To complete my destined path." What a joke.

I rolled onto my stomach and slid my hand between my mattress and the bed frame. I winced when my fingers caught the edge of the cold metal. I slid the blade from its hiding place and studied it. The scrolling writing illuminated momentarily before dimming. "The sword knows what it wants, you just have to have the courage to wield it." Frost's voice echoed through my head.

An ironic smile pulled at my mouth. Bet the darn thing didn't want to put me out of my misery, eh?

Courage. Did I have the courage to end my own life? Maybe that's what I had to do to wake up? I turned the sword in my grip, moving the tip of the blade in position over my heart. The cold metal bit into my skin where it pressed against my pulse. One quick thrust and it could be all over.

I stared down at the blade, gleaming in the firelight. A face reflected back at me in the shiny surface. But it wasn't mine. It was Casey's. Her eyes were sad, her mouth formed the word "No".

The blade dropped from my grasp and tears flooded my vision. Claire was right. Casey wouldn't want to see me like this. She wouldn't want me to do this.

But I hadn't wanted her to die. Not everyone got what they wanted.

The sword somehow was back in my hand and my feet barely touched the ground as I ran for the hidden passageway.

##

I must have blacked out or something, because when I recoverrd my senses, I was in the spot where the plane crashed, sword in hand. With the exception of a layer of snow covering everything, not a tree, not a blade of grass, nothing was out of place. I held up the glowing sword. Cold wind bit at my cheeks.

"What do I have to do?" I screamed at the woods surrounding me. "I completed my path, but I'm still here! What haven't I done?" My voice teetered precariously on the verge of hysteria and my grip on reality begins to slip. Whatever reality that may have been.

"Tori?" White-hot pain seared through me at the sound of Darien's voice.

"Stay away from me," I growled and pointed the sword at him. Tears blurred my vision.

He held his hands up in a defensive gesture, showing he was unarmed.

My hands trembled, the sword wobbling in my grip. I kept the blade raised between us and watched him, my view of his handsome face distorted by the memory of my sister's death as it played before me like on a translucent screen between us.

"This isn't real. You're not real," I whispered.

He nodded. "Aye, you're right. This isn't real. I'm not really here, and you're not really pointing a very sharp blade at my heart." He stepped forward so the point pressed against his jugular. "Do it, then. Prove I'm not real."

I shook my head. "I think I've finally figured it out. I have to kill myself to wake up from this dream."

He raised an eyebrow. "How did you come to this conclusion?"

I took a step back so my blade no longer pressed against his throat. I shrug. "I don't have any other choice."

He took a step to close the distance between us again. "Aye, you do. But that would involve admitting that your sister is really gone, and I d'na think you can, or will, ever truly believe that."

I nodded. He was right.

"So there isn'a anything I can do or say to stop you, is there?"

I shook my head.

His knees hit the dirt at my feet and he stared up at me with those beautiful copper eyes. "Very well. But before you kill yourself, kill me first. Because I d'na want to live in a world where you d'na exist."

I gaped at him with tears brimming my eyes. "Don't."

He shrugs. "I d'na have a choice."

I felt the cloud of numbness, panic and pain ease away as I stare down at his face. Casey wouldn't want this, and I'd kill Darien if I did this. I had to live. For them.

The blade barely made a thump as it fell from my fingers. The grass was soft beneath my knees as I knelt before him. "I'm sorry." I whispered, tears brimming my eyes and spilling down my cheeks.

He raised his sad gaze to meet mine, and I nearly double over as the pain seared through me. His arms were around me in an instant.

He sighed and pressed a soft kiss on my hair before hoisting me into his arms. I barely felt the movement as he carried me back toward the castle. He didn't say a word to me on the way back, and for that I'm grateful.

Once we're back within Aislin's walls, he gently lowered me to my feet. A smile pulled his lips. It doesn't touch his sad eyes.

He brushed a stray lock of hair from my face and tucked it behind my ear. "I must leave Aislin."

He should have let me run myself through. My heart bleeds at the thought of surviving here without him. "What?" I managed to squeak out. My throat burns as I try to fight the tears from springing to my eyes.

"I returning to Kovanic as soon as the snow clears."

"Why?" I'm all about the one-word questions at the moment, since putting more words together would involve me bursting into tears.

"I d'na want to hurt you any more, Tori. 'Tis nay fair to you."

His words stung like he'd slapped me in the face. "Hurt me?"

He continued on his path toward the keep. "I know every time you look at me you see your sister's death. If I am gone, you could find peace."

My mouth fell open as I stared at him. How could he read me so well? "That's not true," I lied.

He smirked. But his eyes were full of sadness and longing. "Aye, 'tis."

I shook my head. Tears filled my eyes and threatened to spill down my cheeks.

Brandon's voice from behind me made me jump. "Victoria, there you are. I have been looking everywhere for you. What --" He stopped short when he noticed the sheen of tears in my eyes. "What is amiss?" He shot Darien a scathing glare.

"Naught. I was just leaving," Darien snapped and stomped toward the stables.

My gaze followed him until he disappeared inside.

Brandon smiled, grabbed my hand and brought it to his lips. "I have something to show you, m'lady." He brushed his soft lips across my knuckles.

I forced myself to return his smile. "Okay." But I couldn't get the thought of Darien's confession out of my head. Nor the fact that had he not stopped me, I'd be bleeding to death in the meadow at this very moment.

Danielle and Claire bounded around the corner at that moment and Claire apparently caught my ashen expression. "Are ye well, m'lady?"

I nodded. Guilt tingled through me as I studied her chocolate eyes. Her words haunted me. "Your sister wouldn'a want this." She was right. And it took me nearly killing myself and Darien stepping in for me to realize that.

"We were just off for a stroll through the gardens," Brandon explained and pulled me along with him.

Danielle and Claire started to follow, but he stayed them with a hand and pulled me with him to the entrance to the garden. I caught the pained look in Danielle's face as I turned the corner with him. Thanks to a gift from the faeries, his leg healed in record time. His limp was barely noticeable and I rushed to keep up with him as we raced through the labyrinth and into the gardens. The snow crunched under our feet as we ran.

"Where are we going?" I asked between pants.

"Here." He stopped in the little rose garden in the middle of the labyrinth. Beside the bench where we shared our first kiss was a new statue of a smiling, little girl with a leotard and tutu poised in a pirouette. It was Casey.

I gasped and covered my mouth to stifle the sob that threatened to escape my lips. "Oh my God! When did you do this?"

"I asked the healer to have it commissioned the day you rescued me. The artist made some drawings of Casey while you had your audience with the king. Casey helped with the um, what did she call it? Tutu?"

I studied her perfect, smiling face in the bright sunlight. The artist captured every inch of her face perfectly. I stroked my hand across her cheek and closed my eyes, pretending for a moment that it was really her standing before me. The statue, warmed from the sunlight, almost felt real.

Tears rolled down my cheeks. It was the sweetest thing anyone had ever done for me. I flung myself into his arms and kissed him on the cheek. "Thank you."

I could feel the smile on his face where his cheek pressed against mine. "You are welcome, love." My stomach soured at the pet name.

He pulled back slightly and his emerald eyes searched mine. "Do you think you could be happy with me?"

It would be too easy to gaze into his gorgeous eyes and pretend everything hadn't happened, that I was still young and naive and that his touches sent my skin tingling.

Could I really just give it all up, give up everything I had gone through, the memories of my time with Darien, the grief of losing my sister again, and live happily ever after with Prince Charming?

No. Deep in my heart I couldn't forget my love for Darien. I couldn't forgive Marcilena for ripping my heart from my chest when she took my sister from me. I couldn't go back to that demure princess happily wasting away her life doing needlework and playing the fiddle, waiting for my Prince Charming to sweep me away. I owed it to my sister, owed it to myself, not to go back to that. And if I wasn't going to end my life, I had to at least live it. I owed her that.

I should tell him no right this minute and put him out of his misery. But I couldn't do that to him. Not just yet. I sighed and told him what he almost wanted to hear: "I don't know."

Pain flashed across his features before he composed himself. "Well, I shall never stop trying. You could be happy with me Victoria, if you would give me a chance." He sighed and plopped onto the bench with a huff. "I c'na be what he was to you, and I d'na want to try. I want our relationship to be perfect because it was meant to be. Not because you are settling for me."

I sat down on the bench beside him, took his face in my hands and looked deep into his green eyes. "I'm broken, Brandon."

He started to speak, but I silenced him with a finger on his lips.

"I'm not the same girl you met on that spring day. I'm not that perfect princess. I can't be that. I've never wanted that." I glanced up at Casey's statue. "When she died, a part of me died with her. It isn't fair to you, or anyone else, to love someone who isn't whole."

His green eyes darkened. "I love you, Victoria. Broken or nay."

A thrill went through me at his words. But it was wrong. "You shouldn't."

"I d'na care. I will take any piece you are willing to give me."

Before I knew what he was doing, his lips were on mine. But it wasn't the tentative, respectful kiss like the last time he kissed me. This kiss was frantic, urgent, and almost desperate.

Confusion raged inside me as his lips danced across mine. If only I could forget everything and be happy with him, here in this nearly perfect moment.

He pulled back slightly, resting his forehead on mine. "Marry me," he whispered.

I froze. "Brandon, I—" My heart clenched and my throat was tight. I'd always dreamed of this moment, when Prince Charming proposed to the fair princess. And her answer was always a laughing, ecstatic "Yes!" So why, now that the question had been asked of me, did I falter?

He smiled gently and pulled away. "You d'na have to answer now. I just want you to know my true intentions. I shall wait for you as long as it takes." He lifted my hand to his lips. "Forever, if I have to." His lips pressed against my knuckles.

"Forever's a long time."

"I have the time." He flashed a grin and stood up, bowing to me before walking away.

I sat there, on that cold stone bench, with my mouth gaping open, watching his footprints in the snow disappear as snowflakes began to fall. I glanced up at Casey's statue. She smiled down at me, as if to say "Ooooh" like she always did whenever she heard me talk about a boy.

"Oh hush," I muttered and got up.

##

That night, when the castle was quiet and the only sound in the world came from a crackling log in the fireplace, I sat up in my bed and glared at the inky black sky outside my window.

Sleep wouldn't come. I couldn't get my sister out of my head. But for the first time since Marcilena's sword had sunk into Casey's chest, it wasn't guilt over the fact that she had died. It was guilt over the fact that I still lived, and I was screwing it all up. My sister wouldn't have wanted me to feel that way. She wouldn't have wanted me to try to kill myself. She would have wanted me to live. She would have wanted me to be happy. But I'd turned this life into a screwed up mess.

Tonight, every time Casey's face popped into my head, it was followed by Darien's. And then Brandon's proposal. The harder I tried to force myself to not think about Darien and Brandon, the more agitated I became. What a freaking mess. One was leaving because of me, the other vowing never to give up until I accepted his proposal. And the one leaving was the one I truly wanted to be with.

If I was stuck in this fairytale world for the rest of my life, I wanted to be stuck with Darien. But how did I let Brandon down without breaking his heart? He'd offered me the world on a silver plate, and, however unintentional, I'd end up throwing it in his face. He deserved better than that. Better than me.

But Darien, sweet Darien. The picture of his coppery eyes as he gazed into mine the night we made love was fresh in my mind. And later, he'd said those three magic words. The words I'd dreamt of hearing since I was a little girl and dreamed of a place like this. But Darien was never in those dreams. Brandon was. Young, naïve me, so focused on the Prince Charming that my mom read to me, that I never took time to consider what I really wanted.

Everything I wanted was summed up in one word: Darien. But he no longer wanted me. Maybe that was for the best. Like I told Brandon, I was broken. Was it really fair to expect Darien to settle for what was left of me?

It was even truer for Darien than it was for Brandon. He deserved to have someone whole, someone who could love him with abandon, who could look into his eyes and see only their life together, past, present and future. And I couldn't look into his eyes without seeing my dead sister.

I sighed and slipped from the bed, my bare feet silent on the rug. I snatched the quilt off the bed and flung it around my shoulders. I cracked open my door and peered out. The darkened hallway was empty of anything but abandoned suits of armor, and they weren't about to bother me.

I wandered down empty hallway after empty hallway, the stone floor icy against the soles of my bare feet. My emotions churned and my stomach twisted like the winding stairways and halls I tiptoed down. They both deserved better than me. But I was so selfish, I didn't want to give either of them up. Maybe if I went away, to another castle somewhere on a princess-exchange program or something, they could move on without me. That would be the best for everyone involved. Tears filled my eyes at the thought of never seeing Darien again.

Something clattered behind me and I lifted my night skirt up and ran, dashing around the corner. I didn't need anyone seeing me running around barefoot and in my nightgown in the middle of the night. I'd become such a recluse since Casey's funeral, for me to finally emerge only to lurk the castle hallways in the middle of the night, they'd surely send me to the healer for counseling.

I stifled a shriek when I slammed face-first into someone. His warm hands wrapped around my shoulders as he steadied me.

"Whoa, there," Darien murmured. "Are you well?"

My blood turned to warm honey as his voice caressed me. My skin tingled where his hands touched me. But he wasn't mine. And I shouldn't allow this. If I wanted what was best for him, I should push him away.

"I'm sorry." I blinked at the tears. I wasn't sure if I was apologizing to him for running into him, or for bringing us to this point, or what I had to do next.

"Are you injured?" His hands ran down my arms and his fingers entwined with mine. His smoldering gaze locked with mine.

My body ached to throw myself into his arms. It took every fiber of my being to remain still. "What are you doing here?"

He blinked and pulled away, running a hand through his dark hair. "I c'na sleep."

"Me either."

His sexy half-grin stretched across his face and he held out his hand. "Walk with me?"

I nodded and slipped my hand into his. Now would be the perfect time to let him go. Set him free. What was left of my heart would shatter into a million pieces, but I would do it for him. If it meant he could be happy.

We made it to the end of the hallway and turned the corner when I pulled him to stop. "Darien." His name was like honey on my lips, sweet and wonderful.

He paused and gazed down at me, his face filled with concern. For the first time I didn't see my sister's death when I looked into his eyes. I saw mine. The thought of life in this world without him was unthinkable. And I was about to do the unthinkable.

"I have something I need to tell you." My heart screamed not to do it, but my head overruled.

"As do I." Darien stepped closer and I took a step back, bumping into the wall I hadn't realized I was standing so close to.

I inhaled in a ragged breath and the air tasted like him. Heady and sweet. "You first."

His eyes darkened as he leaned in toward me. "I love you, Tori. No matter what happens, or what you are planning on telling me next. My heart belongs to you forever. Even after I return to Kovanic, know that you are the only woman who will ever hold my heart."

The tears that I'd been fighting to hold back rolled down my cheeks as he brought his lips down on mine. I kissed him with every fiber of my being, and it was as if my body lost all connections with the world. It was like we were floating, without time, or space, or anything else to anchor us. If this was to be our last kiss, I wanted it to last forever. In that moment, the other half of my heart shattered, like the apple on the floor of the abandoned castle, into dust.

He pushed me against the wall as his kisses trailed down my neck. "I love you," he murmured, his breath hot against my neck.

My shattered heart cried out to tell him, but I couldn't utter the words. I couldn't do that to him, break his heart like his words had done to mine. Without my heart, I would be little more than a ghost, drifting through life. I couldn't do that to him.

The wall behind me shuddered and we tumbled into the darkness.

Darien scrambled off me and helped me up. The hidden room smelled like dust and old hay. He went into the hallway to grab one of the torches off the wall and ducked back into the room.

"What is this place?" I asked.

It was a small, windowless room with a few boxes scattered around, a cot in one corner with an almost threadbare blanket, and a huge spinning wheel in the center.

Darien's eyes surveyed the room. "'Tis a spinning room." He walked over to a stack of crates and pulled out a tuft of dyed wool.

"It looks more like a prison." I pointed to the shackles attached to a long chain, which was hooked into a loop set into the stone.

"There were rumors that Marcilena had an old gypsy woman locked up somewhere for years making her clothes. It appears the rumors were true." He sighed. "Everything about her was true."

My skin crawled at the mention of her name. I squashed the memory of my sister's death into the back corner of my mind, refusing to let the pain overwhelm me again. I approached the cobweb-shrouded spinning wheel and sat down at the little stool. Memories of the day in my spinning class, when Marcilena humiliated me, the day Darien carried me to my chamber and kissed me for the first time, played through my head. My cheeks warmed and I glanced at Darien. His cheeks flushed slightly too. Could he be remembering the same thing right now?

I slid my hand across the wheel, but it didn't budge. It was broken.

Darien's words echoed in my head. "An old gypsy woman". I gasped and touched the little disk on the cord around my neck. "It was Vadoma!"

His brow furrowed. "Who?"

I jumped up from the stool and examined the disc in the flickering torchlight. "The Gypsies in the forest! She knew who I was all along!" I looked at the bobbin on the wheel. "See? It fits here!" I slipped the disc onto the wooden spoke and hooked the fly belt over it. "It's a piece of the spinning wheel!"

He took a step closer, like he thought I'd lost my mind. My fingers ran over the wheel, which sprung to life with its missing part now in place. A thin, gossamer thread wound around the spindle, reminding me of a spider's web.

"It's beautiful." I reached out to touch the shimmering thread and snatched my hand back when the spindle pricked my finger.

Darien grabbed my hand and inspected the wound as a single crimson drop of blood pooled on my finger.

"It's just a prick, I'll be oka—" My head spun and he caught me before I collapsed onto the floor. The room around him blurred and glittery fireworks exploded behind his head.

"I love you, Darien," I murmured as the blackness descended.

30

Chapter Thirty

Copper. The warm, wet taste of copper filled my mouth, like the way wet pennies smelled. I brushed the wetness from the corner of my mouth and fought to open my eyes. My head pounded, intensifying when my eyelids parted, the inky darkness replaced by blinding rays of light slicing through the ceiling like white-hot knives.

Had I been able to take a deep breath, I would have gasped. I was no longer in the spinning room lying in Darien's arms.

I was back on the plane.

I groaned and struggled to un-wedge myself from between the seats. The ringing in my ears receded, and I prepared myself for the silence I was about to encounter.

Electricity arced, crackling and sizzling through the cabin. Moaning. Someone was moaning. Screams and shouting filled my ears. Oh my God.

I slowly lifted my gaze to Mom's seat.

She stroked my hair back with one bloodied hand. "Thank God." She pressed her lips to my forehead.

"Mom?" I croaked. My voice was harsh and ragged, like I hadn't opened my mouth to speak in months.

She smiled and nodded. "It's okay. You're going to be okay."

Relief coursed through me. It really was just a dream. Casey was alive. My parents were alive. We all survived the plane crash and we were going to be rescued.

They were alive.

I shifted back into my seat and gasped, my ribs screaming in pain at the movement. I didn't need to look around to assess the damage. I already knew half the cabin was gone. But even so, I forced myself to look.

Row upon row was filled with bleeding, crying and screaming passengers. Air masks dangled from what was left of the cabin ceiling. Gaping, jagged holes where the cabin had ripped apart. Insulation and wires hung down from the openings. Tiny sparks shot from the wires every now and then. Baggage was strewn everywhere.

I froze when I got to my dad's row. His body was hunched over, but his shoulders rose and fell rhythmically. I breathed a sigh of relief, the action causing a sharp pain to shoot across my ribs. He was alive.

I couldn't see the seat beside him because his wide shoulders blocked the view. "Casey?" I asked. Dad's shoulders froze. My throat burned. Oh God, please no.

Mom shook her head and tears spilled down her face.

My chin shook and tears pooled in my eyes. "No. Please, no!"

Mom pulled me into her arms and hugged me hard. Sobs shook her body. "I'm so sorry Tori."

"It's my fault! I should have fought harder. Not let you come. I should have canceled my trip to keep you from coming!" I buried my face in her hair and let the tears fall, sobbing so hard I couldn't breathe.

"Shh," Mom soothed. "It wasn't your fault. There was no possible way for you to know the plane was going to crash."

"Casey, Casey, Casey." It was all I could do to chant her name over and over as mom rocked me.

She was gone. After all my searching, so long not knowing what happened to her, only to have her so briefly in my arms before Marcilena took her from me. And now she was really gone.

Tears brimmed Mom's eyes and spilled down her cheeks. "I thought I lost both of you..."

She had, I just didn't have the heart to say it.

A flight attendant barked instructions from the front of the cabin. We had to evacuate, in an orderly fashion, out the emergency exits. Row by row, the survivors exited the plane. When it was finally our turn, Mom left first, stopping by Casey to kiss her one last time. I followed behind her, my stomach churning at the thought of being forced to see my sister's lifeless body, this time cradled in my father's arms.

My blood chilled.

My sister was really gone.

Not just in a dream world.

Really gone.

She looked like she was sleeping. Her face was peaceful, the blue tinge to her lips and her lack of breathing the only sign she hadn't survived her injuries. "Oh, Casey." I stroked her chestnut hair back from her face with a gentle touch. Her skin was cold.

Panic rose up in my chest, cinching my lungs closed. "She's really gone."

Dad nodded, the tears falling unchecked down his face. "She's gone." With that, he stood, hefting Casey's limp body into his arms and cradling her close to him. He followed us out the emergency exit and into the bright sunlight.

Numbly I stumbled out of the plane. My feet were like lead, my blood like ice.

Casey was really gone.

Through the fog of my devastation, I absently noted how different the scene was around me from the first time I'd stepped out of the plane. Instead of the unspoiled forest and meadow, the grass was overgrown and prickly against my bare legs. Instead of the almost-painfully clean air I'd encountered when I first stepped out of the plane, the overwhelming scent of jet fuel and burning wire assaulted my nose. Gnarled, ancient trees encircled the small meadow, except for where the plane had torn its path across the ground.

I frowned at the familiar, yet different surroundings. But the fallen log I'd climbed over on the edge of the meadow was in the same spot I remembered it.

Dad laid Casey's body on the grass beside the other victims who hadn't made it. I couldn't bring myself to look at her again. A flight attendant snapped out blankets and laid them over the corpses, hiding them from our view. My stomach roiled as my eyes traced over their lifeless faces. Bianca and her two friends. My blood chilled. Had she not forced me to move, it would be my body laid out next to the other corpses, instead of theirs. Maybe it should have been.

My gaze continued over the deceased. A couple of flight attendants. An elderly woman. A middle-aged man. I choked back a sob. Danielle. I didn't want to look anymore, but I forced myself to. Claire. Oh God. But it was the final two lifeless faces that made me sink to my knees in the scratchy grass.

Brandon's blonde hair twinkled in the bright light. His eyes were closed, hiding his vibrant green eyes, his dark lashes shadowing his strong cheekbones. I'd barely spoken to him in real life, but I'd grown attached to him as a friend in Aislin. Seeing his lifeless body laid out next to the rest of the victims broke my heart.

Finally, Casey, her tiny, ten-year-old body laid so lovingly beside Brandon on the grass, her little hands crossed over her heart.

My chest constricted. I couldn't breathe.

No.

I gasped, trying to take in precious air, but none came.

My sister was really gone.

"She can't be." She couldn't be. This isn't how my story was supposed to end. Not like this. My head spun as I struggled to breathe and the harsh reality of my world crashed down around me. The flight attendant covered the last two bodies with sheets, hiding Casey's face from my sight. A strangled wail ripped through my chest and I sagged down onto the scratchy grass and cried like I'd never cried in my life. Warm arms encircled me, and I sobbed into Mom's arms, her sobs mingling with my own.

No. This can't really be happening. Maybe it's just another dream.

I struggled from my mom's arms and dashed the tears away from my eyes and scanned the meadow.

Dad approached us. "The pilot just got off the radio. The rescue choppers won't be here for a few hours yet. We just have to sit tight until then."

"No!" I snapped and stumbled backwards. "She's not dead. She can't be. This isn't happening."

"Tori --" Dad starts to stay.

"No! I can't do this! I can't be near --" I wave a frantic arm toward the bodies lined up outside the plane.

Dad nodded and pulled me in for a hug. "Shh, there's nothing you could have done."

I shook my head. I could have fought harder for you not to come, I thought.

My blurry gaze scanned the meadow. Everything was familiar, but different, somehow. It felt like a lifetime ago that I'd woken up in that empty plane and trudged through this meadow. But being here now proved that it was all just a dream. My heart wrenched. Darien was just a dream. And my sister was really, truly dead.

I pulled from his arms. "I need to get away from here. Be alone. I-I just can't," I stammered and stumbled away.

"You need to stay here, Tori. You're in shock. And you could get lost." Mom's concern was justified. But I knew these woods intimately. She just didn't know it.

"I'll be careful!" I called behind me as I ran into the forest, scrambling to escape the harshness of this reality. Part of me wished I'd never woken up from my dream world in Aislin.

A deep voice piped up behind me. "I'll go with her just in case."

I closed my eyes and savored the memory of Darien's voice and nearly tripped over a gnarled root in the process. I knew it wasn't really him, but just the sound of his voice was enough to sustain me. Just for a moment. I picked up my pace, even more desperate to see for myself what my mind had conjured up before the real-life Darien could catch up with me and remind me of just how much I'd lost.

I couldn't spend time with him. Not knowing that I remembered a past with him that he didn't.

"Hey, wait up!" Darien called.

I picked up my pace and ran through the brush, tears burning my eyes. I had to get away from Casey, get away from him. I couldn't face either of them or the reality of what this world meant to my relationships with either of them. I turned slightly to shout at him to leave me alone when my foot caught a twisted branch. The earth smelled the same as it had when my face connected with it.

Within a second I was hoisted into strong arms. Tears streamed down my cheeks at the familiar feeling of his arms around me. I finally pried my eyes open and found him gazing down at me with those coppery-brown eyes that never failed to make me melt. He pushed his floppy black hair back from his forehead with one hand and my stomach flip-flopped.

"Are you okay?"

The memory of our first kiss warmed my blood. But taking in his black t-shirt and jeans, I reminded myself that while this guy looked exactly like my Darien, he wasn't. He didn't understand what I'd been through. He didn't understand my loss. And he didn't understand what he'd meant to me.

I shook my head. "No, I'm not okay, but it doesn't matter. Please just go back to the plane." I struggled from his arms. I really had lost more than just a sister. I'd lost love. And worst of all, I'd lost myself.

Every waking second would be filled with thoughts of my sister. Every image in my head would be of the last time I really got to look at her, twirling and twirling in her little pink tutu. That was how I'd always remember her.

Sometimes life was unfair, Mom had said. She was right. Life was very, very unfair. Because of some stupid storm, my mother lost a daughter. I lost a sister. A little girl had her life cut painfully short. She'd never get to grow up, never fall in love.

But when I closed my eyes, Darien's face would haunt my dreams along with my sister's. I knew I couldn't get him out of my thoughts. I'd done what I vowed not to do. I gave him my heart, and no real guy would ever be able to compare to him. But it was worth the loss to have known his love, even if he wasn't real.

"I'd like to come with you," he said.

I closed my eyes again, savoring the sound of his voice, even if it wasn't really *his* voice.

"Okay," I murmured before I could stop myself.

I took off for the fallen tree, not waiting to see if my escort was following me. I had to know if it was really, truly just a dream. If the castle wasn't there, I could at least put my mind at rest that everything that had happened was, in fact, a creation of my subconscious. Maybe I could let it go if I knew it wasn't real. Maybe I could let *him* go.

I had to try.

Darien walked silently beside me, probably wrapped up in his own turmoil about surviving when his best friend didn't. I didn't blame him. I was doing the exact same thing.

My stomach wound in knots as we trudged up the familiar hill. Would the great white castle of Aislin be waiting for me when I got to the top? The frantic pounding of my heart had nothing to do with the hike, even though my ribs screamed in protest. I closed my eyes and stepped up onto the peak.

"Wow, look at that," Darien said.

I pried my eyes open and gazed into the valley below me. A crumbling castle stood proudly in the valley below, a morose memorial to the splendor it once was. Tears burned my eyes. No scarlet flags rippled on the tops of the turrets, which had crumbled to piles of graying stone. Instead of soaring eagles, flocks of pigeons peppered the few remaining rooftops.

A combination of shock and relief twisted through me. I wasn't sure what I expected when I stepped onto that grassy hill, but this wasn't it.

I took off at a dead run for the gate, which stood half-open, hanging from rusted hinges.

It's real.

I followed the path I'd taken so many times before to what should have been the outer garden. I had to see if she was there. It was the one piece that wouldn't have succumbed to time and elements. Thorny vines clawed at my bare legs as I scrambled through the overgrown garden. It was like nature was trying to reclaim what was once hers. Had I not seen it in its original state, I'd never have known it was once a garden.

I stepped under a fallen tree and into the sunlight. Under the thick vines, the shape of an ancient garden wall stood out just enough that only someone looking for it would realize that's what it was.

My fingertips brushed along the prickly overgrowth, like I'd done with the hedges so many months ago. But that was all in my head, wasn't it?

A twinge of sadness trickled through me at the loss of the friends I'd made on my journey, imaginary or not. Especially for one special person, who'd touched my soul in a way no one ever would again.

I sighed, so engrossed in my thoughts that I didn't notice I'd found the entrance to the garden where my sister's statue should have been.

My foot connected with stone and I yelped in pain. A stone figure, completely enshrouded in vines towered above me. I gasped. Could it really be?

I frantically tore at the vines until my fingers bled from the assault.

"Are you all right?"

I jumped at Darien's voice, murmured so close to my ear. I closed my eyes, pretending again for a moment that the person standing behind me, who looked exactly like the man my heart ached for, was really my Darien.

I shook my head, unable to make words come from my lips. I wasn't okay. I was torn between wanting to return to a world I didn't really belong to, to be with the man I loved in a world that didn't really exist or to stay here, heartbroken but with my parents, who had already lost one child today.

"I have to know if it was real."

Darien moved beside me. He studied me with those knee-melting caramel eyes. "What was real?"

I went back to my work, whispering under my breath, "You".

His tanned hands joined in the work, tearing the rogue vines away from the ancient statue. Within a few minutes, the statue was free. I wiped my hands on my shorts and stepped back, shielding the sunlight from my face with one hand.

It wasn't the statue of Casey.

It was of Brandon.

Darien gasped. "What the hell?"

I peered up at the strange statue, confusion swirling through my thoughts. The sculpture was almost an exact likeness of Brandon, all the way to his floppy hair. But the statue wasn't just of Brandon. His arms were wrapped around a woman, her face pressed against his chest, her hands perched on his chest. Her eyes peeked out from behind thick, wavy hair. There was something about the way she looked down at me that felt familiar.

"How is this possible?" Darien asked and approached the statue. "It's Brandon."

I snorted. "Noticed that, huh?"

He frowned at me. "Care to clue me in?"

I shrugged. "You don't remember anything, do you?"

Darien frowned. "What are you talking about?"

I shook my head. "It doesn't matter." Chills chased over my skin. The castle wasn't supposed to be here. That creepily-similar statue to Brandon shouldn't have been there. If it was all a dream, why was this here?

I half-wondered if I'd seen the castle before we'd crashed and somehow my brain had twisted it into some sort of pain-induced hallucination.

Darien watched me like I was possessed. "How did you know this was here?"

I shrugged. I obviously couldn't tell him the truth. He didn't remember, so he'd think I was crazy. "I really don't know."

Confusion washed over his features. He closed the distance between us. "Why did you bring me here?"

I instinctively took a step back. "I didn't bring you here. You followed me, remember?"

His shoulders fell and he took a step back and glanced at Brandon's statue again. "Oh, yeah."

I nodded. "Listen, I am going to keep exploring the castle. Go back to the wreck if you want. I'll be fine here by myself."

"Why?"

I started walking back toward where the door to the main hall would have been. "Because I have to know."

"You said that already. Know what?"

I heaved a sigh, then winced at the pain it caused. "Stop asking questions and either come with me or go back to the wreck, okay?"

Darien sighed, but his footsteps trudged behind me in the grass. I smirked and picked my way through the overgrowth.

The doors to the main hall were exactly where I thought they'd be. Why did my subconscious know the layout of this historical castle? I frowned and climbed the crumbling stairs and ducked under the arch. The huge wooden doors had long since disintegrated.

The once-polished floors held none of their former sheen, instead covered in a blanket of moss and weeds. A phantom Marcilena stood at the base of the crumbled staircase, turning to glare at me like she had done the first time I stepped foot in the main hall. Rage seared through me. She had done so much damage in her reign. I subconsciously reached for my sword at my side, which wasn't there.

"Wow." Darien murmured as he stepped into the hall. The evil faerie disintegrated like a mirage.

"Did you see her?" I murmured.

"See who?"

I shook my head and continued my search. With the grand staircase a pile of rubble, the second floor was unreachable. I wandered through the bottom floor, past the healer's quarters and the torture chamber. Time had not been kind to the castle, and many areas were impassable.

My skin tingled when we turned the corner and encountered a gaping hole in the wall. Sunlight filtered in through gaps in the stone, sending little slivers of light through the circular room.

My heartbeat faltered when my gaze landed on the spinning wheel, enshrouded in hundreds of years-worth of cobwebs. It was really there.

I stepped over crumbled stone and into the spinning room. Chains still hung from hooks on the wall. It was just like I remembered.

"This isn't possible." My fingertips trailed along the huge wheel. My head spun. There was no way I could have known this was here. No way.

"Cool!" Darien said and reached for the metal disc that at one time held the flywheel.

The second his fingers touched the corroded metal, he collapsed.

"Darien!" I shrieked and grabbed for him as he fell. We went down hard onto the moss-covered floor. "Darien!" I checked for a pulse, which beat strongly beneath my fingers. I shook him, but no response.

Helplessness constricted my chest. I held him in my arms and studied him. He was alive, but unconscious. I wasn't sure what to do except wait to see if he regained consciousness. He shouldn't have come. Maybe he had some internal injury he hadn't realized. Now he was going to die in my arms. I couldn't handle losing another person today. It was all too much.

"Oh, Darien." A tear rolled down my face and splashed on to his lip. I brushed it away with one hand. His skin was so warm, so full of life. Without thinking, I leaned over and pressed my lips to his.

A great breath sucked in through his lips, and his arms wrapped around me. My eyes popped open and encountered his melted copper ones. His eyes darkened and slid closed, his hold tightening around me, his mouth slanting across mine as he deepened the kiss.

My eyes fluttered closed and I gave myself over to the heavenly feeling of being in his arms. But it wasn't real. It was, but this was the real-life Darien kissing me now. I pulled back and studied him.

"Sorry," I murmured, brushing my tousled hair out of my face.

"I've missed you, a ghrá."

"Darien?" My eyes widened in shock. "You remember?"

He nodded, a flash of realization lighting his eyes. "I remember everything."

I flung my arms around him and kissed him, pouring my heart and soul into that kiss. He was real. And he was *here*. I kissed him until I was dizzy and had to pull away for oxygen. When I'd caught my breath, I asked "How?"

He shrugged. "I have no idea. I just touched this and I was here."

Darien hauled himself off the floor and helped me up. "Much has happened since you left Aislin."

I frowned. "I just woke up in the plane a few minutes ago.

Darien nodded. "When you collapsed in my arms, we couldn't rouse you. I thought I'd lost you forever."

"How?"

Darien waved to the spinning wheel. "That, I guess. When I touched it here, my memories somehow were transferred. I remember everything, from both worlds now."

I snapped my mouth shut, which had apparently fallen open at some point. "So you're real."

He nodded.

"Oh," I murmured. My thoughts swirled around me like a tornado. Casey's face flashed through my head. "What happened to Casey's statue?"

He paused, considering how to explain. "A gift from the faeries for saving Aislin. They brought Casey back."

I frowned. That didn't explain the statue.

He rushed to explain. "They brought her back. She's alive. But at a cost. For each day she was dead, she aged a year. She's the same age as you are now."

I thought back to the statue. "The girl with Brandon is Casey?"

Darien nodded.

Realization dawned on me. "Casey's alive?"

Another nod.

I flung myself into his arms. "Casey's alive!"

He chuckled and held me. "She's alive."

I hauled him with me out of the castle, back to the garden where Casey's statue stood watch. My fingertips traced her stone cheek. How had I not recognized her? Of course it was her. Only... Older.

The sound of buffeting overhead made my skin tingle. The choppers were here.

"Goodbye, Casey," I murmured and accepted Darien's hand to help me down.

He held something out before him.

I gasped and took my treasured book from him. "Where did you find this?"

"It hit me in the head when the plane crashed."

"Oh, um, sorry." My fingers brushed the tattered cover of my treasured book. The leather warmed under my touch. I clutched the book to my chest, heart racing. My sister was alive! I looked up at Darien, who studied me with love in his copper eyes. I stretched up on my toes and whispered "I love you" before pressing my lips to his.

Shelley Watters grew up in Tucson, Arizona and currently resides in Chandler, Arizona. She graduated from Arizona State University with a Bachelor's in Sociology with a focus on Women's Health Issues, a Master's certificate in Public Health Epidemiology, and a MBA from Capella University. While her days are spent in the corporate world and her evenings driving her equestrian to the stables, she fills every other spare moment filled devoted to slinging words across the page. Her novels sizzle with the heat and passion that only growing up in the southwest can bring.

Visit her website at www.shelley-watters.com
Follow her on Instagram, Threads and TikTok @ShelleyWatters_author

Made in the USA
Monee, IL
14 April 2025